RUTHLESS VOW

WILLOW FOX

1

Antonio

"We have a mess that needs your expertise," Don Moretti says. His steel gaze says more than his words.

"Say no more."

He wants me to take care of the problem and erase any evidence.

Usually, that involves murder or cleaning up the scene. And I must make sure it doesn't tie back to the Moretti family. More specifically, Roberto, the don of the family.

I don't proclaim to be a monster. I've done terrible

deeds, murdered men, ripped children away from their families.

He hands me a slip of paper, folded. I open the page, already suspecting the location, but he's cautious about voicing the command or order aloud.

Scribbled on the inside is an address.

Anyone could be listening.

No one is to be trusted.

The address listed is the docks downtown.

"Take Ardian with you," Don Moretti says.

I nod an affirmative and head out of his office, leaving the door open on my way out. I breeze through the complex, searching for Ardian. He's not at his post at the east entrance. Gian is there instead, Ardian's boss, a capo.

"Looking for someone?" Gian asks.

Does he know my orders at the docks? It's not a secret that we move products in and out of ports, but I don't usually frequent the dock.

Ardian, however, does. That is, I assume, why Roberto suggested that Ardian accompany me. It's not because I need the extra muscle. It's because he needs me.

"Ardian," I say, not further elaborating on my orders.

"He's around back, cleaning up the muck."

That's code for detailing one of Moretti's rides. Someone was offed in the backseat.

I head for the garage. It's heated and comfortable for a winter's day. The vacuum blares across the distance, the hum high-pitched and deafening.

Ardian isn't using the vacuum. The back doors of the SUV are wide open, and Ardian is bent forward, spraying the leather interior.

Monte, another soldier, is cleaning the trunk, scrubbing the suds in with a coarse brush and then vacuuming the interior.

I turn off the vacuum, startling Ardian and Monte.

"What's up?" Ardian asks, only noticing my presence when the high-pitched hum of the vacuum's motor is silenced.

"I've got a job for you," I say.

"Dirtier than this?" Ardian grins. He doesn't let being part of the clean-up crew bother him. There's a smear of fresh blood on the leather seats. The windows have already been cleaned, but the back seat's headrest is disgusting. There are still bits of matter clinging to the leather upholstery.

"Let's hope not," I say.

"Sorry, Monte," Ardian says and steps back from the SUV. "I guess you're stuck finishing the rest of the backseat. Try not to be jealous."

"Wouldn't dream of it," Monte says.

I grab the keys for another SUV off the wall and open the garage. A cold gust of wind whips through the garage. The heat inside doesn't offer enough warmth for a bone-chilling winter's day.

"You guys are assholes," Monte mutters.

It's not like we have a choice. There's never much of a choice when it comes to the don giving orders.

I sit behind the driver's side and hit the gas, hightailing it out of the garage, and before I can shut the door, Monte is already hitting the button, closing it to keep warm.

Ardian laughs beside me as he pulls the seatbelt across his lap and snaps the buckle into place. I drive through the open gates and out onto the main road.

"Where are we heading?" Ardian asks.

"The docks," I say. Ardian handles shipments weekly from the docks. He's familiar with the routine. "Boss mentioned there's a big mess. Know anything about it?"

"Yeah, our last shipment was late. Don Moretti mentioned that the contents might be spoiled."

Contents? I exhale a sharp breath.

"What kind of content are we talking about?" I ask. We dabble in guns, weapons, ammunition. Those types of commodities don't spoil. "Drugs?" I can't imagine a shipment a few days late went bad.

"You don't know..." Ardian says, staring at me, his eyes wide. "Shit. I can't believe you're just finding out. And from me." The grin spreads across his face like he wants to hold this new knowledge over my head.

"Spill it, asshole." I glare at him for a brief second before returning my attention to the road.

"You've heard of the black market," Ardian says.

My stomach tenses. "Yes, is Roberto smuggling humans for organ transplants?" I shouldn't be surprised if he's stolen the market share on harvesting organs. He is involved in plenty of shady business ventures.

"Well, yes, but that's not what this shipment entails."

"Out with it, Ardian!" I'm tired of his antics. What the hell will we be dealing with when we reach the docks?

"Fine," he says and slouches in the passenger seat. "Roberto Moretti owns The Cradle."

The Cradle is the biggest and most prestigious adoption agency in New York City.

"For fuck's sake." I slam on my brakes just as the traffic light hits red. I should have blown through the light. My focus is shot to hell. It's no secret that Roberto is involved in plenty of illegal affairs, but stealing kids is one thing I can't comprehend.

Sure, I've nabbed a child for Roberto Moretti on occasion, but it was because the infant's father was part of the Moretti family, and the mother ran off and stole the child.

At least that's the story I was told.

I'm sure it was true, and this is just something else, more sinister.

I shouldn't care.

I've never cared before.

But the thought of cleaning up children's bodies doesn't sit well with me.

A man like Roberto Moretti has to be stopped, and I'm just the man for the job.

———

I'll never forget the stench of death. The way the fumes permeate every ounce of skin and clothing.

My shirt and pants will have to be burned.

Not because of the traces of remains and blood that caked to the material, but from the stench.

Fourteen children, more than half newborns, were tossed into the harbor. With it, two women had been kidnapped and smuggled along with the children. They, too, had died from dehydration and starvation.

How long had they been locked inside a cargo container?

Where had they traveled from?

We scrub the container down, the interior metal glistening from the thorough wash, leaving no trace of evidence behind.

"How often do you have to clean the cargo containers?" I ask Ardian.

"This happens every couple of months. Usually, Otello helps, but he's out sick."

"Too much vodka?" I quip. Otello can pound it back better than the rest of us, but even he has his limits. The man will ruin his liver, but probably not before ending up dead from the Russians, specifically the Barinov family.

Just as we finish the last of the cleaning, the boss calls.

"When you're finished, I need you across town for a job," Don Moretti says.

I shouldn't care. Their blood isn't on my hands. I didn't murder these children, but the fleeting images of their lifeless bodies and their helplessness burn through me.

"Another container mess?" I seethe.

How could something like this happen?

Why wasn't there food and water with the shipment? What about the weather? It's frigid this time of year. Could they have died of hypothermia before starving to death?

Roberto clears his throat. "No, I need you to head straight to Manhattan Academy."

"The preschool?" I ask.

Is he upset that he lost fourteen children, so he now wants us to start stealing kids from school? He's insane if he thinks we can get away with snatching kids at school.

It will never work.

Besides, Ardian and I will need a shower and a change of clothes before we step foot around another person.

"Yes, Mikhail Barinov's nephew attends Manhattan Academy. I want him brought to our complex."

I pinch the bridge of my nose.

It's not my job to ask why. And it's not just any kid. He wants us to fucking kidnap the bratva leader's nephew? Surely, he's not going to sell the kid. Probably just use him as collateral to get what he wants.

What the fuck does he want that involves using an innocent kid?

We've been battling with the bratva for years, but it's never been an all-out war. Does Roberto know what the fuck he's getting us involved in?

He's my boss. Questioning his authority or his commands is a surefire way to end up like those other kids, dead.

"Do you have a photograph of the kid?" I ask. How am I supposed to know Mikhail's nephew from any other kid at the preschool?

"I just texted it to you," Roberto says. "The kid's name is Liam Barinov."

I glance at my phone. The boy has blond hair and blue eyes. He doesn't look the slightest like Mikhail, but it's his nephew, not his son.

In the photograph, the boy is wearing a blue and white striped shirt and khaki pants. He has a wide grin, oblivious to the horrors of the world.

And he has his mother's eyes.

I would know. I slept with her.

Aleksandra Barinov, Mikhail's little sister, is one hundred percent off-limits.

She's the kind of spice that I enjoy a taste of now and again. And her brother has no idea that we fucked.

Neither does Roberto Moretti, my boss.

The past is best left kept in the past, locked away. It was a long time ago when I was young and foolish, falling into her bed, or rather her shower. We were on vacation and what happens out of the country stays out of the country.

She gave me one wild, insane night with enough fantasies to last a lifetime.

Was it five years ago? Or maybe six when we hooked up?

I can't remember. I still hear her sweet moans late at night when I'm fast asleep.

Aleksandra can't notice me because I'm a dead man if she does.

The entire Russian Bratva will be after me, and I'll never be safe.

————

There's not much time, but we shower and change at a nearby gym that we own, burn our old clothes before arriving at Manhattan Academy. Thankfully, I left my coat in the SUV when we cleaned out the container, or I'd have been forced to burn the leather jacket.

"You ever do one of these jobs?" I ask, staring out the window before slipping on my gloves and stepping out of the vehicle.

"First time," he admits. He shoves his hands into his pants pockets.

We're not kidnappers. I sure as hell don't know the first thing about snatching a kid, other than don't get caught.

The air is frigid, the sun buried behind the thicket of clouds.

It feels like snow.

Ardian is right beside me, shivering. He is underdressed for the weather. Me, I'm just trying not to bring up breakfast. I'm grateful that I haven't eaten anything for lunch. Cleaning up dead bodies and blood, I can stomach. But looking into the eyes of a little kid who's alive and knowing what the fuck to do if he screams, that has me untethered.

I have no intention of harming the boy. And Roberto isn't stupid enough to kill the kid, just put fear into his uncle.

It's nearly three in the afternoon. There's a church bell that rings in the distance, mixed with the wind.

When I'm on the clean-up crew, I don't worry about planning and preparing. It's just a matter of not being noticed.

There's an elegance to being invisible, but having to sneak in and kidnap a child, that involves patience and precision. I don't have candy or a puppy on hand, something to lure the child into the back of our SUV. And that's assuming he's willing to accompany us.

Which means I'll have to do something more drastic.

If Aleksandra ever discovers what I'm involved in, she'll never forgive me. I'm not sure I'll even be able to forgive myself.

When did Don Moretti decide it was okay to kidnap children? Bratva or not, he's just a kid. The boy can't help who his family is. From the looks of the picture, he's, at most, four years old.

Do I want to snatch the boy for Roberto? No, but what other choice do I have? I've always followed orders and done what I was told.

Roberto isn't just my boss. He's practically my father, having raised me as his son.

Ardian and I canvas the surrounding area around the preschool. There is no surveillance equipment to identify us, making the job easier.

The back door of the preschool opens, and a flood of children rush outside onto the playground. They all wear hats and gloves, thick parkas making it challenging to identify the little boy I'm supposed to nab.

I approach the gate and unclasp the latch. There's no lock.

Don't they worry about the children slipping out and running off?

Maybe that's not their biggest concern.

I am.

Men like me, snatching children.

There are worse men. Men who like little boys, and that vile thought is enough to make my stomach flop. Roberto has never proven to be one of those disgusting creatures.

"Liam!" the teacher calls to the boy hanging upside down on the monkey bars. His hat has fallen off, and he throws his gloves to the ground with it.

The teacher, wearing a long, black, button-down coat, hurries across the playground to Liam and bends down, handing him back his hat and gloves.

Liam flips around and jumps down. A bright blue winter hat quickly covers his thick head of golden hair. His hat matches his coat.

"That's the boy," I say to Ardian as he stands beside me. We're not the least bit inconspicuous, but no one pays us any attention.

Maybe they should notice two men standing around a preschool, watching the children play on the playground. But this is a friendly neighborhood where nothing ever happens. It's quiet, tranquil.

Peaceful.

Not for very long.

2

Aleksandra

"What do you mean, Liam's gone missing?" I wrap my turquoise scarf around my neck as I slip on my coat and hurry to the car.

Nikita, one of my brother's guards, is on my toes, following me outside. He snatches the keys from my hands and unlocks the door, indicating that he's driving.

He's a pompous ass, but at least he's a fast driver. "Where to?" he asks.

"Liam and Sophia's preschool," I say.

Nikita drives the twins to preschool all week. He knows the quickest route. I hang up the call, and we're already outside the compound, hightailing it through the city.

Before Nikita has time to shut off the engine, I jump out of the car and rush inside, searching for Liam's teacher.

Sophia is in tears, her face bright red, matching her sweater dress.

"We've contacted the authorities. They should be here any minute."

The police.

I exhale a heavy breath. It's no secret that I'm tied to the Russian Bratva. My brother runs the most prominent and most ruthless organization in New York.

I'd have preferred to keep the police out of this mess, but I want my son back, no matter the cost.

I pick up Sophia in my arms, and her sobs begin to settle. Even if she saw something, she's not capable of speaking right now.

Nikita hurries inside after parking the vehicle. "Who is in charge?" he commands with authority when he speaks.

"I am," a woman with dark brown hair says. "I'm Director Kira Collins," she says, introducing herself.

"Do you have footage, surveillance of the outside perimeter?" Nikita asks.

"I'm afraid not," Kira says. "We don't know what happened. One minute, we have a report that Liam was outside on the jungle gym, and the next minute, he was gone."

"No one saw him leave with anyone?" I ask.

Liam knows not to leave with a stranger. He's smarter than that, and while he doesn't understand what his uncle does for a living, he has enough common sense not to wander off.

"I did," Sophia whispers, wiping away the last remnants of tears.

"Who did Liam go with?" I ask.

Sophia shakes her head. "He was big. Tall and scary," she whispers. Her eyes are wide, and she squeezes me tighter.

I rub her back and breathe only a slight sigh of relief when the authorities come barreling in through the main entrance.

They're here to help. At least that's what I keep reminding myself, but Nikita doesn't seem happy to see them, and Mikhail will be even more upset that they've been brought in to investigate Liam's disappearance.

He'll blame me, and I can't help but wonder if I'm responsible.

————

There are no leads. Two men were seen outside the preschool, but no one could identify them. The best description came from my daughter, "big, tall, and scary," which describes more than half of the men in New York City.

Is it the Moretti family that came after my son?

Could Antonio have realized Liam was his son?

No, I haven't spoken with Antonio in years. His name isn't on the birth certificate. I never told a soul the name of the biological father. It's not possible that he figured it out.

Besides, if Antonio discovered I was keeping Liam a secret, he'd have taken Sophia too. After all, they are fraternal twins.

Staying at the preschool is useless. I answer the police officer's questions and provide my address and phone number, which happens to be the compound's location. Mikhail isn't going to be pleased to have cops showing up at the door. But my children are the priority, whether Mikhail realizes it or not.

Nikita drives me back to the compound.

Sophia is crying in the backseat the entire way home.

My eyes are misty. I'm trying to hold myself together, but I'm struggling. There were no witnesses, but there had to be surveillance footage somewhere in that neighborhood. There were plenty of homes. Didn't someone have a doorbell camera or security camera outside their property? If it was facing the preschool or nearby, maybe we could track down the abductor.

What do they want with my son?

Could it be for ransom?

My phone has been in my hands, while I fiddle with the screen, but no one is calling. It's eerily silent.

"We'll find Liam," Nikita says, assuring me that my son will be fine.

But I don't believe him. He works for my brother, a monster. I should have left the family when the twins were born, or sooner, when I was pregnant. Staying has put my children in danger.

"How?" I rasp, glancing at Nikita. He means well, and I'm sure he's trying to comfort me, reassure me that my son will be fine, but if it's men who took Liam for revenge on Mikhail, then I'm doomed.

Mikhail doesn't give a damn about my son or me. He'd sooner let Liam die than pay any type of ransom. And I doubt anyone is looking for a payday.

This has to be a revenge scheme to get back at Mikhail. Since my brother doesn't have any kids or a wife, whoever it is probably assumed they'd hit him where it hurts.

His biological family.

Except he values the bratva more than his blood.

His family are his men, like Nikita, Dmitri, Yuri, and Luka, his most trusted men.

I fall well below the bottom, far beneath the bratva. He lets me live under his roof, provides for me, but he's not the least bit selfless in his actions. I'm expected to take a husband. It's assumed that I'll marry a man of his choosing. But I've pushed off any marriage, telling Mikhail I will marry the father of my children when he comes back from the war.

It's all a lie.

And whether Mikhail has seen through the lies or not, I'm not sure. He hasn't forced my hand, and I've been grateful.

Nikita answers his phone while he drives. I only hear bits and pieces. None of it makes much sense until he hangs up.

"We have some ideas about who might be behind the abduction," Nikita says. He glances in the rearview mirror at Sophia.

Is he being cautious about what's said in front of my

daughter? Does he not wish to scare her any further? That can't be good.

He lowers his voice. "There's been chatter."

"Do you have a name?" I can't take the silence. Not knowing is worse than anything I could ever experience. I need to do something, to take matters into my own hands if necessary. "Please," I rasp, about ready to beg.

Nikita shoots me a look. "It's just chatter. Men talk."

"What is it?" I'm desperate and will take any glimpse of hope, no matter how slight or insignificant it may seem to someone else.

"The Morettis were seen dumping in the harbor."

My breath catches in my throat. "Dumping what?" I ask.

Could it be Liam? Would Moretti's men have gone after my son and then killed him to dump him in the harbor? It doesn't make sense to me, but men like Moretti and Mikhail don't act rationally. They're impulsive and dangerous.

"Bodies. Children's bodies," Nikita whispers, careful

not to let my daughter overhear his words. "But this was before Liam's abduction."

I want to breathe a sigh of relief, but the only thing that comes out is a choked sob. I should be flooded with ease, but I'm not. The fact that Moretti murdered children has me both angry and shattered inside.

If he is responsible for Liam's disappearance, all hope is lost.

———

We arrive back at the compound, and I usher my baby girl, Sophia, inside. I want her protected from the Morettis and safely tucked away where no one can get to her.

Nikita locks the main entrance behind me, securing the deadbolt and a half dozen other locks to follow.

Mikhail's heavy footsteps thump against the wooden floorboards. "I hear my nephew has gone missing," Mikhail says to Nikita. It's as though I'm not even in the room.

I help Sophia out of her coat, winter boots, hat, and gloves, putting everything in the nearby hall closet.

"Go into the playroom. I'll be in there shortly," I say to Sophia. I don't want her overhearing the conversation between Nikita and Mikhail. She's witnessed enough as it is today.

I spin around on my heels the minute that Sophia has disappeared down the hallway and into the playroom. "He hasn't just gone missing, Mikhail. He's been kidnapped. My son didn't just wander off, away from the preschool on an adventure. Someone came onto the property and snatched my boy. What are you going to do to get him back?" I ask.

Mikhail exhales a heavy breath. He's somber and silent for a long, drawn-out moment. "I'm sure wherever he is, he will be returned safely," he says dismissively.

"I'm not so sure of that, sir," Nikita says. At least he dares to stand up to Mikhail.

It's rare for one of Mikhail's men to speak up in such a way to the boss. Nikita is a Kryshas, an enforcer. He's not an underboss or a Sovetnik.

Mikhail glares at Nikita to shut his mouth. "What makes you think differently?" Mikhail asks. He tilts his head slightly, waiting for an answer. A slew of tattoos covers his arms, chest, and up to his neck. The largest, most prominent, is a snake.

Mikhail is not the least bit a calm or patient man. And the longer it takes for Nikita to answer, the redder Mikhail's face becomes.

"Men talk, sir. I have it on good authority that the Morettis were at the docks this morning, dumping several bodies into the harbor."

"Do you have evidence?" Mikhail asks, stepping closer to Nikita.

Nikita holds his breath, staring up at his boss. "No, sir. I didn't witness it myself. Like I said, men talk."

Mikhail exhales a heavy sigh. "I see. Why does the dumping of several people make you think the Moretti family took my nephew?"

Mikhail pins him with his stare.

Nikita has no choice but to answer. "They were disposing of children, infants, babies, sir. It would only make sense that if a buyer were waiting for a child, they might not wait for another shipment."

"And you think it is a mere coincidence that the Morettis went after my nephew?" Mikhail asks. "Because I don't believe in coincidences."

Nikita's voice trembles as he speaks. "Neither do I, sir." He stares up at Mikhail. The Kryshas might piss himself out of fear.

"If it's true and Roberto Moretti is responsible for abducting my nephew, then we will let hell rain down on the Moretti family," Mikhail says. "We aren't waiting until morning. I want to strike their compound tonight, before they have the opportunity to move Liam."

I want to breathe a sigh of relief, but I'm not the least bit calm or pleased with the fact they're going to attack the Moretti family. What happens if Liam gets in the way, or worse, they use him as a hostage?

Will he become collateral in an excuse for a war with the Italians?

I can't trust that Mikhail will protect Liam. Even if the boy is his nephew, he's never cared about Liam or Sophia in the past. He's provided us a place to stay, but it's only because Papa wrote it into his will that I would be cared for and looked after when he passed.

This feels more like a power play and an opportunity to strike the Moretti family.

Mikhail disappears down the hall. I assume he's running off to arm his men and command them into battle.

"You have to take me with you," I plead with Nikita. "Mikhail doesn't care about Liam. He wants Roberto dead."

"No offense, but you're better off here, where you won't get killed. What good does it do for your children if Roberto or his men shoot you?"

I understand his position, and while he's probably right, I can't just sit and wait. I hurry off to the playroom, to check on Sophia.

"Mommy." Sophia sits on the floor, her stuffed animals around her as she plays school with them.

"I have to go get your brother," I say, bending down and giving her a hug and kiss.

Her bottom lip trembles.

"It's okay. I won't be gone long." I press a kiss on her cheek. "Be good for me. Stay in here, okay?" I need to know that Sophia will be safe. I can't bring her with me.

Sophia's eyes are wide. Her blonde curls bounce as she nods in agreement. "I love you," she says, throwing her arms around me for a tight squeeze.

"I love you too," I say and drop a final kiss to her forehead.

I head to the kitchen and snatch a knife. I don't have access to any other weapons in the compound. Quietly, I grab my coat and am grateful I never removed my boots. I hurry to the garage and slink away in the backseat of Mikhail's SUV.

I need to rescue Liam and make sure Mikhail doesn't betray me. While I don't think he'd sacrifice Liam, I also can't trust that he won't put Liam's safety well below the men who work for him, the bratva.

———————

I'm silent and stealthy. I hide in the back of the SUV, making sure not to be seen. I don't want Mikhail handcuffing me or finding another way to incapacitate me.

I wait for the doors of the vehicle to slam shut.

The bratva aren't the least bit quiet on their approach.

Gunfire erupts from all around, but the vehicle remains untouched.

I'm safe.

But I can't stay in the confines of the SUV and find my son. I wait until the gunfire becomes more distant and poke my head up, making sure there's no one nearby.

I unlock the back door and slip out, leaving it ajar. I don't need to slam it shut. I hurry inside the main entrance where my brother and his men have burst through the open door.

Mikhail brought his army with him, guns blazing.

He isn't here to talk or negotiate. He's here to kill.

Liam was an excuse to attack the Morettis. Any reason that Mikhail can get, he'll take to go to war.

The bratva are bloody savages. They're barely men, interested in only their selfish interests.

I keep the blade of the kitchen knife close. It's the only weapon I have, but it's nothing compared to the guns blasting the men to pieces. I don't want to come close to one of Moretti's men. If I'm lucky, I'll remain invisible as I search their compound for my son.

Gunfire echoes, and men's shouts in Italian follow down the hallway.

More men are coming. I sneak into the nearest room. It's dark, black as night. I'm invisible, hidden from view as several of Moretti's men, armed with guns, hurry toward the firefight.

"Aleksandra," Antonio says.

His voice startles me.

I lift the knife and glance over my shoulder in the darkened room to realize it's an office. "What are you doing in here?" he asks. He's seated at his desk in the dark.

"Why are you in the dark?" I ask.

3

Antonio

One hour after the kidnapping...

The child is behind me, protected until I have the answers that I need, the ones that will satisfy the innate curiosity building within me.

"What do you intend to do with the boy?" I ask, delivering him to Roberto.

I shouldn't care. It shouldn't matter, but it does.

He's a child and not just any child, Aleksandra's son. It's not just another job. I know the woman and the family the boy belongs to, and taking him means we're asking for war. One that we can't win against the Russians.

"You don't ask questions," Roberto says. He glances me over. "You're nothing more than an errand boy, Antonio. Know your place."

My brow tightens. After what I've seen today, I question everything I know about Roberto. "You always told me that my mother left me on your doorstep. That wasn't true, was it?"

Why hasn't the truth dawned on me sooner?

Is that why Roberto kept me from the knowledge of him running The Cradle and being the man behind the smuggling of children and newborn babies?

"You're my son," Roberto says.

I never questioned the adoption. Roberto Moretti was a father to me growing up, teaching me the ways of the mafia.

He still doesn't answer my question.

"Did you abduct me from my mother, like we did the boy?" I ask. I need to know if my family abandoned me like I'd been told or if I was stolen.

There'd always been rumors that I was Russian, how easy it is for me to kill and exact revenge. The fact that I'm ruthless and cunning isn't unnoticed by the mafia. I've never quite fit in with the Italians, but I surmised it was because I was adopted.

They are trained to be cold and cruel by the mafia boss himself.

I was taught by the best to be the worst.

Is it all a lie?

"I brought you into my home, Antonio, and raised you as my son. And this is the thanks that I get? Questioning where you came from?" He stands and steps around his desk, coming to face me. "The bratva are ruthless savages. They threaten our shipments and our families. They're the monsters. Not us."

He's talking in circles, avoiding the question. I stare him down, unwilling to so much as blink. "Did you kidnap me?" I bite, needing to know the truth.

"You weren't dropped off at the doorstep," Roberto says with a laugh. "Think about it. The place is guarded and locked up. How would anyone get past the fence to deliver an infant to the front door? And why would they?"

My hands ball into fists at my sides. I want to slug the bastard, but he's my boss and will throw my ungrateful ass in the dungeon. Or worse, murder me.

"Come here, child," he says to the boy.

The blond-haired little one doesn't step any closer. He's tucked behind my legs and reaches for my hand. My fist relaxes as he grips my hand and clutches it like a lifeline, unwilling to let go.

"This will start a war," I warn Roberto. Does he not worry about the consequences of stealing a child from the Barinov family? He could have suggested that we capture any child, but to go after the bratva's family is ludicrous.

His lips turn upwards just slightly, his eyes crinkling with glee. "Good," Roberto says. "Let them come. We'll burn the bratva. Every last one of them."

I glance at the young boy, practically attached to my hip. "Go outside; stand by the door," I say.

He doesn't question my order. He drops my hand and hurries out of the office. I shut the door behind him. What I intend to do, I don't want any witnesses.

"Don't you see it?" Roberto asks. A smug grin stretches across his face. "The boy is yours. Aleksandra had your son. He belongs with you."

"Lies," I seethe.

He's got no sidearm, and his backup gun is in the desk drawer behind him.

There's a blade sheathed attached to my belt, and my gun is holstered at my hip. There's no silencer attached. The gun will be too loud, bring about too much-unwarranted attention.

I unsheathe the glistening blade, staring into his cold, ruthless eyes.

"I swear, he's your son."

My gaze tightens. "Is that supposed to be you begging for your life?"

"I know who your parents are!" Rather than scream for backup or his men, Roberto says the one thing that has me questioning my very existence.

He's manipulating me, trying to convince me he isn't the bad guy. He reaches for my gun, grabbing it to use against me.

Roberto must be stopped.

———

There's blood on my hands. It's not anything new, except the crimson stains who I am.

There's no relief, no flood of happiness from what I've done. Roberto's men seek a leader, and Mario Moretti is the second in command.

Mario is no better of a man than Roberto.

He is as much at fault for stealing children from their families. While he took orders from Roberto, he helped orchestrate the operation.

How much bloodshed until I can right what's been done?

How many men must die or fall in line?

I remove my blazer, wipe the remnants of my blood-soaked hands, and open the office door. Roberto's body needs to be disposed of, but not before his men know what I've done.

Who I am.

And who I will become.

"Come with me," I say, ushering the boy down the hall and into a closet. I yank open the door. "Stay here. Don't move." I give orders like he's a soldier.

His eyes are wide, fearful. I nudge him back into the hall closet and shut the door. The boy doesn't need to see death and blood, savagery. He's young, innocent, and maybe I can protect him from that life of darkness.

The boy is also a child of the bratva. Stealing him is wrong, but handing him back to men who are far more cutthroat than I am, he's bound to become my enemy one day.

There's little choice in what I must do.

I'm not a man to run, hide, or cower.

"Don Moretti is dead!" I proclaim as I stand in the hallway outside of his office. I open the door, letting anyone who wishes to see the truth with their eyes. "There will be no further bloodshed of babies, stealing newborns for profit, or kidnapping innocent children."

"Who put you in charge?" Mario asks, stepping down the hallway.

"I did," I say, staring him down. There's a splatter of blood on my crisp white shirt. I don't dare look in the mirror and see if my face or neck has any of the don's remains on me. "I killed Roberto, and I will kill any man who gets in my way."

I've initiated a challenge, a call for the next don.

————

It's only a matter of time until the Barinovs come barreling through the front door. The hours tick by, with Roberto dead and the other men invoking a challenge. We aren't the least bit prepared for war.

Mario challenges me, leading to a severe puncture wound in his abdomen, in his chest and a broken leg. No more men must die today, but if they stand behind Roberto, there's little choice but to fight and prove I'm the next don to take the Moretti throne.

The fighting inside ceases at the sound of gunfire erupting just beyond the doors. It's time to lead my men in victory.

Mario is wounded along with a half dozen other men and the capos who fought with Roberto. I shout orders to arm the soldiers and stand ready for a firefight.

I want to lead the battle, but the boy is who they're after, the young child Roberto ordered me to kidnap.

The men know their places during an attack. There have been many drills training the men at the complex where to stand and what to do in battle to protect the don.

Will they protect me?

I'm not sure. I don't intend to find out. The soldiers rush to the armory and procure weapons. I grab the little boy from the closet and bring him into the darkened office. The lights are off. Roberto's body has been moved, but blood stains the marble floor.

"Under the desk," I order him to hide, shuffling him out of sight as I sit in the boss' chair at my new desk.

My gun remains unholstered in my hands, the safety off. I'm prepared to shoot any soldiers who enter the office, anyone I deem a threat to myself or the child.

In the darkness, the office door creaks open. The room remains dark, but I recognize her when she steps inside, as the light behind her cascades over her briefly.

I'd recognize her anywhere.

Aleksandra Barinov.

I can't help but stare, transfixed by her presence. She's the last person I expected to show up. "Aleksandra," I say.

She lifts the blade in her hand and spins around to face me, the desk between us.

Does she think she has a chance with that weapon against me? How many men has she killed?

"What are you doing in here?" I ask. It's no surprise that the bratva broke through the main entrance, but Aleksandra, I didn't think her brother, Mikhail, would have allowed her to tag along.

Unless he wants her dead?

"Why are you in the dark?" she counters.

The little one under the desk bolts out when he hears Aleksandra's voice.

"Mama!" the child squeals from beneath the desk and hurries around me, rushing to his mother's aid.

"Liam," Aleksandra clutches her son, breathing an enormous sigh.

"Quiet," I warn the two of them. The last thing I want is to put Aleksandra or Liam's life in further danger.

Aleksandra lifts Liam into her arms, keeping him against her hip.

"I can get you out of here, but you have to promise me something."

She stares at me, her eyes bright and wide, but she doesn't make any promises. "Please, help us."

"Keep him far from the bratva and your brother, Mikhail."

She exhales a heavy breath. I'm asking a lot of her. They're family. And why would she listen to me? Is it the shiny metal of the gun in my hand that would persuade her to abandon the only family she's ever known?

"It's not like I have much choice," she mutters under her breath. "Do me a favor and ask your mafia boss to stop kidnapping innocent kids." Aleksandra isn't afraid of me. Most women would cower at the sight of the gun in my hand, the threat of what it means.

Why doesn't she fear me?

"Roberto will no longer be a problem," I say.

Her brow tightens, but she doesn't respond. She probably doesn't believe me, but I'm not about to confess to her that I've killed our mafia's leader. I don't need the Barinovs discovering that we're vulnerable in our hierarchy as we establish a new chain of command.

"Follow me," I say as I usher her out of the office. We don't get far. Mikhail and six of his men are coming at us; guns are drawn, ready for a fight.

"Don't shoot!" Aleksandra holds up one hand to her brother and his men. The other is wrapped around Liam's waist, keeping him tight against her.

"What the hell are you doing here?" Mikhail shouts at his sister.

"Rescuing my son," Aleksandra snaps.

4

Aleksandra

"How the hell did you get to the Morettis'?" Mikhail asks as he ushers us outside into the cold, blustery air.

I carry Liam to Mikhail's vehicle and open the back door. "I rode in the backseat," I say.

The guards retreat as word spreads that we've recovered my son alive.

Climbing into the back with Liam, I ensure his seatbelt is secure. There's no booster seat which worries me.

"The hell you did," Mikhail huffs and slips into the front passenger seat. One of his men, Nikita, drives us back to the compound.

"Did you find it odd that there was no sign of Roberto Moretti?" Nikita asks.

"He was probably holed up, hiding in one of the upstairs rooms, like a coward," Mikhail says with a chuckle. "The man fears his own shadow. Deserves to be hanged if you ask me, for what he did to my nephew."

"Liam, your nephew's name is Liam," I shout at Mikhail. Neither of my children ever get any attention from their uncle, not on birthdays or Christmas, but the minute he can use them as an excuse to wage war, he's family.

Mikhail glances over his shoulder at me. "Why are you getting your panties in a bunch? You found the kid. Who was that Italian with the sharp nose and scruff?"

Is he trying to get under my skin? Because it's working well. "Do you mean Antonio?" Maybe I shouldn't admit to knowing a Moretti.

"They share the same nose, facial structure," Mikhail says, pinning me with his stare.

Fuck me.

"I didn't notice," I say.

"Yuri mentioned that Liam may have been taken because his father wanted to be with his son. I thought it was a far-fetched idea, but after seeing Antonio today, I can't help but wonder if there's something there, little sister."

Yuri, his second in command, is a dick. There's no way he knows that I slept with Antonio. If he did, he'd have gone to Mikhail the moment he had suspicions.

Silence fills the vehicle. I'm not having this conversation with Mikhail and certainly not with Liam seated beside me in the backseat.

———

When we arrive back at the compound, I lead Liam into the playroom with his sister.

Mikhail follows behind us. I can feel his presence without so much as turning around to look at him.

"I'd like a word with you, Aleksandra," he says. There's disgust in his tone; the way he says my name drips with annoyance, like I've inconvenienced him today.

"I'll be right back," I say, giving Liam and Sophia a hug and kiss before following Mikhail out of the playroom and down to the study.

He slides the pocket door open, flips the light on, and gestures for me to step in first before shutting the door behind us.

"You told me the father of your children was overseas," Mikhail says.

I bite down on my tongue and give an exasperated sigh. "I said he was at war." It wasn't a lie.

"Antonio is the children's father," Mikhail says. It's not a question but an observation.

I don't answer.

"I'll take your silence as confirmation." He emits a heavy sigh. "Does Antonio know he's the father?" Mikhail steps farther into the study, approaching his decanter and grabbing an empty glass on the silver tray beside it.

He pours himself a glass of whiskey, swirling the amber liquid before tasting.

"I haven't told him," I say. "There's no father's name on the birth certificate." He can't know. I didn't tell anyone.

He takes another swig of whiskey and exhales a heavy sigh. "You've put me into a difficult position, little sister."

I don't dare ask him how. I remain silent. It's safer not to irritate him. He has a short fuse, and I don't want to be on the other end of his anger.

"All along, have I not told you I want to protect you?" Mikhail asks.

"Yes, I don't understand." What is he getting at?

"You told me when the father of the twins returned from war, you intended to marry him. I suppose that was a lie to bide your time, keep you from marrying a man of my choosing."

"I don't have any intention of marrying Antonio," I say. "Nor will I marry one of your bratva brothers."

"The decision of whom you will marry isn't your

choice, Aleksandra. Father entrusted me to choose your suitor, a man who will protect you."

"And you honestly believe a Russian is capable of protecting me?" I laugh at the absurdity of his suggestion. "You'd sooner marry me off to one of your men than let me live freely under your roof."

"That's enough!" he bellows.

He's won my silence.

My mouth shuts, and I take a step back toward the door. "Am I excused?" I know better than to leave until I've been given permission. I'm lucky Mikhail hasn't berated me for sneaking out with his men this evening.

He offers the flick of his wrist for me to leave.

I don't ask twice. I hurry out of the study and to the playroom to check on the twins.

Antonio is right. Living among the bratva isn't good for Liam or Sophia. But what other choice do I have? Mikhail forbids me from working and leaving the twins, aside from the couple of hours they spend at preschool per week.

Where would I go?

Antonio is Italian Mafia, my sworn enemy. I can't exactly show up at his front door asking for help, nor would I want to admit to him that he's the father of my children.

That would be like setting off a nuclear device.

I don't have enough money saved to provide for the twins and myself, let alone afford a roof over our heads in New York City. Property is expensive. Apartment buildings are outrageous.

I exhale a heavy sigh and fold my arms across my chest, staring at Sophia and Liam as they play house together. It's any wonder Liam isn't scarred from today's events.

A child shouldn't be kidnapped and then practically unfazed by his surroundings when he returns after enduring whatever happened.

I approach Liam, bending down to the twin's level. "How are you doing?" I ask, my question pointed at Liam, but I'm also concerned about Sophia. She witnessed her brother's abduction.

That couldn't have been easy to see or process.

Liam glances up at me, his bright blue eyes wide, his lashes fluttering as he stares. "I don't like the dark."

I pull him into my embrace for a hug. "I know, babe." I assume he's referring to the darkened office and how he had to hide under the desk at Antonio's feet. Why was Antonio protecting Liam?

My head aches, and my neck is sore, making my stomach tumble. At least being inside the compound, the twins are safe. I don't need to worry about their well-being.

But what about mine?

"Aleksandra," Luka says, announcing his presence at the door of the playroom.

I glance over my shoulder, my arms folded across my chest. "Yes?"

"You should know Mikhail has gone behind your back." Luka keeps his voice low, careful not to be overheard. He's one of the most loyal guards, and while his allegiance is to Mikhail, we've grown close over the years while he's been entrusted as my bodyguard.

I had assumed at some point that Mikhail would demand Luka to marry me, but that day hadn't come. A small part of me is relieved. He's a decent guy for a member of the bratva, but he's not exactly my type.

Anyone my brother picks out isn't my type.

"And what are you doing?" I point out. He's going behind Mikhail's back, coming to me, telling me whatever secret he intends for me to hear from him.

"Hoping you won't get me killed," Luka says and quirks a wry grin. "I heard him on the phone with the Italians."

"Why would he do that?" I ask. "What purpose would he have to call Roberto Moretti?"

"From what I overheard, Roberto is dead, and Antonio is their new leader."

The air is sucked from my lungs. "No." It can't be true. Antonio is rough, dark, and probably would stab a man in the back if he weren't looking. Is that how he became don?

"No one saw Roberto during the attack," Luka says.

"Did you happen to see him when you were sneaking around?"

"Only Antonio and Liam." I'd intentionally avoided as many soldiers and men as possible. "Why?" I ask.

"I wouldn't have said anything, shouldn't—but if Antonio is the father of your twins, I thought you should know."

Why is he being so damn cryptic?

"Know what?" I'm trying to remain calm and keep my voice down. I don't want to alert the twins to our conversation, especially since it regards their father.

"That your brother, Mikhail, intends to take out the Italians. All of them. He's exacting revenge because they kidnapped your son."

5

Antonio

Six weeks later...

Most of the men have followed in line with my leadership. They've accepted my new position as head of the family, don.

I didn't kill Roberto to become the ringleader of a fucked-up circus. But that's what I got.

I dismantled the operation involving The Cradle. I refuse to kidnap children and be a party to their illegal affairs.

It turns out that Roberto's most lucrative schemes were stealing and selling newborns. He had his hand in a dozen or so other illegal enterprises that I'm working to grow more capital, but it doesn't come easily, especially when our shipment of arms is repeatedly stolen at the dock.

Three weeks in a row.

It's not a coincidence.

Someone is working for the other side, the Russians. If it were the Feds, we'd have been busted and brought in by now.

We still have our drug trade, smuggling narcotics in, paying customs agents to look the other way. It's enough to pay the bills, but my men like living lavishly, and I don't need them questioning my tactics.

I'm constantly being watched. I have to prove my worth to the organization that I run.

Ardian has become my most trusted ally, from soldier to second in command. The other soldiers fell in line when I stepped up and won the seat on the throne. But Mario, who was second to Roberto, I worry that he'll betray me.

He pledged his allegiance to me when I fought him for the position. I could have killed him, maybe I should have, but there was enough bloodshed that day. He is now a soldier and guard for the complex.

Ardian slumps into my office. He looks like shit.

"Got a minute, boss?" Ardian asks.

"Come in and shut the door," I say.

Ardian closes the door as he shuffles into the office. It used to be Roberto's office. It's mine now. The desk has been replaced with a darker wood, more extensive and taller to fit me better. The floor has been scrubbed, with no evidence of Roberto's demise.

"The Russians are intercepting our weapons shipments at the dock," Ardian says.

I pinch the bridge of my nose. "They're after our organization," I say.

I killed Roberto because I had no other choice. I had to stop him from kidnapping children. It wasn't out of honor or desire. I did what no one else was willing to do. I didn't want to be the fucking boss.

"There are rumors that the Russians aren't just hitting the Italians in New York. Men talk, sir. They say they're moving in on all the mafia complex's houses across the country."

I exhale a heavy sigh. It's nothing I didn't already know, but hearing it makes it official.

There have been reports of fires, kidnappings, and threatening our women at gunpoint. It all started the day after Roberto snatched Liam. It can't be a coincidence.

But what I can't get out of my head are Roberto's final moments.

I swear he's your son.

Could Liam be my child? I had thought it'd been longer since Aleksandra and I had first met and stumbled into bed together. It had been on vacation, far from New York City, a fluke that we'd bumped into each other.

I'm not the beach-going type of guy. Sand gets everywhere, not to mention it's hot and humid. My clothes practically stick to my skin.

But the ladies on the beach, topless at that, make the grainy morsels of sand worth the hassle.

I sit at the nearest hut, nursing a beer. The outside of the glass perspires from the heat. It's how I feel, sticky and wet.

There are dozens of women of different shapes and sizes fanned out on the beach. The water is warm, clear, bright, and blue farther out to sea.

I want to jump in, cool off, let loose.

But I'm here on business.

And there are no fun times to be had. My boss is a stickler, setting up the arrangements for our activities. I'm here as the muscle.

My presence is enough to threaten these men into submission.

But I don't care about the business or the illegal dealings. It's the girl stalking across the sand, her long blonde hair. She doesn't fit in—her skin tan from the long hours she's lain out on the beach under the sun.

There's something about her that's caught my eye. Looks aside. Not that she isn't gorgeous and the complete package. It takes every ounce of effort not to stare at her perfect body.

"Take a picture. It'll last longer," she smirks as she strides right on by me.

I shift on the stool, my beer growing warmer by the second. I swig the rest of it and stand, sinking into the abysmal sand.

"Hey, wait up!"

"I wasn't actually offering you to take a picture, perv," she quips, glancing at me over her shoulder.

I shuffle through the sand, and it's like lead as I try to hurry to catch up. She doesn't slow down in the least for me. Why would I think she'd do me the honor of having a conversation?

"I'm not—okay, I was staring," I admit. I hold out my hand. "Antonio," I say, introducing myself, hoping we can try this again.

She purses her lips together, and her eyes squint under the bright afternoon sun. "You're Italian," she remarks, quiet for a second before finishing her introduction. "I'm Aleksandra."

Russian.

We should be enemies, but we're on vacation. Besides, it's not like she's part of the bratva. Right?

She glances me up and down. It's like she's deciding if I'm worth her time or not. "Let me guess, you're here on business and want to have a little fun?"

She isn't wrong.

"Is it that obvious?" I ask.

"The white button-down shirt and black slacks," she says, pointing at my outfit. "Gosh, you look like the Italian Mafia. The least you could do is remove your shirt and pants. If you're going to stare at a beautiful woman, give her something to look at too."

There's something about her that draws me to her. I've never met anyone like her. She's outspoken and fierce. Strong and determined. I ignore her mafia comment. She's pegged me based solely on looks, and while she isn't wrong, I don't need to tell her whom I work for. It's not like she knows the name Roberto Moretti. We're far from New York City and the criminal enterprises we left behind.

"You look hot," she says with a wry smirk. "How about we get out of here?"

That should be my line. I should be the one wooing her, convincing her to come back to my hotel room.

"Where to?" I ask. *I have a dozen thoughts fleeting through my mind of places I'd love to experience with her, like ravishing her beneath a waterfall or fucking her on a yacht.*

She yanks on my tie, dragging me to follow her back to her cabana.

My lips slam against hers in a hungry frenzy. I've wanted to touch her, taste her, feel her skin against mine.

She's soft and a perfect fit as I strip down. I no longer care about the sand on my toes or the tiny grains against her body.

"Shower?" she asks, grabbing my hand as she leads me farther into her cabana to the bathroom. *The place is vast, gorgeous, and I'm jealous that I'm not staying in one of these little huts on the beach.*

"Nice place," I say, admiring it briefly on the way to the bathroom. *My gaze never left her naked body.*

"It's my brother's for the summer," Aleksandra says. "Mikhail doesn't know I stole a key."

My mouth goes dry.

Mikhail Barinov?

"So, he's out of town?" I ask.

"No." She smirks and nudges open the bathroom door. "He's at lunch with his—friends," she says like she's trying the word out for the first time to describe them.

"The Russian kind of friends who are family?" I don't want to be right, but I have it on good authority that the Russian Bratva is in town from New York.

We're both meeting with the same angel investor.

Aleksandra gasps as she turns on the shower spray. I'm not sure if it's the temperature or my remark.

"You're Italian Mafia?" she glances at me over her shoulder. "I was joking earlier, out on the beach. Damn."

She spins around to face me, her gaze pinning me. The desire hasn't been diminished in the slightest by this newfound knowledge.

Being with her is dangerous.

And it makes the encounter between us a thousand times hotter. At any moment, we could be discovered and found out.

She slides the glass shower panel aside and steps in beneath the spray, dipping her head back.

"Your brother is Pakhan, head of the bratva?" This isn't just dangerous. Being with her is deadly. She could have me murdered.

Aleksandra squeezes the water from her hair as I yank her hips against mine, crushing her to me. I'm rough with her, and she emits the quietest purr, her eyelids heavy.

"Yes, if he catches us, you're dead. We're both dead," she whispers. Her pale blue eyes match the color of the sea. I'm transfixed by her stare.

"Then we can't get caught," I say. I cover her mouth with mine and guide my leg between her thighs, listening to the heavenly moans that spill past her lips.

She tastes like strawberries and whipped cream. Her skin is soft like velvet and warm from the shower's heat. It takes every ounce of strength not to pound into her, break her.

"I've been in contact with the dons in Chicago, Los Angeles, and Breckenridge. They will be staying at the complex while we assemble."

"What would you like me to do, sir?" Ardian asks.

Is the complex warm, or are my thoughts of her making me perspire? It's easy to pretend she doesn't mean anything to me, that it was just a fling. But the child, the boy, Liam, could he be mine?

"Sir?" Ardian clears his throat in a mild attempt to get my attention.

"Make sure the rooms are adequate and ready for company. I've invited their families and anyone who's been threatened by the bratva into our home for protection."

"Do they not have suitable protection of their own, sir?" Ardian asks.

I don't know. I am not usually the one who handles looking after each mafia group. There are many across America, at least one in each major city. We run independently, but on occasion call on each other for help when it is necessary.

I've never had the pleasure of sitting in on a meeting with the other dons. That had been Roberto's responsibility. But he's dead, and I'm in charge.

———

Private flights have been chartered. Arrangements have been made to bring the bosses and their most trusted advisors to our meeting, scheduled for tomorrow morning.

But I can't get Aleksandra out of my head.

Mikhail Barinov's head will be called for, and his complex burned to the ground. It doesn't take four of the most powerful men together to know that we're not waging war on peace.

The men will want vengeance for what Mikhail has done, threatening our families and homes, our livelihood.

And I'm okay with that. I know it's coming.

But Aleksandra is innocent in all this, so is her child, Liam. Warning her would be a grave mistake. I can't do that, not without putting my own family in danger.

I grab the keys for the SUV and hurry out to the garage.

"Where are you heading?" Mario asks. "The guests will be arriving soon."

"I have something to take care of before they land," I say cryptically. Mario hasn't proven himself to me, not where I might divulge secrets to the man who used to be Roberto's second.

"I'll keep the complex in order until you return," Mario says.

I want to trust him. He was a good man to Roberto, but I don't know where his allegiance lies. Did he surrender to me because he was a coward and chose his life above all else?

"Appreciated," I answer. I grab my coat from the hook and slip it on as I hurry out into the garage.

Monte and Ardian are detailing another SUV. "What are you doing out here?" I shout at Ardian above the sound of the vacuum's roar.

"Getting ready to pick up the Barones," Ardian says. "Their flight lands in a couple of hours."

"Thanks," I say. I open the door to an unoccupied SUV and climb into the front.

Ardian doesn't ask where I'm heading. I doubt he knows, but he also respects my privacy. If I want him to know something, I'll tell him.

I hurry across town, weaving in and out of traffic as I rush toward the preschool.

6

Aleksandra

"We're going to be late for pickup," I say.

Nikita ignores me, his phone shoved against his ear as he listens to my brother babble on about something.

Nikita is driving in the opposite direction of the preschool. I doubt it's because he's not paying attention. Mikhail is ordering him to take care of business. Whatever that means.

Even with his ear tucked against the phone, I can hear bits and pieces of the conversation. Mikhail raises his voice every so often, and it echoes through the phone into the car.

Grumbling, Nikita hangs up the phone, shoving it into the cupholder while he weaves in and out of traffic.

"Pickup is in fifteen minutes." I'm not going to make the twins wait.

"And as soon as I handle what the boss asked me to do, we'll swing by and get the kids."

"No," I say and fold my arms across my chest.

"No?" Nikita glances at me. He's not used to me being less than obedient.

"Liam and Sophia will be upset when I'm not there. Drop me off, and I'll take a rideshare back to the compound."

Nikita snorts under his breath.

"What?" I ask. It's a simple solution and will fix both problems. Why can't he see that?

"I'm supposed to be guarding you," Nikita says.

"And you're supposed to be picking up my kids," I retort. "Can't another one of Mikhail's minions do whatever it is he wants to be done? What about Luka?" I ask.

My brother has plenty of men who can handle the job. Why Nikita?

"I'm the closest to the target. And believe me, you don't want your kids seeing what I'm about to do to the Italians."

I rub my forehead. "I swear if you don't drop me off at the preschool on time, Mikhail isn't going to be your biggest problem. I will."

Nikita curses in Russian and rolls his eyes at me. "Fine. Do you have your phone?"

"Yes, when don't I carry it with me?" I ask. "As soon as I have the kids, I'll get a ride straight to the compound."

It's not like there's anywhere else I want to go today. It's freezing outside. Too cold for the park, and it hasn't snowed in days, so there's no chance for sledding.

He grumbles and hits a hard right at the next street, hurrying to the preschool. "Stay out of trouble," Nikita warns as I hop out of the vehicle.

"I should be telling you that," I say, staring at him. "Do yourself a favor, and don't get caught." I slam the door shut and button up my coat as I head for the main entrance. The sidewalk is crunched with salt, leaving a white powder on the bottom of my black winter boots.

Nikita rushes off, not even waiting for me to get inside the front door.

"Ms. Barinov, Aleksandra Barinov," a woman says, approaching me. She's in a dark black coat down to her knees. Her hair is dark, slicked back in a ponytail. She should be wearing a hat, but she probably hasn't been outside very long. Her cheeks aren't red yet.

"Can I help you?" I ask. I don't recognize the woman as one of the parents from the preschool. The lady looks older, more mature, and professional.

If I had to guess, she's a cop.

But she's not in uniform. Maybe she's a detective? She wasn't one of the officers who helped with Liam's abduction. Mikhail informed me that he took care of it with the local police department, explained it was a misunderstanding and a relative had picked the boy up.

"I'm Agent Melinda Malone with the FBI," she says.

"I'm sorry, I have to pick up my kids from preschool," I say. "I think you must have me confused with someone else."

"Your brother runs the Russian Bratva. We've been watching Mikhail for a while. Eventually, he'll slip up, and when he does, you don't want your children or yourself around."

She reaches into her pocket to hand me her business card. "Call me if you want protection. We can get you out of New York and give you a new life."

"You have me mistaken for someone else," I say.

I don't intend to take her business card, but she shoves it into my hand. "You need a friend, Aleksandra, and I can protect you and your children."

She's foolish to think she can protect us from Mikhail. It doesn't matter where I go. He'll always find me. He's got men in every city who report to the bratva. There's no escaping Mikhail's clutches.

I glance at my watch and brush past her as I head for the front entrance of the preschool. The FBI agent retreats to her vehicle.

I buzz the front door and hurry inside for pickup.

Ten minutes later, I have Liam and Sophia at my side as we head back out into the brisk winter air.

Agent Malone is nowhere in sight, her vehicle gone. I'm relieved. The twins aren't the best at keeping secrets, and I don't want Mikhail knowing that the feds talked to me, even if I didn't say anything in return.

I punch in the rideshare request and wait with the kids outside for the vehicle.

Liam has his thick winter gloves on, along with his blue hat. His nose is red, but otherwise, he doesn't appear the least bit bothered by the cold.

Sophia is very much my daughter, shivering and jumping in place as she tries to get warm.

"Put your gloves back on," I say with insistence and lower her hat around her head, making it snug. The damn thing has a way of falling off. Although I'm not sure, it isn't from Sophia lifting it.

"I don't like wearing gloves," Sophia whines. "Then I can't use your phone."

I give her a pointed stare. "My phone is staying with me," I say. What makes her think I'm going to hand over my phone so that she can play games on it while we wait outside?

"But you don't have your gloves on," Sophia says.

I exhale a heavy breath, trying not to show my frustration. "That's enough, Sophia. Gloves, now."

Her nose twitches as she pushes her gloves onto her hands. "But they're cold," she whines.

"I'm going to kill Nikita," I mutter under my breath.

"What's that?" Antonio asks.

I don't see him approach. I'm too busy fussing with Sophia and my phone, waiting for our ride.

"What are you doing here?" I ask.

Do I even want to know the answer to my question?

He leans in close, so that the kids can't see, and flashes his gun at me. "I'm giving you a ride."

A small part of me wants to leave the twins behind, protect them from the Italian mobster, but I can't abandon them, and I doubt he'd let me.

"You're not giving me anything," I say.

"Are you sure about that?" He pushes the barrel of the gun into my hip, his jacket keeping the weapon out of view from my children. "I'd hate to have to harm a hair on either one of their heads."

Is he seriously threatening my kids?

Fuck him.

I'd stomp on his toes and bolt down the street, but how far would I get? He has a gun, and he's not the kind of man to give empty threats.

"You're an asshole," I sneer as he leads the twins and me to his SUV parked around the corner.

He opens the back door for the twins, and they climb into the backseat. He flips the child lock switch before he slams the door shut behind them and opens the passenger door for me.

He corners me, blocking any chance of escape. If I fight now, he has my children. I won't let him leave without me.

"Where are you taking us?" I ask.

"Get in the vehicle." Antonio doesn't answer my question. He's gruff and forceful. He pushes me into the front seat when I don't get in quickly enough. "Was that so hard?" He leans in and yanks the seatbelt across my waist, securing the buckle before slamming the door shut.

I glance back at the twins. Do they recognize Antonio from Liam's abduction?

"Buckle up back there," I instruct. I don't want anything happening to either one of them.

Antonio climbs into the front seat and starts the engine. The vehicle purrs to life, and heat flows freely out the vents. He hasn't been waiting for long.

"Why are you doing this?" I ask, glancing at Antonio.

He pulls out into traffic. I don't expect him to take us back to the compound where I live with Mikhail. Antonio didn't grab us just to give us a ride home.

"Not that you'd believe me, but I'm protecting you."

I snort at his answer. "Yeah, right? Since when is kidnapping suddenly protecting someone?"

He bites down on his bottom lip. He's silent.

There's something he isn't telling me. Well, two can play at that game. I don't need to divulge that Nikita is heading after the Italians to attack them. But where?

I don't know where their compound is located or where Nikita was headed.

Either way, I don't want to be in the middle of a firefight.

I clear my throat. "If you're planning on taking us to your house, the kids don't have anything. No clothes. No toys. We should stop for a few things."

Antonio glances at me briefly. "Why? So, you can try to escape? I don't think so."

Okay, he's going to be harder to convince than I thought. I press my lips together, trying to come up with an excuse for him to take us some place safe.

"Do you really think your compound is safe for my kids?"

He lets out a soft humph. "They're both yours?" he asks, glancing in the rearview.

Shit. Did he not realize that I have twins? Is that why he only snatched Liam a few weeks ago?

My silence is my admission.

The heat blows throughout the vehicle, and Antonio reaches for the thermostat, turning down the fan.

"I thought the girl was a friend of his or another Russian's kid."

"The girl is mine," I say, giving him a pointed look. If he so much as harms a hair on her head, I'll kill him with my bare hands.

"Wow, you really got busy there, having two kids so close together in age."

"They're twins, you fucking asshole." I don't care that the kids can hear my language from the backseat. It's the truth. At least I didn't say they were *his*.

"You weren't saying that when we—"

"Shut up!" I snap at him.

"Twins, huh? Do I need to worry that the father is going to come after us?" He glances over at me as we sit in traffic, taking a long look at my left hand.

"Yes," I brazenly lie.

Is he looking for a wedding band?

I cover my hand. Not that he hasn't already seen the absence of a ring.

"Well, he certainly didn't do the honorable thing and marry you."

I shift in my seat, staring at him. He has no idea that he's the father? Can he not do the math? Or maybe he thinks that his swimmers can't produce one, let alone two kids.

It's safer if he thinks the twins aren't his, isn't it?

But would the threats against us diminish if he realized he was their father?

No, I can't tell him the truth. I don't want him in their lives. There's enough danger with Mikhail and the bratva. I don't need to add the Italian Mafia to fuck up their lives further.

"What do you want, Antonio?"

He smirks and glances at me. "You still remember my name."

His attention returns to the road as traffic begins to move at a snail's pace before picking up speed through the traffic light as we cross-traffic and veer a hard left.

"You haven't answered my question," I say. He has a way of avoiding giving me answers.

"Where's your bodyguard?" he asks and pulls over on the side of the road.

He reveals his gun, pointing it at me as it lies across his lap.

I glance at the kids in the backseat. He child-locked the doors. It won't do much good if I shout for them to run. I'd have to get out first, open their door, and hope that he doesn't shoot one of us.

"I don't know."

"Don't lie to me," Antonio says. He raises the gun slightly but keeps it out of sight of the twins. "A bratva princess never goes without her bodyguard."

I hate that he refers to me as a princess. There's nothing luxurious about having my brother run the bratva.

He stares, waiting for my answer, the gun making me uncomfortable. Not because he could hurt me, but because no one can protect the twins from him. "Mikhail called him in on an assignment."

"What assignment took precedence over you?" Antonio asks.

"He didn't say." It's not a lie. I may have overheard a few things, but I don't know where they were heading, only that it involved the Italians, which isn't a surprise.

My answer must be enough to satisfy him because he darts back into traffic.

Antonio reaches for his phone and voice dials Ardian, whoever he is.

"Be on the lookout," Antonio warns. "It's possible you have the bratva coming." The conversation is short, and he ends the call abruptly.

"Where are we heading?" I'm growing tired of his lack of answers and explanations.

"I'm the one with the gun," Antonio says, reminding me that he's in charge.

I fold my arms across my chest. "You were nicer the last time I saw you."

"When I handed over your kid?" he quips, glancing at me. "You're welcome."

I meant the beach, in St. Martin, but there's no sense in bringing that up.

"Why'd you kidnap him, anyway?" I ask. "You snatched him, let him go, and then grabbed all three of us. For an abductor, you suck."

He cracks a grin. "Do you think I like doing this? I killed Roberto. Took over the entire damn Italian organization in New York."

"Do you want congratulations?" I glare at him.

Is that what Mikhail had been blabbering about, how the Italians were in disarray, and now was the time to strike?

"Wait, you're seriously the new don?" I ask.

The idea is crazy. He was a soldier, the muscle for Roberto. At least that's what I'd assumed when we'd met. That's what he'd led me to believe. Had he lied to me?

"I'm the one asking the questions," Antonio retorts. He glances in the rearview mirror as he drives us in the opposite direction of our home. "Are the twins mine?"

7

Antonio

She's uptight, pissed, and I don't even attempt to console Aleksandra. Instead, I ask the one question that's been nagging at me since Roberto's death.

I hadn't even known there were two kids, twins. Hell, the little boy had been a surprise.

"Are the twins mine?" I glance at her out of the corner of my eye as we head for the complex. I'm bringing her home, to my fortress, where she'll be safe.

I hope to turn her and convince her to divulge anything she knows about her brother's business and his plans. But I don't suspect that she knows much. She's likely on the outside, given no responsibility from the bratva.

"No," she says a little too quickly. "You're not their father."

I bite down on my bottom lip.

"I don't believe you," I say.

"Your name isn't on the birth certificate," Aleksandra says.

I'm not surprised. I had tasked Ardian with checking, but he hadn't returned to me with any information. He's been overwhelmed with his new position. We all have taken on more responsibility.

"Semantics. That doesn't mean they're not biologically mine. There's a test for that," I remind her. Just because she insists that they're not my kin, I can find the truth out myself.

And what will I do with the results?

I pulled them from harm's way because there's a chance the boy might be mine. And now twins?

Even if they're not mine, Aleksandra and her

children don't deserve to be caught up in the war. They're innocent.

She purses her lips and glances out the side window. It's the quietest I've ever seen her, which has me rattled. The twins must be mine, or she'd push for me to run DNA tests and prove I'm not their father.

I approach the gate, and Otello opens the wrought iron, allowing us entrance inside the property. He closes the metal doors once we're inside.

"This is your home," Aleksandra says. She stares out the window, glancing up at the three-story accommodations.

"I hope you'll find it satisfactory," I say and pull into the garage. I shut off the engine and open the back door while Aleksandra steps out from the passenger side.

There's a heavy stillness in the air, and I walk up to the entrance. "Come with me," I command. I don't open the door yet. I snatch the children's backpacks, glancing through them to ensure there are no hidden weapons inside.

"I need to make sure there isn't anything you can use against my men or me."

Not that I think the twins would know how to use a knife properly, but that doesn't mean there isn't one buried away for Aleksandra.

The bags contain nothing more than their scribbles and a half dozen markers. Again, I check their plastic lunch boxes. There is no sign of a weapon.

"Do you think I gave them a knife or a gun?" she snaps.

"I'm going to have to search you," I say to Aleksandra.

She rolls her eyes and puts her arms straight out. "Get on with it."

I check her coat pockets and run my hands along her body, feeling over every curve to ensure that there isn't a weapon tucked away. Although if she had one, wouldn't she have attempted to use it on me sooner?

She's clean, except for her phone, which I snag.

"Hey!"

"Who do you plan on calling? Your brother, the bratva?" I shut off her cell phone and remove the sim card.

"Jerk," Aleksandra mutters under her breath.

Does she think that I didn't hear her?

I ignore her remark and open the door, leading her and the twins inside.

"Come with me," I say and lead them up the back stairwell to the third floor.

"Planning on locking us up in your dungeon?" Aleksandra grumbles loud enough for me to hear.

"No, that's down in the basement. I could give you a tour sometime," I say with a smirk.

The little ones follow us up the stairs, and I escort them to a bedroom with two twin beds. "There's an adjoining room through there." I point to the wooden door between the rooms and open it to allow Aleksandra a glance into her bedroom.

"Stay here," she tells the twins and shuts the door behind me, leaving the two of us in her bedroom.

A wry grin tugs at my lips. "Couldn't wait to get me alone?" I tease.

Aleksandra rolls her eyes. "What do you think you're

doing? How long do you intend on us staying with you?"

"As long as necessary," I say. "Mikhail is a dangerous man."

She scoffs at my remark. "And you're not? He's my brother. He'd never hurt the kids or me."

"No, he'd only hurt other people's children. Do you know he's involved in attacking the Breckenridge compound? He ordered the bratva to threaten Nova, a six-year-old girl, the daughter of Moreno, the Italian's second in command."

"He wouldn't do that." Aleksandra shakes her head in disbelief. "Besides, Breckenridge is on the other side of the country. The bratva doesn't control that territory."

"Don't they?" I ask. She knows that there are other bratva groups in different cities. They may not be as organized as the Italian mafia, but they are more than capable of working together, especially when wanting control over a city.

"Your brother also ordered a hit on Luca Ricci, the son of mob boss Dante Ricci."

"Enough!" She takes several strides, moving farther away, keeping her distance. "It's all lies. I don't believe you."

"Then hear it for yourself from the families and their children. They're on their way here right now," I say.

"The children are coming too?" Her breath catches in her throat.

The color drains from her cheeks as though she's seen a ghost.

"What is it?" I ask. There's an urgency in my tone, and when she doesn't answer, I step closer, invading her personal space. My hands fall to her shoulders. "Tell me what you know."

Her lips part, and a soft puff of air expels past the ruby red. "Not much. The guard who was on duty dropped me off at the preschool because he had to deal with the Italians."

"Did you hear anything else?" I need to know which caravan they intend to attack. Three planes coming from three different cities: Los Angeles, Chicago, and Breckenridge. They were all due to arrive at different times but at the same regional airport.

I release my grip on Aleksandra, but I don't give her any farther space between us. There's an urgency to the closeness. I need answers.

"No, just that Nikita, my guard, was in a hurry. I had to practically beg him to drop me off at the preschool first."

I run my fingers along my jaw. I've already contacted Ardian and warned him with what little information I had while in the vehicle. "Stay here." I head out the main entrance of her room and lock the door behind myself.

I step down the hall, secure the twins' bedroom as well, and pull out my phone. I need to find out what's going on at the pickup site.

Are my men in danger?

Can I still warn them before Nikita and the other members of the bratva show up for a fight?

With Aleksandra locked in the bedroom upstairs, I don't have to worry about her escaping or causing trouble. There's no phone in either room, and it's too high for her to escape out the window.

She's trapped.

I dial Ardian, wanting an update on his status, but there's no answer.

"Damnit!" I curse as my footsteps are heavy, coming down the stairs to the main foyer.

"Sir?" Mario says, noticing my frustration. "Is everything not up to your liking for our guests?"

Is he oblivious to the danger, or is he basking in his enjoyment of me struggling to keep my men alive?

"Ardian is in danger. I have it on good authority that Mikhail sent at least one man to attack our convoy."

Mario's brow tightens. "Surely, Ardian and the men on the plane can handle one man."

It's not that I don't think Ardian is up for the challenge. He's a great marksman and can consistently hit a target, but up against the bratva, he's inexperienced. The bratva doesn't fight fair. They're filthy and notorious for their brutality.

"I want Gian, Monte, and you to provide backup for Ardian." I hope I'm not wrong about trusting Mario. "Ardian is supposed to run the families back and forth. I want to ensure their safety. They didn't come all this way to get attacked by the bratva on our turf."

"Yes, sir," Mario says.

He hurries to gather Gian and Monte. They head to the armory to pack up the SUV before rushing out the door.

Silence fills the complex, although I'm not alone. There are dozens of men on the premises securing the facility, ensuring that no one comes in or out without expressed permission.

I grab a pen and a pad of paper. I head back up to the third floor and knock briskly as I unlock the door, allowing myself into Aleksandra's room.

She's nowhere in sight. The connected bathroom door is ajar. I trample through the bedroom and poke my head into the twins' room. She's seated at the edge of one of the beds.

"Forget something?" she asks, glancing at me.

She's calmer than I might expect. Has she come to accept that she will be staying here for a while?

"I thought you might need a few things for you and the kids," I say, handing her the pad of paper first. The pen could be used as a weapon, although I don't worry that she'll overpower me.

"How long are we going to be staying with you?" she asks.

"As long as necessary." My answer is ambiguous. "Write down what size clothes you need, and I'll have one of my men go to the store."

"What about Sophia and Liam?" she asks. "You can't lock them in here indefinitely. They have school, and they need to interact with other children."

"They have preschool," I clarify. "If they miss a few days, it's not the end of the world. There will be other kids here shortly, assuming the bratva doesn't murder them when they land."

"They wouldn't do that," Aleksandra says, although she doesn't look too convinced.

———

I leave Aleksandra and the twins locked in the upstairs bedroom. It's safest to keep them out of the way until I find out what the hell is going on.

My phone rings on my way back down the stairs.

"Ardian, what's going on?" I answer the phone. The caller ID showed his name.

"There's been an explosion at the airport."

"Where?" I ask and hold my breath. Did they hit the plane? The terminal? Something else?

"They targeted an airplane. They hit the wrong one. I'm guessing it was bad intel. Jace and Olivia's plane took off late. It probably saved their lives."

Sweat beads on my brow. "I sent a team to help you out: Mario, Gian, and Monte. If the bratva intends to take out the family, they're going to strike hard."

"Why not hit the complex?" Ardian asks. "We're bringing every top-level member of the family together. Seems like the perfect time for the bratva to attack."

"Yes, that's why I've kidnapped Aleksandra and her kids."

"Shit," Ardian gasps. "I hope you thought this plan through, boss."

8

Aleksandra

Antonio hasn't come back to visit me tonight. I'm not sure why I thought he would. He's made it clear that he's swamped, and I'm not his top priority.

Fine, but why keep us here against our will?

Antonio sends a guard to my room a few hours after I've turned over my list.

There's a rough knock, and I wait for someone to come barging in as Antonio did earlier.

"Ma'am?" a voice travels through the wooden door.

This guy has manners. I stand and head for the door with a heavy sigh, tugging at the handle.

It's unlocked.

"For you and the kids," he says, handing me four full bags of clothes. How long does Antonio plan on keeping us locked up inside his home? There's several weeks' worth of clothes in these bags.

"Is that all?" I'm mildly joking, and I don't expect anything else, except maybe an answer that I'm not likely to get from Antonio or his men.

"No, there are several more bags and a few boxes of toys downstairs," the guard says.

He doesn't so much as crack a grin.

At least the kids will be relieved to have toys, something to do. A few sheets of paper in their backpacks kept them occupied coloring for an hour. It's longer than I expected for the two of them to stay out of trouble.

I bring the bags into my bedroom and toss the contents onto the bed, sorting through everything. The sizing is correct, and I'm sure my cheeks are burning when I notice the undergarments buried in the new clothes.

They're colorful and lacy. Now, why the hell would he think I'd need matching panty sets that are sexy?

There's no way Antonio is ever seeing me naked again.

The kids' clothes fit into a separate bag that I've dumped onto my bed. I fold their clothes and stack them to carry into the adjoining room.

"I'm bored," Sophia whines as I carry her new outfits into the room.

"Me too," Liam joins in.

"Great, you can help put your clothes away inside the dresser." I open the bottom drawer and let the twins shuffle their clothes in, although they spend more time unfolding each item and admiring it before stuffing it into the drawer.

Sophia is enthralled with the bright purple sparkly sweater and colorful shirts. Liam is amazed by the T-Rex and dinosaurs on his new pajamas. Somehow, Antonio has managed to win them over.

"Ma'am," the guard calls from the other bedroom. He must be standing near the door.

I head through the adjoining door to greet him. He's carrying a huge open cardboard box with new toys filled past the top.

"Wow, you guys really overdid it," I say.

I'm not sure what to say. For a kidnapper, they're being too nice. Are they trying to win over my kids' affections?

"Don Moretti wanted the twins to be well cared for, and you as well," he says.

"Antonio?" It's strange to hear him referred to as don.

"Yes," the guard says.

"I didn't get your name," I say as I take the box from him. Perhaps if I try to win him over, he can help us get out of here.

"I didn't give it," he answers curtly. "I'll be bringing you dinner in a bit. Stay out of trouble, ma'am."

"It's Aleksandra," I say.

"I know."

He shuts the door abruptly, leaving me standing in my bedroom, a box of toys in hand. I carry the box into the kids' room, placing it on the floor for them to explore. I have half a mind to withhold the gifts. I don't want Antonio buying their affection.

But there's already so much happening, and at least a new box of toys will keep their minds off what's happening around them. I hope.

———

We're served dinner from the same guard who brought the toys and clothes to the room. He cleans up our trays when we're done, locking the door when he leaves, keeping us captive.

Why is Antonio doing this?

What does he want?

It isn't easy to sleep, and the moment the sun comes up, I'm out of bed and in the shower. There are new toiletries in the bathroom and a fresh fluffy towel hanging on a hook by the shower.

I clean up, dress, and wait for the twins to wake. I don't want to startle them. At least they're calm and quiet. Pretty soon, they're going to grow antsy, being cooped up inside the bedroom.

How long are we prisoners with the Morettis?

If Antonio is expecting Mikhail to offer up something to trade for us, he'll be sorely mistaken.

There's no television in the bedroom. There's a window at the far opposite end of the room from the door. It overlooks the courtyard, which is relatively barren this time of year.

There isn't much to do. There are no books in the room, no obvious form of entertainment. Is Antonio trying to bore me to death?

At least he had the kids' interests in mind.

They remain asleep as the sun shines through the curtains. I keep the adjoining room door slightly ajar if they need anything or stir. Besides, I want to know if someone attempts to sneak into their bedroom.

I don't trust Antonio or his men.

Why should I? They kidnapped us.

There's barely a knock at the entrance to my room, and the lock clicks. Antonio invites himself in without waiting for my permission.

It's his house. I suppose there's no privacy for me as his prisoner.

"How long are you going to keep us here against our will?" I ask, folding my arms across my chest. I stand from the bed, not trusting that he won't hurt me.

I need to protect myself and my children. At least they're asleep, and I don't hear any movement from their bedroom.

"As long as necessary," Antonio says. "When the children wake, get them dressed and let the guard know they're ready. They'll have breakfast downstairs with the other children."

He has to be mad. "You've kidnapped other kids?"

He emits an exasperated sigh and steps farther into my room.

I don't want him in here, not that I have a choice. I take a tentative step back, keeping the distance between us. I don't want him to trap me in the small space.

"You have a penchant for not listening." His gaze never wavers as he pins me with his stare. His tone is forceful. "As I mentioned before, your brother threatened the family, including *children*," he emphasizes. "They've been invited to stay under my roof until the matter is resolved."

"Resolved?" I repeat. "How do you plan on doing that?" I ask. "Mikhail will never negotiate with you. And if you think holding me here for ransom will help, you're wrong. He'd sooner sacrifice his niece, nephew, and me than give you anything."

The bratva doesn't care about the family they were born into. All that matters is their brothers, the family they've been accepted into by spilling blood.

"I'm not keeping you here as a tool, *Tesorina*. You're not being held for ransom," he says. "As I told you before, though you may not have been listening, you are here under my protection. If you were anything less than a guest in my home, do you think I'd be bringing your children toys, new clothes, and offering a warm bed to sleep in?"

I stare into his dark brown eyes. "I don't know what to think. You've held us against our will."

"Sit," he commands, backing me up toward the bed.

The power he evokes, the stance of his walk, his roughness and proximity force my feet to stumble backward.

He exudes authority, and while I don't want to do as he says, my body yields to him.

"Good, *Tesorina*."

He's pleased that I've sat on the edge of the mattress. He towers above me.

I shouldn't let him get this close. It's dangerous.

"Quit calling me that," I snap. I want to anger him. I yearn to throw him off his game, and if I upset him, maybe he'll decide we're not worth the hassle.

Will he let us go?

The corners of his lips tug upwards. "Are you not my little treasure?"

"I'm not your anything!" How dare he think he can own me and that I belong to him.

His hand reaches up, and at first instinct, I recoil, afraid he's going to smack me across the face. It's what Mikhail does when I challenge him.

Instead, his hand is strong but gentle, capturing my jaw, forcing my gaze to meet his.

I want to turn away, deprive him of his desire to make me listen, but even if I shut my eyes, I'll hear him. Do I plug my ears and sing loudly to tune him out?

"You are mine, *Tesorina*, and until you accept it, your stay will be—unpleasant."

"Is that a threat?" My top lip twitches as I stare up into his dark gaze.

He never flinches. Antonio is calm, steady, and calculated. It's like he's perfected this moment, thought about it a thousand times, and knows exactly how it will go and what will happen.

"It's a truth, one that you will come to see, eventually," he says. His grip is tight on my jaw, and his other hand grabs my hair, fisting it into a ponytail.

He has me at his mercy.

Antonio tilts my neck upwards.

Is he going to kiss me? I'm trapped, and while the thought of kissing him by force I find revolting, there's also something stimulating about his strength.

Besides, it's not as though we haven't kissed before. And from what I remember, it was hotter than a thousand suns.

But he doesn't kiss me. At least not yet.

He watches my reaction, studies my lips, and leans closer.

His breath teases me, lingers against my satin lips. "Did you know your men bombed the regional airport? They tried to kill a child, a little boy just a few years older than Liam."

His words sting like venom. "I don't believe you," I say. "Mikhail would never hurt a child."

"No?" Antonio pulls back and drops his hold from me. His legs nudge mine as he's still poised at the edge of the bed above me. "He ordered multiple kidnappings on high-level members' families and their children."

There's a heaviness that fills the room.

I don't want to believe Antonio, but Nikita had

warned me that Mikhail was acting dangerously, seeking vengeance for what happened with Liam.

"This isn't Mikhail's fault. You stole my son," I lash out at Antonio. I stand, and my fist slams into his chest as I push him away, wanting him out of my room. "You started this war!"

He grabs my wrists, but I don't ease up.

Tears burn my eyes. "You took my son! This is all your fault!"

Antonio doesn't loosen his grip as I fight him with all my force, my hands bunched into fists.

He spins me around, my back pressed tight against his body, my arms tucked against my chest, my fists just beneath my chin, and he traps me, holding my arms and me in place.

I struggle against his strength to break free.

His breath is warm as it tingles against my neck. "Are you done?" he whispers.

"Never!" I slam my foot onto his toe, but he doesn't so much as flinch.

Why should he? He's got boots on, and I'm barefoot. I attempt to spin around to knee him in the groin, but he doesn't let me move.

"Enough!" he barks.

"I don't take orders from you."

He grumbles under his breath and pushes me against the mattress before heading for the door. "Mario will be back to check on the children, as well as get a DNA sample from each of them."

"What?" He can't be serious. If he thinks there's any chance of him gaining custody, he's sorely mistaken.

"If they are my children, then you can't honestly believe I'll hand them back to the Barinovs and let the bratva raise them."

He slips out of my bedroom, slamming the door shut abruptly behind himself. The latch clicks, and I'm sure that he's locked me in.

"Mama?" Sophia's voice carries through the open adjoining door. Of course, he woke her. The way he stormed out of the room, he probably woke the entire compound.

———

After the twins are bathed and dressed, I try the door handle. It's locked.

I give a firm knock. Is there a guard standing on the opposite side of the door?

The lock clicks, and the same guard from yesterday is waiting outside the bedroom door.

"Are you Mario?" I ask.

He straightens his shoulders but doesn't answer my question. "I'll take the children down for breakfast," he says, gesturing for them to accompany him outside of their bedroom.

The children?

I don't ask. I step past the threshold, and the guard shakes his head. "Sorry, my orders were to accompany the children downstairs."

"They're not going anywhere without me!" I push the guard backward and grab Sophia and Liam by the arm, forcing them back into the bedroom.

"Mama," Liam whines. "I'm hungry."

"Me too," Sophia pleads.

"I come with you, or I force you to listen to two screaming kids who are hungry," I threaten the guard.

He grumbles under his breath. "I swear you're not worth the headache. He should have left you and the little brats behind."

"Excuse me?"

9

Antonio

Aleksandra is exhausting to be around.

I pop two ibuprofens on my way down to the office. Our guests are in the dining hall. The children are having breakfast at the main table. We've extended the leaf and added a few seats, but we don't entertain often.

There are plenty of bedrooms in the complex, but this isn't a hotel or bed-and-breakfast.

"How are you doing this morning?" Ardian asks, as he accompanies me to the office.

Is it that obvious that Aleksandra is putting me through the wringer? I exhale a sharp sigh. I'll survive. I've dealt with worse. "Any news about the Russians?" I ask, steering the conversation far from the girl upstairs and the two, possibly my, kids.

"Gian led a team of soldiers into the Russian compound before daylight," Ardian says. I ordered the attack, and I'm aware of the circumstances. I don't know if Mikhail was captured, killed, or escaped. There's been no word from my men on Mikhail's whereabouts.

"And? Any news on Mikhail?" I ask.

"Gian radioed in about an hour ago. They interrogated a half dozen Russians onsite, but no one was talking. Mikhail wasn't at the compound. We don't know where he is, and he isn't likely to return if he knows we're watching the place."

I bite down on my bottom lip, tasting the metallic zing of blood. "He can't stay away forever," I say.

I sit down at my desk, and Ardian grabs a seat opposite.

"Agreed, but he's probably in a safe house," Ardian says.

"And we have no one who can tell us the location?" I ask.

"You tell me," Ardian says, his hands folded in his lap. "You've got the girl upstairs. She probably knows best of anyone."

"I'm not interrogating the girl," I say. "And no one else is, either."

"Understood," Ardian says. "But if we don't find Mikhail and stop him, we don't know what he'll do next. If you don't mind my candor, sir, all of us in one location, it's concerning."

My gaze tightens. It's not a problem that hasn't crossed my mind. It's one of the reasons I insisted on bringing Aleksandra under my roof.

"What do you suggest we do?" I ask. We've convened so that we can stop the Russians, not give them a target to obliterate all of us in one blast easily.

"We need the location of the safe house. Mikhail is calling the shots. He's working with the other Russians, but he's the leader. If we take him out, we have a chance to stop the war," Ardian says.

"I'll get it. I need time."

"Time isn't on our side, sir," Ardian says.

———

I head out of my office and into the dining room. Sophia and Liam are seated at the table. Aleksandra has grabbed a chair against the wall and is situated by herself.

She found her way downstairs without my permission.

Against the opposite wall, are several of the dons from different cities, Dante, Alessandro, and Jace, conversing with one another. Their wives are standing near the window, Olivia, Nicole, Paige, and Karina, having a bite to eat while chatting.

Aurielo and Moreno stand together, a small plate in each of their hands as they finish the last of their breakfast.

Stepping into the room, Aleksandra stands and heads right for me.

"Are you holding all of them against their will, too?" she asks, practically biting my head off.

"They are guests in my home. These are the families that your brother, Mikhail, threatened," I say, pinning her with my stare. "Do you know anything about them trying to kidnap Nova?" I ask, pointing at the little girl with strawberry-blonde hair and the brightest baby blue eyes.

Aleksandra glances at the six-year-old.

"That girl's been through hell, and to think your brother ordered her death."

"He would never do that," she scoffs.

I grab her arm and drag her out of the dining hall, leading her to my office. I shut the door behind her, allowing us to speak freely.

"He ordered multiple hits on the children of mafia families. Mikhail is a ruthless man."

"And you're not?" Aleksandra steps closer. She doesn't appear the least bit afraid of me. If she is, she hides it well.

"I do what is required of me," I say. "I removed Roberto from his position because he was kidnapping children, selling them to families so that he could make a profit."

Her ruby lips close, and she stares at me, her eyes tight. "Why are they here? Why bring them closer to danger? If my brother is responsible, it seems unwise to have them under the same roof."

That's why she's here, as my insurance policy, so that he won't murder the entire Italian mafia. Would it be easy for him to sacrifice his sister and the kids?

"Then help me stop him," I say, closing the gap between us. My voice is calm, soft, reassuring. I'm trying to reason with her.

"Even if I could help you, why should I? You're keeping me here against my will."

"I'm keeping you and your children here to protect you, *Tesorina*."

Has she not realized the danger that returning home puts her in?

Aleksandra folds her arms across her chest. "Locking me in a room. How is that protecting me? You kidnapped my son. This is all your fault. This war that's going on, you started all of it. And now you want my help?" She laughs darkly and takes a step back. "You're on your own."

"*Tesorina*," I say, trying to reason with her.

"I'm not helping you, and I'll never help you. You're a monster." Aleksandra turns and heads out of my office.

I let her go. I don't chase her. There's no need. She can't leave, and there are other ways to get information.

If she doesn't talk, I'll use the children.

The children are all gathered in the living room near the hearth.

I've let Aleksandra accompany the twins. It's wrong to keep a mother away from her babies. And while Sophia and Liam aren't newborns, they are still her children.

The fire sizzles and crackles. I have Mario and Monte bring the toys that I purchased for the twins to share with the other children staying over.

The other dons and their close associates join me in the office.

"Tell me you have a plan. Better than sitting around and waiting for Mikhail to order his next attack," Dante says.

He's frustrated and fed up with the situation.

We all are.

"I know you're worried about your families. That's why we've come together, to stop the bratva from coming after our families and destroying our businesses," I say.

"And the Russian girl at breakfast. Who is she?" Dante asks. He has the darkest eyes I've ever seen, cold and brutal.

"She's off-limits," I warn. "A guest under my protection." I don't need the men getting any ideas about what they might do to get her to talk.

"A Russian girl under your protection?" Moreno scoffs at the notion. He's Dante's second and was extended an invitation because his daughter, Nova, was recently threatened by the bratva. "She sounds like trouble."

"She has children of her own," I say, not confiding in the men that they very well are my kin too. "And if putting her under our roof keeps Mikhail from attacking us, it's a wise decision to make."

"You kidnapped the girl?" Don Rinaldi asks.

"Alessandro, I assure you that she won't be an issue for you or your family." I don't need him up in arms or his muscle and interrogator he brought along, Aurielo, to react.

"Alessandro doesn't have family outside of the Rinaldis," Aurielo says. He folds his arms across his chest. A grimace crosses his features. "It's my son I'm worried about, Ashton. One of the bratva came at him on the playground with a knife. Threatened my boy, which is a threat to all of us."

Aurielo drops his hands and balls them into fists at his side. "I'll kill Mikhail if he's behind the ambush. Let me in a room with him, and I'll be the last thing that man ever sees."

My responsibility is to keep them calm and allow us to come together to stop the bratva. We all have a common interest and a common enemy. But we must use our brains, not brawn, to outsmart the Russians.

I hold up my hands. "Aurielo, if we kill Mikhail, there are other Russians who will take his place."

"What do you suggest? A truce?" Alessandro asks. "You're crazy if you think the Russians are willing to uphold a cease-fire."

"They will if we offer them something they want," Dante says.

"Like?" I ask, wondering what he has in mind.

"You mentioned we have a Russian girl and her children. What relation are they to Mikhail?" Dante asks.

He's too intelligent and cunning for his good. "I already told you, she's not a bargaining chip."

"You're already using her to secure our safety. Suppose we offer her back to the Russians for a truce," Dante says.

I grumble. This meeting wasn't supposed to involve a discussion on Aleksandra. "That would never work," I say.

"It's worth bringing the Russian girl in, finding out what she knows," Moreno says. "There's no way she's completely innocent. She's Russian."

As if that makes her the enemy because of her bloodline.

"That's enough! She is my guest, and those children are possibly mine," I seethe. "She is not a bargaining chip. I won't be handing her back to her brother."

There's a silence that fills the office. A few of the men exchange stares.

It was unlikely that any of them knew she was Mikhail's sister. I stand from the chair at my desk. "We'll reconvene in ten minutes." I need a break and a stiff drink.

———

"Sir." Mario steals my attention the moment I step out of the office. He was waiting for me but chose not to interrupt the meeting.

"Yes?" I ask and gesture for him to walk with me as I head down the hallway.

"You asked me to go keep an eye on the girl," Mario says.

I did ask him that, specifically when he was upstairs guarding their rooms, which he didn't do the best job, considering that she's downstairs with the children.

"And?" What's his point?

"I believe her children may know the whereabouts of the Russian boss, Mikhail," Mario says. "They were speaking about a log cabin in the forest, a special house, outside of the city."

"That doesn't exactly narrow it down," I say. "And they're four. I doubt they know how to drive to the cabin."

"You're correct, but the house has solar panels installed, and it's in Saugerties, not too far from the Hudson River."

"Narrow it down. Have Gian get a drone up there if you have to and figure out which property belongs to the Russians," I say.

"Yes, sir."

"Good work," I acknowledge, before walking past the living room. Perhaps keeping Mario around wasn't such an awful idea.

Aleksandra is situated on the floor, her back against the wall. She's reading a book that she must have found on the bookshelf. Her knees are bent, her focus on the pages. She doesn't seem to notice my presence just outside of the door.

The amber light of the fire cascades her in a soft, warm glow. She's beautiful, and the silence from her is even more delightful.

I hurry to catch up to Mario as he's headed in the opposite direction, away from my office. "Did you get DNA samples from the twins?" I ask, trying to be discreet, although it seems like everyone already knows my secret.

"I did not," he says. "I can do that now if you'd like."

There's no sense in making a scene in front of the other families. "That isn't necessary. This evening, I'd like you to make sure you do DNA swabs and send them in to be tested right away. I've already done my sample. It's in my top desk drawer."

"Do you want me to go through unofficial channels?" Mario asks.

"I want the results as quickly as possible." If that means that he needs to use a source to do it, a soldier who greases a cop, I don't care.

The twins are likely mine, based on Aleksandra's remarks, but I need confirmation. She could be playing me, thinking that I'll keep them safe if they're my kin.

10

Aleksandra

I pretend to read, seated by the fireplace. It gives me the best vantage point, with the wall to my back, to see the twins and the door.

The kids are seated on the floor, telling stories, sharing tales of their recent adventures, which happen to all be terrifying encounters with Russian men.

Mikhail is behind the threats, the fears that have been instilled in these kids. And while I'm not happy that Liam had been snatched, I'd have never wished that on anyone else.

The book doesn't hold my attention, but I keep it propped on my knees, my legs bent as I turn the page every so often. I don't want anyone to know that I'm listening in on their conversations.

I don't think the kids would care, but there are a few adults, women I don't know. Which means I can't trust them.

I catch a glimpse of Antonio by the door. I stare at the pages in the book, feeling his presence and his attention on me.

He hasn't stepped into the room or called out to me. I flip the page as I pretend to be interested in the contents.

He disappears down the hallway, and I wait a beat before standing. The twins don't seem to notice or care that I've gotten up from the floor.

I saunter to the door and head out into the hallway, curious about what is happening. Why bring all the Italian mafia families together? Are they intending on waging war with the bratva?

I'd reach out to Mikhail and warn him, but if what Antonio and the children said was true, then he's behind the vicious attacks.

Antonio rounds the corner, slamming right into me. "What are you doing, *Tesorina*?"

"Looking for the bathroom," I say, attempting to come up with a reasonable excuse. No one noticed that I'd left the room.

Am I no longer under house arrest? Or are the guards too busy to keep an eye on me?

"I'll take you there," he says, grabbing my arm. He leads me in the opposite direction, across from the living room I had just occupied with the children.

Antonio waits for me to go into the bathroom.

"Okay, I don't have to go," I say.

His eyes twinkle. "I know. You were snooping."

"I wasn't snooping," I counter. "What may have looked like snooping was mild curiosity."

"Let me guess. You want a tour."

Is he mocking me? "Are you offering to give me one?" I ask.

His jaw is tight, his lips a straight line without any hint of humor. "No," he says. "If you'd like, I can escort you upstairs to your room, or you can return to the living room with your children."

"Not much of a choice," I say and glance at the room with the kids. "Is it true?"

Antonio looks at me like a child who's stalling for bedtime. He glances at his watch. "Is what true, *Tesorina*?"

"Mikhail is responsible for traumatizing all the children in there."

He leans back against the wall, his arms across his chest. "It's a lot of power for one man to claim responsibility when he works out of New York City," Antonio says. "But yes, he has affiliated with other bratva organizations to terrorize the Italians, specifically their children."

I don't want to believe it, but with what Luka has told me, it all fits together. "Mikhail isn't at the complex," I say.

"We already know that. We hit the building early this morning, before dawn."

I gasp. "Were there any casualties?" While I'm not

fond of my brother, there are a few men I still have respect for, like Luka.

"I can't discuss that with you," Antonio says.

"Maybe they're just soldiers to you, but I grew up with those men. They're my family."

His gaze tightens as he leans closer. "We took a few men hostage, interrogated them in their own home," he says and cocks a grin. "But they're alive. Most of them."

"Most of them?" I croak.

"We kill only when it's absolutely necessary. Not for sport," Antonio says. "Do you have the address for the safe house in Saugerties?"

I stall for a moment. I'm betraying Mikhail and the bratva. If I tell Antonio, I can never go back.

He stares at me, waiting for the address.

"I'll take you there," I say.

He snorts at my suggestion. "The hell you will. You'll stay here with your children. My men don't need to babysit them."

"There are plenty of other people around to keep an eye on them," I suggest. It doesn't have to be his guards.

"The answer is no." Antonio is firm with his decision.

"Fine, then you'll have to find another way to get the address."

He grabs me by the arm and drags me across the hall, shoving me inside a room. He slams the door behind us, leaving the two of us alone.

It's a library, with built-in bookshelves towering on two walls and a window ledge turned into a cubby to read.

I don't peg him for a man who reads. Let alone in a room that feels this inviting and sunny. "This was Roberto's library?" That doesn't fit my understanding of the Italian mobster, the monster who ordered my son to be taken and sold.

"No, it was created long before Roberto became don," Antonio says. "This house, the complex, has been in the family for generations. According to Mario, this used to be a playroom. When Roberto chose not to have children, he converted it into a library. He wanted the window boarded up, and any evidence of what this room was destroyed."

"But the window is still there, so is the nook," I say, pointing out the quiet place to read.

"Mario hired contractors to redesign the room, but he always believed that the don would desire an heir."

"Why would he think that?" I ask. A man who kidnaps children for a living doesn't strike me as father material.

Antonio steps toward the window. "It's not unusual for a don to desire a child, to hand the throne onward, but Roberto never forged a relationship with anyone."

He stares out the window and has me perplexed.

Does Antonio want a relationship? Is he hoping that Liam will take the don position when he's no longer capable? That's years away, but the nagging thought still fleets through the back of my mind.

"And you're different?" I ask.

"I hope I am," Antonio says. He shifts to meet my stare. "The address for the safe house, *Tesorina*. I need it." The gruffness has returned.

Betrayal burns through me as I whisper the address to him.

He hurries out of the library, leaving me alone.

Do I mean anything to Antonio, or did he use me to get the information he wanted?

I stand there transfixed, in a daze.

What have I done?

Did I contribute to Mikhail's execution?

Antonio isn't going to be kind or warm to my brother. He's a mafia don. I can't expect him to show up, ring the doorbell, and ask to talk like men.

I rush out of the library. If I warn Mikhail, then Antonio is as good as dead. But if I remain silent, my brother will be tortured, or worse, murdered.

There are no winners, and I've handed Antonio the treasure map to find my brother.

I have to do something, and sneaking into the back of his vehicle isn't going to work this time. Perhaps I can call Mikhail, suggest that he surrender before the war escalates and everyone dies.

The bratva doesn't surrender. I don't imagine that the mafia does, either, which puts me in a predicament.

Blood is blood. Mikhail might be a monster, but he's the monster I know, the one I'm most familiar with, and he's not keeping me against my will.

I should never have told Antonio where Mikhail is hiding.

Antonio is nowhere to be found. There's a rush of commotion at the opposite end of the hallway. I sneak into a nearby room and search for a phone.

There's no sign of a landline.

Do they only use cell phones on the property? Antonio snatched mine when he brought me here.

I sneak from one room to the next. Again, no sign of a landline. I can't leave, and even if I could manage to escape, my children would have to come with me.

Maybe I can steal one of the guards' phones without them noticing?

"Aleksandra, what are you doing in here?" Mario asks. His eyes narrow as he glances me over, his gaze examining my empty hands.

I haven't stolen anything. Is that what he is worried about?

"Minding my own business," I say. "Why do you have a fondness for following me around? Is there any place for me to go? There are dozens of guards and a state-of-the-art security system, by the looks of it. Even if I wanted to leave, I doubt I could get out."

There's no sense in telling him the truth. He isn't likely to hand over his cell phone, and if he's distracted, maybe I can slip his cellphone from his pocket. I step closer; if I'm going to snatch his phone, I can't do it from the opposite end of the room.

"It would be best if you'd return to your room upstairs," Mario says.

Now is my chance. My bottom lip juts out in a pout as I stalk across the room, closing the distance between us. Intentionally, I knock into him with my elbow, distracting him while I snatch his phone.

Mario grabs my wrist and spins me around, his phone in my hand.

"I'll be taking that," he says and releases his tight grasp on my wrist, only long enough to grip my arm and drag me out into the hallway. "I have half a mind to toss you into the dungeon."

I ignore Mario's threats.

At the opposite end of the hall, is Antonio. I need to get his attention. "Antonio, wait!" I call after him.

He spins around, hearing my voice, and tells the gentleman he's with to hold on a moment. Antonio closes the distance between us. "What's going on?" he asks, glancing at Mario for an explanation.

"I found her sneaking around the complex. She tried to steal my phone, sir."

"And why would you want Mario's phone?" Antonio's gaze latches onto mine.

I swallow nervously. Mario's grip remains strong against my arm. He hasn't lightened up his hold, even with Antonio standing just inches away from me.

"I need to call the twins' preschool if they're not going to be attending classes today," I say, hoping that I've bought my way out of this unpleasantness with a lie.

Antonio doesn't move from his position. "Nice try. You were going to warn Mikhail that we're coming, weren't you?"

He can see right through me, and it scares me. "Please, don't hurt my brother."

"Lock her upstairs," Antonio orders.

"What about the twins, sir?" Mario asks. "What would you like me to do about them?"

"They can stay downstairs with the other children, so long as they're keeping out of trouble and are not doing Aleksandra's bidding. The minute you see them trying to lift a cell phone or sneak out of the room, you send them upstairs with her at once."

My children have no idea what's going on. They're young and innocent, and I intend to keep it that way.

But it worries me, leaving them alone, unattended with the other mafia players. Whether they're dons, wives, or children, I'm not too fond of the thought that I can't watch over my kids.

Mario drags me up the stairs, escorting me to the third floor, leaving Sophia and Liam in the living room with the other children, oblivious to what's happening around them.

"Please, I want to be with my children," I beg Mario.

He rolls his eyes and unlocks the door to my bedroom on the third floor. "Get in," he orders. "If you behave, Antonio might let you out when he returns."

11

Antonio

My men head to the armory and load the vehicles with enough assault rifles and weapons that we are well prepared.

Mario returns from locking Aleksandra upstairs.

"It's done," he says. "Where would you like me, sir?"

"Keep an eye on the children. I don't want any trouble from them. If the twins take after their mother, they might go snooping, looking for secrets." While I doubt it's likely that the four-year-olds would get into much, except perhaps making a mess, I also won't take any chances.

"Sir," Nikki steps out from the living room with the children. She's Dante's wife, Luca's mother, and from the stories I've heard, quite fiery and fierce. She's been through quite a lot early on, when Dante and she met.

I respect her, not something I can say about everyone.

"Yes, Nikki. What can I do for you?" I glance at my watch. My men will be ready to head out any moment.

"I'd like to arrange a meeting with the Russian girl, Aleksandra. We have quite a bit in common, and I think I might be able to help."

"Who says I need help?" I stare Nikki down, awaiting her answer.

"No one said anything, sir. But it's obvious she's upset, and locking her upstairs is only going to infuriate her further."

Had she overheard the conversation about sending Aleksandra upstairs? I hadn't intended to make it common knowledge throughout the complex that we're not necessarily on the same side.

I hate that Nikki is right. "Go on," I snarl. I don't like being wrong, and it's worse when someone else points it out.

"I've been in her shoes, the daughter of an opposing mafia family, and while her family is Russian and not Italian, I can relate to what she's going through."

"And what do you think talking to her will accomplish?" I don't doubt that they share a common situation, but Aleksandra is strong-willed and isn't going to bow down to my authority or listen to some girl tell stories about her past.

"For starters, it might invoke trust. sir. While I want Mikhail dead as much as the rest of us, killing him doesn't solve the fact that he's already conspired with other bratva organizations across the country. She might be a valuable resource if we turn her."

"And you think you have the ability to turn her against the bratva?"

"Out of everyone here, I have the most experience with being estranged from family," Nikki says. "What do you have to lose?"

My pride, for starters, but no one needs to know.

And she's right. If I need Aleksandra's help, she won't give it to me until I've gotten through to her.

"Keep it between us. You have until I return," I say, glancing at my watch.

————

"You should stay here," Ardian says as he grabs the key from the hook. "I know you want to be on the front lines and take out Mikhail, but you're no good to the mafia dead."

"I don't plan on dying," I say without a hint of amusement. "Are you questioning my ability as a soldier? I'll have you know my life's blood and sweat have been on the streets."

"I don't mean any offense." Ardian is quick to backtrack. It's not wise to piss off a don. "The leaders are all here to converse with you and draw up a plan to end the war that Mikhail started."

"Roberto started it," I admit to Ardian. It's not a discussion that I'd have with just anyone, but he's my best man, my most trusted ally, and my advisor. "Stealing kids, running The Cradle, this is all his fault."

"Not to mention that we stole that boy, Liam, from the Barinovs," Ardian says. "I get it. You're trying to atone for your sins."

I raise an eyebrow. "I never said that."

"Bringing the girl under your roof. You're either protecting her or in love with her. Maybe a little of both," Ardian says.

The nerve of him! "Don't get yourself killed today," I retort. I'm not in the mood to discuss Aleksandra with anyone. It was bad enough Nikki had the audacity to come to me with her suggestion, but now I've got Ardian adding his input. He's lucky I don't put a bullet in him to shut him up.

"I'll do my best not to, boss." Ardian grins and gives a wave as he heads toward the SUV.

I order my men to head out, taking six vehicles as the soldiers prepare to infiltrate the Russian safe house.

While I want to lead the pack into war, Ardian is right. The other dons have come to New York to end this tyranny, not join our forces to fight. Leaving them to stop Mikhail isn't the best use of my time as boss.

"You're not leaving, sir?" Mario asks as he brushes past me with Nikki at his side.

"I've got other matters to tend to. Take Nikki upstairs, but don't tell Aleksandra I'm here."

"Yes, sir," Mario says. "Come with me." He escorts Nikki up the stairwell and out of sight.

I pinch the bridge of my nose. Why have I let Aleksandra creep into my heart? She is just a girl I shared a wild night with nearly five years ago.

"Oh, and Mario," I shout at him as he hits the top of the landing, where I can no longer see him.

He retreats two stairs down so that I have his attention. "Yes, sir?" He obeys orders well. Is that why Roberto liked having him around?

"Get that test we discussed done ASAP."

"Of course, sir."

I need to know whether the twins are, in fact, mine. The sooner I have the answer, the easier it will be to decide about Aleksandra.

12

Aleksandra

There's a soft rap that echoes against the wooden door.

I don't respond, but it doesn't matter. The door clicks and is opened by one of the young women from downstairs.

"Can I help you?" I ask tersely. It's not like she got lost on her way to her room and ended up in the wrong suite. The door was locked from the outside by one of the guards.

Besides, I haven't heard a sound from the nearby rooms on the third floor. The other guests are probably being kept on a different floor.

"I'm Nikki," the young woman says, introducing herself. Her long black hair and deep-set amber eyes are striking. She's a bit older than I am, though probably not by much.

"Aleksandra," I say, although she likely already knows my name. I'd imagine I'm the talk of the town. Well, downstairs anyway.

It's not every day that a Russian associates with an Italian.

"Do you mind if I come in?" Nikki asks. Her hands are clasped in front of her. She's wearing a black pair of leggings and a dark maroon sweater that goes down to her knees. It's oversized and looks relatively warm and comfy.

"Knock yourself out," I say and gesture for her to come in.

Do I even have a choice?

What does she want?

She strides across the room like she owns the place and leans against the edge of the windowsill.

"Did Antonio send you up here?" I ask. It would make sense to try to get information out of me. I'm not looking to make friends while I'm here. It's not like I want to be here, cooped up in this room, locked in the Italian compound.

"He gave me permission to come and visit you, but it wasn't his idea for me to come upstairs," Nikki says.

She appears genuine, but I've just met the woman. Earlier, she was downstairs with the other guests, but I had done well to keep to myself and avoid an uncomfortable conversation. Which it seems I'm now going to have to endure.

"Plan on telling me I'm a horrible person for consorting with the Russians?" I'm anticipating a fight. The girl didn't come up here to mingle and make friends. She has plenty of that downstairs.

"They're your family," Nikki says. "No one can fault you for the family you were born into."

Why do I get the distinct feeling that she does fault me for consorting with the Russians? Even though they are my family, I choose to be with them instead of what—on my own?

"What would you know about that?" I glance her over. "You're married to a don. Am I right?" I don't have to know who she is to see the power she exudes. While I can't remember her husband's name, I'd recognize him after witnessing the two of them chatting earlier.

Does she think I'm a threat now that I know all the Italian families?

If I wanted to betray them, return to the Russians, I'd have information on the dons, their spouses, children, and close associates.

But I'm not out for blood.

I want my kids safe and to return home.

"Dante didn't always love me. When we met, we were enemies from two different feuding mafia families," Nikki says. She pushes herself off the windowsill and paces the length of the room from the locked door to the window on the opposite side.

I roll my lips together, silent. I let her speak.

"I left my family, chose Dante over my blood, because he had my best interests at heart. My father was a monster, threw me into his trafficking operation and was willing to sell me to his enemy, to get me off his hands."

"My brother isn't like that."

Nikki stops pacing. Her gaze locks on mine. "Good, because I wouldn't wish that on anyone, even my worst enemy," she says.

Is that what we are, enemies? I wouldn't consider us friends or even acquaintances, but I've just met the woman, and I don't have any issues with her. She isn't the one keeping me here against my will.

"Thanks?" I'm not sure what she's looking for, why she came up to speak with me and tell me about her family.

"I haven't known Antonio for very long," Nikki says as her gaze meets mine. "But if he brought you here, he's protecting you."

She's crazy if she buys into the fact that Antonio is a hero. He's a monster, ripping my children and me away from our home.

I refuse to give her any indication of what I'm feeling. I don't trust her. "What makes you say that?" I ask.

"Men like Antonio, they don't bring pretty ladies into

their homes with their children, unless they're saving their lives."

"He snatched us at gunpoint. That doesn't seem very chivalrous to me," I say.

Did Antonio leave that tidbit out when explaining who I was and how I wound up under his roof?

She stands in front of me, a few feet away, giving me plenty of personal space. Nikki isn't forceful or overbearing, which I appreciate.

"And Dante bought me at a marriage auction," Nikki says. "I didn't exactly see eye-to-eye with him. For the longest time, I thought of him as my captor."

"Sounds like he is your captor to me," I mutter.

"He's not," Nikki says, her gaze narrowing. "We might not be equals concerning the mafia. I certainly don't run the mafia, and I wouldn't want to, but he's a good man. He treats me right, protects our son Luca, and is a wonderful father. It might be difficult to imagine the don of the family being a doting father, but he's a good man. And I suspect if you let Antonio into your life, you'll find he isn't so different."

"Antonio kidnapped us," I snap.

Why does she think I'll forgive and forget what he did?

"Besides, I'm not looking for a father for my twins and certainly not one who is the mafia boss," I say.

There's no reason to elaborate that he is their biological parent. If she hasn't heard the rumors, I don't want to give her any extra information.

Nikki offers a tight-lipped smile. She doesn't argue with me. Instead, she heads for the door and gives a firm knock, indicating to the guard that she is done speaking with me.

"Think about what I said," Nikki says, glancing back at me. "Consider what is best for your kids."

"That's what I'm doing."

Doesn't she realize all I want is to protect them from danger? How does that protect them by bringing them here, under Antonio's roof, with dangerous men brandishing weapons?

The guard opens the door, and Nikki steps out into the hallway, shutting the door behind herself. I contemplate charging through the open door, pushing past her, and breaking out of the bedroom.

But how far would I get? My kids are downstairs, and the last thing I want is to put them in danger.

———

I sit alone in my bedroom. There's no sign of the twins, and no one else comes to visit except the guard, to deliver a tray of food into my room for lunch.

"Where is Antonio?" I ask.

"He's busy," Mario says, not answering my question as he places the silver tray with food on a small table in the bedroom.

"I want to see him."

"Eat your lunch," Mario says. "I'll be back to retrieve the tray in an hour."

He shuts and locks the door. I'm alone with only my thoughts. Maybe I should be grateful that he's keeping me in warm and comfortable quarters. I have a bed, a bathroom, and a separate room for my children.

My brother wouldn't nearly be as generous to a hostage. They'd be thrown into a prison cell.

I've seen Mikhail's atrocities on several men who have betrayed him. And what I haven't witnessed firsthand, I've seen the remnants of body parts that littered the prison basement.

Antonio hasn't threatened the children. And while he's taken us against our will, he hasn't physically harmed any one of us.

That doesn't make me grateful to him. He's still a monster, but maybe he's less awful than my brother, which doesn't say much.

I finish the sandwich on the tray and am surprised when Antonio comes into the room.

"*Tesorina*," he says, glancing me over.

My heart quickens at his presence.

"I want my children," I say, standing from the edge of the bed. I step closer to him, unafraid.

"Our children," he says, correcting me.

I pinch my lips together. "I need to see them." I don't answer his remark.

"And you will when I know you won't do something stupid, *Tesorina*," Antonio says. He steps closer, closing the distance between us.

"Quit calling me that," I snap.

Why does he think he can bestow a pet name on me? I'm not his anything.

A smirk crosses his features, pleased with my outburst.

Why does this delight him? Is it that he's found a way to bother me? Am I better pretending that I don't care and let him call me whatever he wants?

He guides his hand up to my cheek, and his thumb brushes a strand of hair behind my ear. He's gentle and attentive.

I smack his hand away.

"Get your grimy paws off me."

His eyes crinkle as the corners of his lips turn upwards in a smile. "I require your assistance," Antonio says.

I take a step back, needing space, and fold my arms across my chest. "And why would I ever help you?" I glance at the silver tray on a nearby table. Could I use it as a weapon, knocking him unconscious, and then take him as a hostage with his gun?

He doesn't so much as glance behind him. "Don't even think about it."

"What?" I ask innocently. He couldn't know what I'm thinking.

"Hitting me over the head with that tray," he says. "Don't even think about it."

Well, he isn't wrong on the first part of my plan. I bolt around him for the tray. It's the only feasible weapon I can use.

Antonio grabs my wrist and spins me around, pinning his body against mine, restraining me. "Something tells me you like this position, *Tesorina*," he whispers into my ear.

"I don't like anything about you," I mutter.

"That's not what you were moaning in the shower."

I stomp on his toe and spin around to face him, slamming my knee up into his groin. "That was a long time ago." I reach for his gun attached to his belt. It's my only chance out of this hellhole.

He groans in pain and releases his grip on me, pushing me away, knocking me backward onto the bed. The gun remains holstered. He's stronger than I am and quicker.

"The guard isn't going to just let you go," Antonio says and straightens up. Any residual pain from my assault is hidden from me. "And do you honestly think I would let you get ahold of my gun?"

He towers from above, and I scramble backward to keep from being trapped. I bolt off the side of the mattress for the locked door.

"How far do you think you can get?" he asks. "The door is locked. My men aren't going to let you parade through the complex to retrieve my children and send you on your merry way."

"They're not your children."

"We'll see," Antonio says. "I had Mario send in DNA tests. You're not leaving until the results come in."

I don't dare ask how long that will take or what will happen when he finds out he is their biological father.

"Is that why you kidnapped us? Because you want to be a father?" It seems far-fetched even for Antonio.

"As I told you before, I brought you here to protect you." Antonio grows more annoyed with my questions. "Would you rather I hand you over to your brother and let you share a cell in the basement together?"

My stomach drops at his admission. "You have Mikhail here?"

"It's why I came up to your room," Antonio says. "I was going to ask you to talk to him, but maybe I should put you both in lockup together. Does he know that I'm the twins' father?"

"You're not their father," I say. Even biologically related, that doesn't make him their father. He's not in their life, and I don't expect him to be around as they grow up.

Antonio grabs my arm. He's forceful as he drags me across the room.

"Where are you taking me?" I try to break free, but he's too strong. I use my other hand to attempt to reach across him for his gun, but he slams my back up against the wooden door and forces my hands above my head.

"*Tesorina*," he whispers into my ear.

His proximity forces my body to shiver. I pray he doesn't notice my reaction.

"I know you want me," he breathes into my ear, pinning me against the door. His body is tight with mine, and it's not his weapon I feel against my crotch.

"Seems you want me too," I say, forcing my eyes to meet his as he pulls back just slightly to stare into my gaze.

Is he going to kiss me?

His breath mixes with mine, teasing me. His proximity excites me, and as much as he's a monster, he hasn't hurt me. Antonio hasn't forced me to do anything yet.

"If I wanted you, I'd have had you," he says. "Do you think I can't get any girl I want, or whom I desire?"

"I'm not yours to have," I say and rock hard against him, attempting to break free. All that happens is his hold on me tightens against my wrists, and his body is pressed harder against mine.

"Your body isn't saying that, *Tesorina*," Antonio says with a smirk.

13

Antonio

I have Aleksandra pinned between her bedroom door and me. It's like a fierce inferno blazing a thousand degrees, and I'm the only one capable of putting out the fire.

Do I want to put it out?

No, but I'm not about to burn alive, either.

"Get off me," she snarls at me.

"Do you promise to stop chasing after my gun?" I don't need her getting ahold of my weapon and using it on me or any of my guards or guests.

She snorts.

I guess that's a no.

"Promise me that you'll behave, and I'll walk you down to see your brother."

Her blue eyes are dark and intense. Her cheeks are a similar shade to her ruby lips as she expels a soft puff of air. "Fine."

I'm not sure I believe her, but I take her words at face value. I relinquish my grip on her wrists and take a step back, ensuring my weapon is out of her reach.

"Next time you decide to get feisty, I may have to get the handcuffs," I threaten.

Her eyes widen, and I can't tell if she's excited about the prospect of being restrained or horrified.

I knock promptly on the door. "I'm done," I say to Mario and wait for him to unlock the door and let me out of the room.

Mario opens the door, and I step out first, escorting Aleksandra to accompany me downstairs. I grab her forcefully by the arm, not letting her far from my grasp.

"Can I see Sophia and Liam?" she asks as I lead her down the hallway to the stairwell.

"After the visit with your brother," I say. If I give her what she wants now, I'm unlikely to earn her cooperation.

She's silent, which I can only ascertain is her agreement. We head down to the main floor and wind through the hallway until we reach another locked door. I relinquish my grip from around her arm, retrieve the key from my keyring, and slide it into the door, giving it a forceful shove.

Aleksandra is right behind me. I can feel her presence on my heel. "You first," I say as I open the door and gesture for her to walk down the basement stairs first.

"Now you're being chivalrous?"

She steps down the stairs, one at a time. The basement takes a moment, with the dim lighting, for our eyes to fully adjust.

Mikhail is in a nearby prison cell, alone. We didn't capture any of his men. He was the only one at the safe house. We left after getting everything we wanted out of the men we had interrogated.

Otello guards the prison. He's situated a few feet from the cell, keeping an eye on the prisoner.

"Give us a few minutes," I say to Otello.

"Sure thing, boss," Otello says. He heads up the stairs for a break.

Why had Mikhail been the only man at the safe house? Had his guards fled? Why had they left him behind?

"Mikhail?" her voice cracks as she approaches the prison cell.

He stands on the opposite side, coming forward toward the door. "You're working with *him*?" Mikhail's dark eyes widen as he takes a step backward. He runs a hand through his dark hair. "I trusted you, sister, and you betrayed me."

I step closer, standing beside Aleksandra.

"Call off your men and the other bratva leaders, Mikhail, to end the tyranny on the Italians."

His dark eyes shine under the overhead lamplight. "I'd sooner die than help your men," Mikhail says. He stares at Aleksandra, and his top lip snarls as he glances her up and down. "Traitor."

She folds her arms across her chest. "I'm not

working with *him*," she says, pointing at me. "I'm a prisoner too."

"Right." Mikhail rolls his eyes. "You seem like quite the prisoner. Where is he letting you stay, his bedroom?"

"How dare you!" Aleksandra turns to face me. "Let me in there. I'll kill him for you."

While I don't think she means it, she's undoubtedly feisty enough to try, but I'm not about to watch her spat with her older brother.

"That's not going to happen," I say. She can't really want me to let her into his cell. It has to be a trick so that she can aid in his escape. I wouldn't put the idea past her. She's already tried to steal my gun.

Mikhail takes a step back, and he doesn't appear the least bit unsettled. He laughs under his breath and shakes his head. "I never expected a Barinov to fuck a Moretti. You're no longer one of us, little sister."

"What?" Her voice catches in her throat, and I swear there's a tear glistening in her eyes. "I'm not—we're not together," Aleksandra says.

"You're just on the other side of the prison cell to convince me to talk?" Mikhail asks with a laugh. "You're dead to me, Aleksandra. Enjoy playing house with your new family. And if you decide to return to the compound, I can promise you that those little brats won't see the light of day."

She turns to run up the stairs, and I consider stopping her, but instead, I let her go.

"Do you enjoy tormenting women and children?" I ask as I approach the prison cell. I don't open the wrought iron doors. If I did, I might kill him with my bare hands.

Mikhail stretches his arms and interlocks his fingers behind his head. A moment later, his arms drop to the side. "It beats being cooped up in a prison cell. When I get out, Antonio, you can count on me coming after your entire organization."

"You've already come after us. Why do you think you're locked in our prison?"

"For sport?" Mikhail chuckles and plops down onto the floor. There's no cot and no bed.

I don't trust that he wouldn't hang himself with bedsheets if given the opportunity. And while the idea is tempting, Mikhail dead doesn't help the situation.

I haven't heard any indication that they intend to retaliate, but the longer he stays in our prison, the higher chance of the bratva invading our home. And keeping Aleksandra on the premises isn't going to save us in the slightest.

I leave Mikhail. There are enough mafia dons and interrogators under our roof to handle one man.

I find Aleksandra at the top of the steps, heading up the stairs, the door shut. I don't say anything, not wanting her brother to overhear us. I open the door and let her step out onto the main floor. I lock the door behind us. Not that Mikhail is capable of escaping, but just in case, it's an extra level of security.

"Antonio," Aleksandra's voice is soft and fragile. Her eyes are crinkled, and she's holding back her sobs, at least outwardly.

I pull her against the wall, out of earshot of my men, for a bit of privacy.

Otello stands outside the entrance to the prison in the main hall, chatting with Mario. "Catch you later," Otello says to Mario as he gives me a nod and hurries down to the prison cellar to watch Mikhail.

His job is to make sure nothing happens to the prisoner unless I order. I'll send Aurielo, one of the mafia's finest interrogators, whom Alessandro brought with him, and let my interrogator, Jacopo, accompany him.

Between the two men, I anticipate swift results.

"You're safe here. None of my men will lay a finger on you or your children." Is that what she's worried about? I try to quell her nerves, but I worry it's something I can't quickly fix.

She rolls her lips together and glances away, her gaze far and distant. "Please, don't hurt Mikhail. I know he's a bastard, but he's my brother." Her voice cracks as she finally catches my stare. Our gaze locks on each other.

"I assure you that I won't lay a finger on him."

I won't promise that my men won't torture him to get him to talk.

Her brow is knitted, and her bottom lip trembles.

"You have my word that he will be treated far kindlier than any man the bratva detains," I say.

"That's not reassuring," she whispers. "They'd skin a man alive to get information out of him."

While we have other methods, I don't deny that our interrogators can be brutal. "If he answers our interrogators' questions honestly and divulges information, then he has nothing to worry about."

"He won't talk," Aleksandra says. "He's too proud to betray the bratva. He'd sooner die."

I disagree. We've had men divulge secrets when held against their will, threatened and tortured. And while he might not care about his own life, he would be devastated if we destroyed the entire bratva organization, his legacy.

"Don't worry about Mikhail," I assure her.

I escort her across the hall to my office so that I may have a moment alone with Aurielo and Jacopo. My hand is on the small of her back as I usher her inside, flipping the light on after I open the door.

"Planning on locking me in here?"

"No, I just need to have a moment alone with my men."

"Can I see my children?" Aleksandra asks.

"I'll bring them to you. Just wait here." I gesture for her to stay put while I head to the living room. The twins are seated with the other children. "Sophia, Liam, do you want to see your mom?"

They jump up from the floor and follow me, bouncing in the hallway, down the corridor to my office.

I open the door, ushering them inside and shutting it before I head back down to find a team that can interrogate Mikhail successfully.

While I can do the deed, I don't want his blood on my hands. Not with Aleksandra under the same roof.

———

"She hasn't tried to leave, sir," Mario says as I approach the office.

I decided it wasn't necessary to lock her in

physically. The door is shut, and a guard is standing outside the door.

She isn't going far, and with two noisy kids, she isn't going to get by without being seen.

"Good," I say.

"Any news about downstairs?" Mario asks, remarking about the prisoner.

"My men are on it." I won't elaborate. There isn't anything specific to tell until the interrogation is complete, and I'm not sure Mario is a man I'd confide in, either.

While I trust him standing guard in front of a door, he's not someone I'd divulge our secrets to. At least not yet.

I open the door to my office and stand at the entrance, stunned by the amount of chaos from only a short time.

"I wasn't sure how long you were planning on keeping me in your office," Aleksandra says.

"Well, it didn't take long for you to let your children run through here like two little tornadoes," I quip.

The kids have gotten into practically everything that wasn't locked up in the desk. Papers are skewed over the floor; paperclips are tossed freely; pens are stacked like a woodblock tower.

Did Aleksandra permit them to make a mess of my office?

"I prefer to think of them like a hurricane," Aleksandra says with a sly grin.

"Do you think this is funny?" I glance at my watch. "Fifteen minutes. That's how long I was gone."

"I know," she says with a smirk. "Do you think they did all this? Next time, you won't keep my children from me."

She's giving me a headache. I rub my forehead and glance down at the two children attempting to dismount the pens to make a racetrack for their paperclip vehicles.

I should punish her, but what good would it do? She already has it in her mind that I've kidnapped her. And I can't let her go, not if the kids are mine. I'd never see them again if it were up to her.

"Would you prefer to keep company with your brother downstairs?" I threaten.

The twins have no idea what I'm talking about, but the color drains right out of Aleksandra's face. "You wouldn't do that," she says.

"I don't do that with guests, but you seem hell-bent on believing that I'm not keeping you as a guest. If the accommodations aren't to your liking, then I can have you moved downstairs."

"Please don't do that," she rasps. She doesn't beg, but I'm sure it would come to that if I dragged her down the basement steps.

I gesture for her to step out of the office for a moment. I don't want Sophia or Liam to overhear our conversation.

She stands from behind the desk and comes around to the door, accompanying me out into the hallway.

"Sir," Mario says.

"Give us a moment," I say, and he heads across the hall but close enough that should I need to call him back, he's ready at a moment's notice.

"Tell me, where would you go if I let you leave?" Her brother has made it clear that she's no longer welcome with the bratva.

"Home."

She's foolish to think she can return, and there are no consequences. "Your brother may be imprisoned, but the guards we interrogated won't take kindly to your betrayal."

"How did I betray them?" she asks.

"You've been staying as a guest at my residence. Don't you think they won't take kindly to your disloyalty?"

Does she not realize they'll disavow her as Pakhan's sister? The bratva isn't a forgiving group of men.

"Coming here wasn't my choice," she says and points at my chest, poking me. "You forced me to come here. You've held me against my will."

"That's not what your brother believes. As he said, you're not imprisoned."

She drops her hands and folds them across her chest. "Doesn't mean I'm not being held against my will."

"If you want to go, then leave," I say. We have her brother. It's what we wanted and one of the reasons I required her to come with me.

"Fine," she brushes past me and heads for my office.

I shove my hand against the door, refusing to let her open it. "You can leave, but the children remain under my roof until the DNA tests come back."

"What? Antonio, no."

I'm as sure as the sunrise. "They're my children."

Her eyes glisten. "Please, don't do this," she begs me to let her leave with the twins. "You can't separate them from their mother."

"I wouldn't dream of it," I say. "You are welcome to stay, but the twins aren't going anywhere until their DNA tests come back."

"And then what?" she whispers. "What happens if you're their father?" Her cheeks are rosy, her eyes glassy. She's at the edge of her breaking point.

"I'll want custody," I say. "I can't very well let them leave. The bratva will be after them. As soon as your brother realizes they're my children, he'll use them to hurt me."

"He wouldn't do that," she whispers. "Mikhail wouldn't hurt the kids. Everything he's done has been because my son, Liam, was kidnapped by the Italian mafia."

She can't believe that everything that's happened can be forgiven. "And now, the threats he makes?" I ask. "Do you believe they're empty? That you can return home, and he will let you live with him at his compound?"

She's silent, and her back is pressed up against the door. "I don't believe he'll let us return home."

Aleksandra isn't foolish enough to lie to me.

"I'll have to find someplace new and safe. But he won't hurt me if I leave you. He does not need to protect me."

I don't think it's as easy for Aleksandra as she makes it out to be. "Mikhail is out for blood and revenge. The minute he discovers the twins are mine, it's leverage for him to hurt me. He doesn't care who gets in the way of his dirty plans."

There's an internal struggle, like a fog that settles over her eyes as she squints and struggles with the right choice and what to do.

"Please, you can't keep me locked up here."

"I wouldn't dream of it if you can keep yourself in line," I warn her. "I won't be made a mockery of in front of my guests. Is that understood?"

Her gaze falls to my lips, staring at them for a long moment. "Yes," she whispers, glancing up into my eyes. "I won't disappoint you."

"Good." I take a step back, letting her retreat into my office.

She opens the door, and the kids are doodling on my desk with the permanent marker that they found.

Wonderful.

"How about you three clean up this mess, and then you can join everyone in the living room?"

I leave the door open and gesture Mario over.

"Keep an eye on them. They need to clean up the office, and when they're finished, they can join the other guests," I say.

Mario peers into the office, his eyes widening at the sight in front of him. "Yes, sir."

———

I've made a promise to Aleksandra that I wouldn't personally harm Mikhail. But my interrogators will do what is asked of me, and I expect to have information that we can use against the bratva.

With Aleksandra and the twins in my office, I hurry across the hall and back down the locked stairwell to the prison.

Otello leans against the concrete wall facing the prison cell with Mikhail inside.

Mikhail's hands are bound behind him, and he's seated on a wooden chair.

Across from him, Jacopo and Aurielo have laid out several instruments for torture on a nearby folding table that they've brought into the prison cell.

Jacopo holds a blow torch, fire blazing as he threatens Mikhail. The bratva leader's face is bloodied, his eye blackened. Numerous bruises are covering his skin, and they've only just begun.

"You can end this, Mikhail," I say as I approach the prison cell.

Otello unlocks the gate, letting me inside.

"All we need is your cooperation to end this war."

"A war that you started," Mikhail says with a snarl. "This is your fault, Antonio! You stole my nephew."

"Roberto ordered the abduction of your nephew, and in case you haven't noticed, he's not calling the shots anymore. He's dead."

"Does my sister know that you're a cold-blooded killer?" Mikhail smirks, and there's a smear of blood on his teeth from his gashed lip.

"I don't think she cares, considering it runs in your family. Tell us how to stop the attacks on the other mafia families. If you want a war, you have it with me. Leave the children out of it."

Mikhail's eyes are icy. "We intend to slaughter your sons and daughters. Every one of them. And if I don't report to my men within the hour, the bloodshed will escalate."

14

Aleksandra

Two days later...

I pull Antonio aside after breakfast. He's been busy entertaining the other mafia families, which has spared me from dealing with him too many times over the last forty-eight hours.

The twins have been with me in the living room during the day and the bedroom in the evening. Thankfully, Antonio hasn't separated us again.

We have meals with the other guests, and Sophia and Liam seem to get along with the other children. Me, I keep to myself. Nikki has been polite, offering a warm smile, but I can't help but wonder if she's trying to get information for the mafia.

"Yes?" Antonio asks as I grab his arm and lead him just outside the commotion with the other families.

The guards breeze past as they clean up the dishes from breakfast, ignoring the conversation between the two of us. Although I don't feel like there's any privacy, I don't want to be away from my children, either.

"I want to see Mikhail," I say.

Antonio's gaze meets mine. "That isn't a good idea, *Tesorina*." He brushes a strand of hair behind my ear. The gesture is intimate, and I should push his hand away, but I don't.

"Why not? Why can't I see my brother?"

He's been in their custody for just over two days. What have they done to him?

"You wouldn't like what you'd see," he says.

I shouldn't be surprised, but it's a punch to the gut. "Because you've tortured him?" Mikhail can be an asshole at times, but I wouldn't wish anything bad on him.

"I kept my promise, *Tesorina*. My hands are clean," Antonio says.

"Ordering a man to be tortured isn't keeping your hands clean," I retort. I'm not blind to the fact that he has interrogators downstairs, causing Mikhail to suffer. The bratva would be doing the same if we were under their roof.

"Precisely why you don't need to see Mikhail," Antonio says. "Go, enjoy the company of your children and our guests. They will be returning home soon."

"And me? When might I be allowed to return home?"

I don't care about when his guests leave. They're not prisoners. And while he's been generous with letting me roam his estate, I'm still held captive. Just because I have a nice bed and a warm meal doesn't detract from the fact that I'm without my freedom.

"You heard Mikhail the other day. He's not inviting you to return to the bratva compound," Antonio says.

I tug my bottom lip between my teeth. I heard him, but I didn't want to believe it. "He doesn't mean it," I say. "I'm welcome in my own home." I'm certain it was a show, for Antonio's sake.

"And if you're not? What will that mean for your children?" Antonio asks.

Would Mikhail or his men murder me because they believe I've consorted with the Italians? The bratva doesn't take prisoners. Instead, they kill any man who gets in their way or interrupts their plans.

Is that a risk that I'm willing to take?

It's not only my life, but my two children. There's no sense in lying to Antonio; I suspect he can see right through the facade. "I don't know," I say. "If you don't let Mikhail leave, then I suppose I could return, and my safety would be ensured."

"Who would take Mikhail's place as the bratva leader?" Antonio asks.

Is he asking because he wants information? There are always two underbosses for the Pakhan, spies who watch over the captain, the Brigadier.

Yuri is one of Mikhail's underbosses, but so is Dmitri. And if one were to take Mikhail's place, I'm not sure which it would be. I'm not privy to the politics of the bratva. I'm kept out of their meetings.

Would they fight for the position of Pakhan?

"I don't know who the next boss would be," I say. It's not a lie, but I also don't want to jeopardize the lives of any more bratva men. Assuming they're still alive after the Italians attacked my home.

I've heard nothing from the Bratva. There have been no attempted rescue missions. Are they leaving Mikhail behind and assuming that he's dead? Do they not care about my children or me?

Antonio is silent. "The test results will be back this afternoon."

"Test results?"

"The DNA tests I had run comparing my sample to the children's."

I expel a heavy sigh. There's no chance that the twins aren't his. Antonio was the only man I'd been with that summer.

And I've run out of time stalling.

"What are you intending to do after you get the results?" I ask. I don't see him as a warm father figure for Sophia and Liam. I'd settle with letting him send them presents and a card on their birthday, but I suspect he'll demand more.

He avoids answering my question. "What do you intend on doing about your brother? He made it clear that you're not welcome to return to his home. You've also heard the kids from different families. He's responsible for the attacks on the other complexes."

"You give him too much credit."

"He orchestrated the attacks," Antonio says. "Even if he didn't physically abduct a child, he is responsible."

"Just like you're responsible for kidnapping Liam." The vicious cycle continues. Will there ever be an end?

His jaw tightens. "And I regret that decision."

"What about bringing me here against my will, with my children? Do you regret that too?"

He guides me farther down the hall, away from listening ears. We're alone. I'm not the least bit afraid of Antonio, unlike when he first forced me into his vehicle at gunpoint. He hasn't hurt me, not physically. And while I'm not happy to be here, he hasn't harmed my children, either.

His hand is on the small of my back, and he stops just outside of his office door. He doesn't lead me inside. Instead, he backs me up against the frosted glass door. The glass is cold and sends an involuntary shiver down my spine.

"I'm sorry that you didn't have a choice in coming here," Antonio says. His apology appears genuine. He's not the least bit squirrelly or trying to weasel his way out with an excuse. "I wanted to keep you and your children safe."

"And?"

There must be more than just protecting us. We barely knew one another.

"With the Hell brought down on the other mafia families, I needed a bargaining chip in case Mikhail decided to attack our complex."

"You used me," I say and fold my arms across my chest. "How did that work for you?"

"The bratva didn't attack the complex, but I'm not sure they even knew that you were in our possession. Honestly, the whole operation was a fuck up from the beginning." Antonio runs a hand through his hair.

I want to know what he means, but I don't ask. I just wait and listen, hoping that he'll expand on what he says.

"How did Mikhail know that our mafia family was flying into New York? They targeted the airport and attempted to obliterate one of the Italian's private planes when it landed."

"I don't know. Nikita received a call with private orders, direct from Mikhail," I say. "He was in a hurry and was going to make me late for picking up the twins from preschool."

"Boss!" A gentleman wearing a white dress shirt rounds the corner of the hall, quite disheveled. On further inspection, there's a smattering of blood on his sleeve.

Was he with Mikhail?

My mouth goes dry, and I want to hurry down the hall, run into the basement, and find out what the hell is going on.

Antonio steps back from me and turns to give the gentleman his undivided attention. "My office?" he suggests.

"Please," the man says.

"We can continue this discussion later," Antonio says to me.

I step aside, unblocking the door, and Antonio opens his office door, gesturing the gentleman inside. The door shuts abruptly behind him.

The frosted glass makes it impossible to see anything. The room appears soundproof as well. Even standing outside, I can't hear a word exchanged between the two men. Not even muffled words.

I wander down the hallway past the entrance to the basement prison. Even if I wanted to sneak down, it would require a key to enter the premises.

Besides, a guard was always on duty, which would make it impossible for me to speak with Mikhail alone. But at least I could know for sure his condition and if he's alive.

The bratva wouldn't have tortured a man for two days. They'd have killed him by now.

I wasn't exactly invited into the holding cells and interrogation rooms. But it was no secret that prisoners were brought in and didn't stay long.

"Aleksandra," Nikki says, spotting me as she steps out of the living room. "You look like you've seen a ghost. Is everything all right?" She approaches me, and I have nowhere to go, no place to escape from her onset of questions.

"I just was having a word with Antonio when one of his men needed him," I say.

"Come on; keep us company." Nikki wraps an arm around my shoulder and escorts me back into the living room with her and the other guests.

Their chatter ceases as I enter.

Were they talking about me? Or are they just uncomfortable with my presence? I'm not exactly thrilled to be around them, either.

Nikki offers me a seat beside her on the sofa. Up until now, I'd been keeping to myself or spending time solely with the twins.

"Hi," I say and give an awkward smile as I sink into the couch.

"This is Paige, Karina, and Olivia," Nikki says, introducing them to me. "Everyone, this is Aleksandra."

I'm sure they already know who I am. There's probably been chatter about me for days. I've smiled politely but avoided conversing with strangers. I don't intend to stay very long, but I can't help but wonder when I will be able to leave.

"Where are your—husbands, boyfriends, masters?" I'm not quite sure what the men are to these ladies, whether they're being kept and held against their will like I am or happy to be with these men.

If they are being held against their will, perhaps we have something in common, and they'd be willing to fight for their freedom alongside of me.

"Handling business, and Aurielo is my husband," Karina says. "While it wasn't exactly a wedding that I dreamed of as a child, Aurielo saved my life. I can't fault him for the past. We're happy together, but protecting our son is of the utmost importance."

"I don't think any of us shared a typical romance with our husbands," Paige says. "I met Moreno when I was hired to be a nanny for his daughter."

"Nova?" I ask, knowing more about the children than their parents after sitting with them for the past two days.

"That's right," Paige says. "I had no idea what I was getting myself involved in at the time, but I honestly have no regrets. I'd do it all over again."

"Your husband is a murderer," I whisper. "All of them are. That doesn't bother you?"

Olivia leans back in the glider, the chair rocking as she speaks. "Your brother is bratva and attacked our families. I don't think you have room to speak." There's a hardness behind her exterior, and a chill runs through my body.

These women have undoubtedly seen as much as I have, if not more, by their husband's hands. Have they witnessed murders, kidnappings, and interrogations?

While I've been sheltered from the atrocities that the bratva embarks on, I'm not unaware of the suffering that men cause onward to other men. I just never imagined that they'd involve children.

"Olivia," Nikki says, scolding the blonde. "I've invited Aleksandra to join us as our guest. We've all been in her position, not knowing whom to trust. And questioning whether we've been betrayed by someone we care about."

The blonde scoffs under her breath. "And we're supposed to trust her? She's the sister of Mikhail Barinov. For all we know, she's taking notes about our families that she can report back to the Russians."

I shift on the sofa and lock eyes with Olivia. "I wouldn't do that. Contrary to what you might have heard, not everyone who is Russian is a monster."

"I wasn't implying all Russians are monsters, only ones who are bratva," Olivia quips. "And you, my dear, are a bratva princess, the sister of the bratva boss."

"Bratva princess?" I can't help but laugh at the title,

like I'm wearing a crown and living luxuriously because of who I am.

They think they know me, know my family, and what my life is like. But they're wrong.

"My brother may be the Pakhan, but he doesn't spoil my children with presents or allow us to live lavishly under his roof. Some guards accompany me everywhere I go, but that's protecting me from men like your husbands," I say. "The enemy."

"Do you still believe our family is the enemy?" Paige asks. "We've welcomed you with open arms. Even Antonio has given you quarters away from the rest of the guests."

I chuckle at her remark. Does she believe that we're guests? Maybe they are, but a guest means I can come and go as I please, which isn't the case.

"What is so funny?" Paige glances at me and then at the other ladies, waiting for an answer.

Nikki clears her throat and breaks the awkward silence. "Aleksandra wasn't brought in by invitation."

"I was forced at gunpoint into Antonio's vehicle," I

say. "My children and I had no choice but to follow his orders."

"From what I can see, he cares about you," Nikki says.

"He cares about Liam and Sophia." I doubt he gives much thought about what might happen to me.

"Because they're his children?" Paige asks. The other women glare at her like she let something slip that she wasn't supposed to divulge. "What? It's true, isn't it?" Her gaze locks on mine.

"Leave her alone," Nikki scolds Paige. It's like the two of them know each other, more than just for the past few days.

"How about we talk about you and your kids?" I challenge, wanting the spotlight far from me.

"Sure, what do you want to know?" Nikki's eyes light up, a wide grin on her face. "Ask me anything."

"Anything?" I repeat.

The woman appears to be an open book, but I doubt she'd tell me her most intimate secrets. Not that I want to know about her dirty details in the bedroom with her husband, but there has to be something worth learning.

Paige is the first to speak, staring at Nikki. "Do you resent your father for selling you to Dante?"

"I was letting Aleksandra ask the questions," Nikki says, glaring at Paige to shut her mouth.

This is a sensitive subject. Good, now she can feel like she's sweating under a sunlamp for a bit. "What she said," I quip, wanting Nikki to answer the question since it seems to be making her uncomfortable.

"Fine," Nikki says and stretches, taking a second to answer. "I hate the old man. He didn't just sell me to Dante. He would have sold me to anyone to get me out of his hair. He handed me over to his associates to auction, drug, and poison me. He's a fucking bastard. I'd gladly do a jig on his grave and maybe leave some dog shit behind."

I can't help but chuckle at the image in my head. Maybe the two of us can be friends if she can help me get out of this place.

15

Antonio

I head up the stairs after visiting the prisoner, Mikhail, and having a word with Aurielo and Jacopo.

For now, we have what we need—targets for the bratva compounds in Chicago, Los Angeles, and just outside of Breckenridge.

I hurry to find Dante, Alessandro, Jace, and their close associates, to discuss our tactical advantage. We need to strike while we still have the element of surprise.

Except Mikhail has been held for over two days. Won't they be expecting an attack? Have they moved all their influential leaders to another off-site location?

We don't know all their safe house locations, only outside New York, where we found Mikhail.

The leaders discuss what they think is the best course of action. We've already attacked the bratva compound in New York. I leave the decision entirely up to them. It's their men at risk going in and leading the charge.

We don't want to open ourselves up to another attack. The message is evident amongst the group. We need to end this tyranny once and for all.

Mario comes into the study where we're discussing strategy and a calculated response.

"This came just a few minutes ago for you," Mario says as he hands me a sealed envelope.

"Thank you," I say, dismissing him. His responsibility is to keep a close eye on Aleksandra and make sure that she doesn't attempt an escape or sneak down to converse with her brother.

Are the DNA results inside the envelope?

"Excuse me," I say and step out of the study, heading for my office and shutting the door. While the privacy of my office is ideal for a meeting with one or two individuals, it isn't set up for large-scale events like the one that we're having at the complex.

I don't worry about the guards overhearing our discussions. They are men I have little choice but to trust, and if they betray me, they're dead.

I fiddle with the envelope in my hands. I'm not ready for the truth, whatever it may be.

If I'm Sophia and Liam's father, what then?

Aleksandra will hate me if I force custody on her.

But if they're my children, they should know their father. And I'm nowhere near the monster their Uncle Mikhail is. He's a bratva boss who likes to flex his muscle and threaten anyone who looks at him the wrong way.

I grab the letter opener from my top drawer and tear the envelope. Sliding the folded sheet of paper, I open it to reveal the results.

They're my children.

I slump into the chair at my desk. My heart hammers in my chest. I thought relief would flood through me at the news, but instead, it's a rush of adrenaline.

I'm a father.

I'm their father.

What do I know about children? Let alone having two of them.

"Fuck!" I curse, grateful that no one else can hear my outburst within the closed space.

I drop the results on the desk and pinch the bridge of my nose.

Sophia and Liam are mine. I should be ecstatic, thrilled, delighted.

My hands tremble, and I swallow the bile that rises to my throat. I can't ignore it any longer, and burying my head in the sand won't do a lick of good.

I stand and clomp through the office and down the hall, making my presence known as I approach the living room.

The kids are on the floor playing with a new train set that I had delivered. They all seem to be getting along, which is a pleasant surprise.

Not that the kids weren't playing well together the past few days, but Sophia and Liam had been keeping to themselves quite a bit. I wasn't sure if it was because they're twins and prefer each other's company, or they're just a bit socially awkward.

Aleksandra is seated on the couch beside Nikki. Olivia, Paige, and Karina have pulled up chairs as they sit in a circle gabbing about who knows what.

Hopefully, it's not regarding me.

I should have put Mario in the room with them, not just as a lookout, but to feed me back any information that's shared.

"Aleksandra, a word," I say and gesture for her to get up and come over to me.

She gives the girls a look before standing. "Is everything okay?" she asks. Her voice travels, probably back toward the girls, as I lead her out of the living room and down the hallway.

"The twins are mine," I say, shoving the DNA results at her as proof that she kept the truth from me.

"I know," Aleksandra says. Her demeanor is calm, and why shouldn't it be? She's had more than four years to process this information. I've had only a few days to accept what might be a fact.

And now that it's official, my world has been turned on its axis.

"Maybe we should sit down somewhere and talk," she suggests.

I nod. It's all I can do. Words don't seem to form, and I lead her down the hallway to a private corridor and into one of the many rooms in the complex. It would have been simpler to extend her an invitation into my office, but I'd read the DNA results and had felt suffocated in such a small space.

This room has more windows, is brighter even with the gray clouds blanketing the sky. There is an assortment of books scattered amongst the shelves and a sofa near the window. I take a seat and leave space for Aleksandra to join me.

She sits at the opposite end of the couch, turning

toward me. "I didn't expect for you to find out this way." Her voice is soft, hardly above a whisper.

"How did you intend for me to find out? Were you ever going to tell me that I had twins?" I pin her with my stare, and her cheeks burn.

"No, as far as I was concerned, you were the enemy."

We've always been on two opposing sides, since the day we met.

"And you still feel that way about me?" I'm not sure why I bother asking. I don't expect a sudden change of heart after forcing her to come live with me.

"To be honest, Antonio, I'm confused." She slides her legs up on the sofa, shifting to face me. "I never imagined Mikhail would hurt children."

Her gaze tightens, and her bottom lip juts out just slightly with a pout.

I'm silent as I listen, wanting her to open up to me.

She fiddles with her sweater and stares at her pants, speaking but putting distance between us by not making eye contact. "It makes me rethink everything I thought I knew about my family and the bratva. I'm not saying I'm disowning them," Aleksandra clarifies her position, "but I never thought they'd target children."

"For what it's worth, I want to be part of our children's lives, but I won't hold you captive."

She brushes her hand over her pants as she glances up at me, filled with hope. "You'll let me go?"

"Yes, but Liam and Sophia stay here with me."

"No," Aleksandra gasps.

"You kept them from me for four years. You can stay or go, but the kids aren't leaving." I don't point out that it's dangerous for them to leave as they are easily a target.

She pulls her legs up against her chest, wrapping her arms around her knees, protecting herself. Aleksandra doesn't get up. She doesn't flee. Is it because she realizes there's nowhere she can go and hide from me?

"You're a monster."

"Maybe I am," I say, giving her the insult, letting her win this battle. "Your brother is no better. You were living under his roof with my children, putting them in harm's way."

"That's not fair!" Her eyes widen, and her jaw drops. "I never put the kids in danger."

"How do you think Mikhail would have handled discovering that a member of the mafia fathered the twins?"

Her tongue darts out to lick her ruby lips.

"You were a soldier when we met. I told him the truth, that you were at war. I just happened to leave out the part that you were a soldier for the *mafia*."

Aleksandra gives me the most endearing smile and glances down at her knees tucked against her chest. Her cheeks burn. Is she embarrassed?

"What is it?" I ask. My hand is soft and gentle as I touch her arm. I don't want there to be a wall between us or an icy void any longer.

"I may have mentioned to Mikhail that I'd marry the father of my children when he returned home," Aleksandra says.

My heart quickens at her admission. There's no doubt in my mind that she didn't mean what she'd said. It had been to keep her brother, the leader of the bratva, at bay.

And yet I can't help myself. "I'm back, *Tesorina*," I say with a smirk. "I'd hate to think that's what's stopping a truce between the Russians and Italians, marrying you. Do you intend to follow through with your promise?"

She gives me a half-hearted grin. "You can't be serious. Not without a full-blown proposal. I expect flowers, wine, maybe even an airplane in the sky."

"Oh, is that all it will take? Me, down on one knee with a grand gesture?" I'm joking with her, but I want to do right by her. She's the mother of my children.

"Yes, that might work." Aleksandra is laughing and covers her face.

I lean forward for her hand, bringing it down from her face. "You are sexy and beautiful when you laugh. Don't ever cover it up."

She tugs her bottom lip between her teeth.

I could easily kiss her. And a massive part of me yearns to taste her lips, feel her body against mine, but not like this. Not while she's here against her will. "If you don't want to stay, you can leave," I whisper.

"I can go? The children and I—"

"No," I say, cutting her off. "You can go. The children are staying here with me, under my protection."

"I can't leave the twins, Antonio," she whispers. "Please, don't make me leave them." Her eyes burn with tears.

Doesn't she realize that I don't want her to leave? But I refuse to keep her against her will. She's not a hostage. She was here to keep her safe and the mafia families secure.

"You don't have to go anywhere," I say, bringing my palm to her chin to meet her stare. "I want you here, but I don't want you to resent me for keeping you under my roof, in my home."

Her lips part, and a soft puff of air escapes past. "I can't leave my children." She exhales a heavy breath and pulls back from my touch. "We will stay, but only under certain conditions."

A wry smile sneaks out of me. "You have demands?" This ought to be good.

"If you want to put it like that, yes, I have demands," Aleksandra says. She straightens her back. She wants to appear in control, taller, stronger, and I give her credit for trying to negotiate with a don.

"For starters, absolutely no sex between us. We are here, together, to co-parent."

To say I'm disappointed is an understatement, but I didn't think she'd just sneak off into my bed, either. There's so much disdain in her gaze when she watches me.

"Yes, what else?" I ask.

"I declare the entire third floor as my wing of the house. Your guards aren't to follow me around or invade my personal space."

I try to suppress a laugh at her tone and suggestion. No one else is currently residing on the third floor. It's an easy request. "What else?"

"Sophia and Liam will be enrolled in preschool at Manhattan Academy and are to have a normal life. They need a playroom with toys, fresh air outside, and friends over."

"They have friends?" I'm trying not to mock the kids, but they're four.

"They could have friends," Aleksandra counters. "When they're older, they'll have friends, and I'm not going to keep them under lock and key."

She makes a valid argument.

"Any other conditions?" I ask.

"Yes," she says, "I demand my freedom to come and go as I please, and lastly, I do not want Sophia or Liam to know that you are their father."

"Is that all?" I mock, and my eyes crinkle with a faint smile. "I can work with you on most of your demands, but in time, the children will discover that I'm their father, and I won't lie to them if they ask."

She grumbles under her breath.

"What was that?" I ask. I'm sure it was a snide remark, but I didn't quite catch what was said.

Aleksandra presses her lips tight together. "Nothing," she mutters.

"Good. Now that we have that settled, you should be aware that I have several conditions of my own."

Aleksandra groans, and her eyes are glassy but not

from sadness. There's a frustration brewing, an annoyance with having to follow my demands.

"Go ahead," she resigns with a sigh as I've defeated her.

Except I haven't, she's had her say, and I've met her with my own set of conditions.

"Any guests must be approved by myself or my second, Ardian. That includes for the children or yourself."

She opens her mouth, but then shuts it and gives a weak nod. "Fine."

I suspect she's holding something back, but I don't push. "This goes without saying, but you are not to consort with the police, feds, or anyone else regarding our business dealings and what you may or may not overhear."

"I'm not a rat. If I wanted to have your organization destroyed, I wouldn't go to the police."

"Good to know," I say and pull her closer, her knees against the sofa, my gaze locked on her. "You're not to see, speak, or communicate within any form the bratva or any of the men who associate with your brother."

"I don't want to see them," Aleksandra says. "What else?"

"When you or the twins leave the complex, you will bring a bodyguard with you. I don't trust that your brother's family won't come after you or my children."

She tilts her head, resting it on the top of the plush sofa. "That's nothing new. I'm used to having a bodyguard. Next?"

I'm surprised that she isn't fighting my demands, but maybe she's given up all hope.

Gently, I guide her legs from being squished between me and the sofa onto my lap.

She tenses at first until my fingers caress her feet. "What are you doing?"

"Trying to help you relax," I say.

"Antonio," her voice holds a tinge of warning.

But she doesn't tell me to stop.

"The final rule that you must abide by under my roof, you cannot bring another man home."

"You expect me to be celibate?" She rolls her lips between her teeth, but she doesn't pull away.

"I never said that." I watch her squirm against the sofa.

Have I made her uncomfortable?

"I'm not having sex with you," she stammers and pulls her feet from my grasp, bringing her knees back to her chest.

"Of course," I say, "you've made your rules clear. We will be co-parenting."

Her gaze tightens as she pushes her legs off the sofa and stands. "What about you? Do you intend on bringing random women home to fuck?"

I chuckle at her remark. Is she jealous? "Who said anything about them being random?"

Aleksandra's eyes widen in horror. "Oh my gosh. Are you seeing someone?" The color drains right out of her face as she steps farther away, pacing the length of the room.

The afternoon light cascades in through the windows, shining down on her. "Come sit," I say and pat the sofa beside me.

"Are you?" she asks again. There's an urgency in her tone.

Why does it matter to her if I'm seeing another woman? She's made it clear that nothing will transpire between the two of us. Is it because of the twins?

"I'm not," I say and stand from the sofa. Methodically, I approach her, slow and patient, as I reach for her hand. "Sit with me." I try again to get her to calm down.

What has her in such a tizzy?

She pinches her lips together, and a soft sigh spills out past her mouth.

"You seem relieved that I'm not dating anyone."

Aleksandra avoids my stare and fiddles with the single piece of lint that she's managed to discover on her black leggings. She picks at it as though she were picking apart a flower, petal by petal.

"It's not that."

"Look at me," I say, and I wait for her attention to return to my gaze.

After a moment, she must realize I'm staring, and she glances up at me. "Yes?"

"Why would it bother you if I were dating someone else?"

"It wouldn't," she blurts. "I mean, I don't care. It just seems unfair that you get to traipse women through this place, and I don't."

A smirk etches my face. "Oh, you can bring all the women into your room that you want, but I get the privilege of watching."

Aleksandra's cheeks burn, and she rolls her eyes. "That's not what I meant, and you know it."

It may not be, but a guy can fantasize. "I'd have thought after having twins, you wouldn't have cared about bringing random men into your bedroom."

Her brow furrows, and she folds her arms across her chest. "You don't have the right to dictate my life or with whom I sleep, Antonio."

"Don't I? You're living under my roof, free of charge. You're eating the food that my staff cooks for you.

They clean up after you. Wash your laundry. You have it pretty damn good if you ask me."

"Well, I didn't ask you," she snaps, and her top lip scowls with indignation. "And tell me how much I owe you. I'll pay my fair share."

I glance her up and down. "How do you intend to do that?"

She's never mentioned a job, and from what I had gathered, she lived under Mikhail's roof without any expenses.

"I'll get a job," she says.

"I'd rather you stay home with the twins, and I'll provide your room and board, along with a stipend."

She scoffs at my suggestion.

"What?" I ask.

"They're four. Pretty soon, they're going to be in elementary school."

"Yes, but they need someone at home to help them with their homework when they're done at school. I either hire a nanny to look after them or let you do it."

"Because you're too busy."

"What do you think?" I snap, tired of her antics. I've tried to be kind, warm, open to her suggestions and what she wants.

It's not exactly easy for me, to show this side to someone else. I've locked it away all my life, and for her to think anything else would be foolish.

16

Aleksandra

Three days later...

"Is it over?" I ask Mario. The mafia families pack their bags and head out into the garage to be shuttled to the regional airport.

"It will be soon," he says.

While I'm allowed throughout the house, he's been my appointed bodyguard if I leave the premises.

I haven't left yet.

Not until I feel it's safe for me to leave the premises, will I venture out. I understand my brother is still being held downstairs.

Is he alive? The basement prison is soundproof. I've heard no screams, no shouts, not a peep from downstairs.

Which should bring solace to my mind. But the mafia doesn't take a bratva leader and give him spoils. No doubt he's suffering, but I don't want to think about what they've done to him. The bratva would be crueler in their punishments and interrogations.

He helps carry the luggage for the guests to the vehicles. I wait inside near the living room, watching the twins as they stack wooden blocks as tall as themselves.

I shouldn't care that the guests are leaving. It's not like we became friends, but Nikki had been warm and open, comforting.

And now I'm going to be alone with Antonio and his men.

I run a hand through my hair, my stomach in knots.

"You're going to miss them," Antonio whispers as he comes up from behind.

He doesn't touch me, but his presence still makes me shudder. I silently pray that he doesn't notice the reaction he elicits.

"It was nice to have someone to talk to," I confess.

I spin around to face him.

"You know, *Tesorina*, you can invite friends over. Just not of the male variety."

"Worried you'll have a little competition?" I smirk.

Why does he care about me inviting a man under his roof? Unless he's the jealous type, which fits with being a don.

My stomach is topsy-turvy as I stare up into his eyes.

It's like I'm in high school all over again, except this time, the stakes are much higher.

"No, because I respect the rules you've put into place," Antonio says.

There's a tinge of disappointment that flutters through me. I shouldn't care whether he dates another woman or the entire city of New York.

Except I don't want his sights set on anyone else. I

pinch my lips together. "Are you saying that I don't respect the rules?"

"I wouldn't dream of it, *Tesorina*," Antonio says. His breath teases my lips. He's so close that I can practically feel his warmth against mine, his body grazing my skin. "And when I said no men coming into the house, I also meant that you aren't to shack up with one of my men."

I pretend to pout. "Shucks, you figured out my grand plan. I was going to invite Mario into my bedroom and—"

"I swear you'd better be joking," Antonio seethes. He's not the least bit amused by my sense of humor.

Not even a hint of a smile grazes his lips. Gosh, he is the jealous type.

"Relax," I say and pat his arm. "My body is solely for my pleasure. No man under this roof is going to touch it."

I swear Antonio whimpers at my remark. "Say that again, *Tesorina*."

His eyes have darkened deeper, richer chocolate. I

lean in, wanting to kiss him, taste him, explore his mouth with my tongue.

But I refrain from letting my desires and impulses win. I slip past him and head into the living room to check on the twins. Not that they need my attention, but I need them right now, or I'd do something that I might regret.

———

I can't sleep. I haven't been trying for very long, but I'm not tired. It's like my feet want to move, to dance, to be set free.

And I'm still just a caged bird.

At least my cage is a little bigger. I have the entire third floor, but aside from the twins' room right next door, the rest of the suites are empty.

Antonio has agreed to turn one of the rooms into a playroom for the twins and another, he intends to make a surprise for me.

I don't know what he thinks I want him to do with that room, but I'm curious to see the results.

It's just after eleven, and I should be winding down.

But I'm wide awake, like I had a double shot of espresso.

I sneak out of my bedroom, carefully closing the door behind myself without so much as a squeak.

There's no sign of Mario outside my door, which is a welcome relief. Are there surveillance cameras set up throughout the inside of the complex? I haven't seen any, but that doesn't mean they're not hidden away, out of sight.

I know better than to snoop. I'm bound to get caught, even late at night; some guards are awake watching the house all night.

My footfalls are light and silent as I slip quietly down to the main floor and into the kitchen. I'm bored, and my mind is under-stimulated, which is probably why I can't sleep. Being cooped up in the complex hasn't helped me in the slightest.

And the fact it's snowing outside doesn't give me relief that I'll be able to go out soon and enjoy a walk in the warmth.

I don't have snow boots or a coat warm enough for the frigid temperatures outside.

At least the complex is warm, comfortable. I saunter into the kitchen and peek into the fridge. Nothing grabs my interest.

I'm not hungry. The meals have been adequate.

Okay, if I'm honest, they're more than just passable. They've been quite tasty, and I hate to admit that Antonio's chef is far better than Mikhail's. Not that I'd ever say as much.

I shut the fridge and sneak down the hall. There's a liquor cabinet in the corner of one of the rooms I'd seen earlier in the week. I hadn't checked to see if it was locked.

The house is dark, and I stumble unceremoniously as I attempt to find the light switch.

My hand smacks the wall, finally flipping the switch.

Antonio is seated on the couch, a glass of scotch in his hand. "What are you doing?" he asks.

"I could ask you that," I say, breezing past him as I head for the cabinet and make myself a drink. I pour half amaretto and half sour mix into a glass.

"Have a seat." Antonio invites me to stay.

I sip my drink, making sure it's to my liking before I collapse onto the sofa beside him.

"How often have you been coming down here, sneaking my alcohol?"

Does he think this is a regular occurrence? Is he accusing me of stealing from him?

I can't help but feel offended at his accusation. "Just tonight. You had guests recently in your house—"

"I'm kidding," he says and quirks a grin. "Relax, *Tesorina*."

The prospect of him joking about anything feels foreign.

"Right," I say and gulp the amber liquid. It's sweet and tastes perfect. And for the briefest of moments, I allow myself to relax and unwind while I pour a second glass for myself.

I grab a seat beside him on the sofa with my second glass. I swear I'm already buzzing, but it's probably his proximity and scent that has me reeling. Or maybe it's because I've been cooped up in his house and I'm growing even more sexually frustrated every passing day.

Some days, I hate Antonio, and other days, I want to rip off his clothes and fuck him.

I toss my head back and down the liquid faster than I can pour it.

"Slow down there, *Tesorina*."

"Don't want to," I say and stand, sauntering toward the liquor cabinet to grab a third drink. My lips tingle, and I sway my hips just slightly when I feel Antonio's gaze on my ass.

Maybe I imagine it, his desire for me.

I brush past him with my drink in hand when he grabs me by the wrist and pulls me onto his lap.

"What are you—"

"You've had enough to drink. I'm cutting you off."

"Why?" I whine and bring the glass to my lips before he can take it from me. "It's not like I have to drive upstairs."

"Yeah, well, I'm not sure you can walk up to the third floor," he says, sounding more amused than upset about the situation.

I shift on his lap, and my hips gyrate as I try to reach behind him for the liquor cabinet, but there's no use while I'm seated. And Antonio isn't about to let me get up.

His hands are firmly planted on my hips.

"How much have you had to drink?" I ask. He's been seated in here long before I came in, but was he nursing his first glass of scotch, or was that several in when I found him?

"Enough," he whispers, staring into my gaze. I can feel the bump between us, his cock growing from my hip movements.

And I should stop. Get up. Move onto the other side of the couch.

But I don't.

I press my lips together, my gaze locked on his as I straddle his hips and grind into his cock.

"Quit doing that unless you want me to fuck you on the sofa," he grunts.

It's like I went from a minor threat, a teasing gesture, and he just had to up the ante. Do I want him to fuck me? God, yes. I want to feel his cock buried deep inside of me.

What's stopping me?

I can't remember.

I don't care.

My mouth crushes his hard and fast. My fingers pull at his crisp white shirt, ripping the buttons, tugging it from his trousers.

The only sounds I hear are his moans and my heart pounding wildly, the sound deafening in my ears.

His tongue pushes its way into my mouth, hungrily taking control as he flips me onto my back on the sofa.

"Is this what you want?" he whispers, staring down at me.

"Yes," I answer eagerly, giving him permission.

Fuck the rules.

Fuck every one of them.

Rules were made to be broken.

17

Antonio

Aleksandra tastes like honey and vanilla. There's a sweetness on her soft skin that makes me yearn to sink my teeth into her flesh.

But I'm not a monster.

My fingers delve beneath her shirt, my palm presses against her stomach, grazing her skin, inching my way over and across her breast.

"We shouldn't—" she whimpers against my lips, but she doesn't stop kissing me. She tugs my bottom lip between her teeth, encouraging me onward.

"We definitely shouldn't be doing this," I say in agreement. My other hand teases at the waistband of her pajama bottoms.

I trail a soft, warm path of kisses from her lips across her neck.

Aleksandra moans and shifts, giving me greater access to her neck. Her legs trap me, wrapping around me, keeping me against her.

"Tell me to stop," I say, allowing her to end what's been started. My destination of kisses teases her collarbone as my fingers inch her t-shirt higher to expose the smooth, creamy complexion of her stomach.

She sucks in a breath as I lift her shirt up and over her head, letting it tumble to the floor.

Her gaze meets mine, but the words don't come. There are no pleas to stop, no admissions of guilt, only sounds of pleasure as my lips caress her navel.

I guide my tongue across her navel and gently plant soft kisses over her abdomen, inching her bottoms down slowly, methodically.

Aleksandra loosens her grip on me so that I can help guide her pants off. Soft whimpers and moans emit from the back of her throat.

"Do you want me to stop?" I ask, her pajama bottoms halfway down her hips. My breath is warm against her panties.

She smells divine, and I want to discover how wet she is for me already.

"God, no. If you stop, I'll kill you," she grumbles at me.

I love how eager she is, how much she wants me.

I yank her bottoms off in one swift motion, pajama pants and panties, tossing the items across the room.

"I'm going to make you scream my name, *Tesorina*." I grab her by the hips and shift her around so that I can kneel on the floor.

She moans her acceptance.

"What was that?" I ask, bringing her legs around my neck. I drag every second out, making the moment last and listening to her sweet pleas for more.

"Tell me you want me to lick your pussy." I stare into her gaze.

She struggles to keep her eyes open, and the words seem difficult to form. "I want you," Aleksandra begs.

My fingers circle her lips, teasing, exciting and arousing her. "I like it when you talk dirty, *Tesorina*. Tell me what you want me to do to you."

A whimper murmurs from the back of her throat. I drop soft, slow kisses along her inner thigh.

"That."

"What's that?" I smile deviously, nibbling on her inner thigh as I move in the opposite direction that she desires. I kiss a soft path near the back of her knee, bending her leg.

"Fuck," she mutters.

She's glistening for me. Already wet, and I've barely touched her the way I intend.

"You want me to fuck you, *Tesorina*?" I whisper just above her pussy. I'm teasing her, wanting to hear her plead and beg for my cock.

Aleksandra is restless against the sofa, shifting her hips, indicating her answer.

"Answer me," I command. She's mine, and she will do as I demand.

There's an inward struggle as she tries to speak, but the words are raspy and rough. It's difficult to hear what she's asking of me.

"Try again," I say and try not to smile, but it's near impossible. I love that I've made her speechless.

She takes a heavy breath, a gasp as she finds her voice, though shaky. "I want you to fuck me with your tongue," Aleksandra says.

I drag my tongue down her slit and hold her steady as I lick, suck, and taste her sweetness.

Her moans are heavenly, and she does little to silence the whimpers that spill past her lips. I give her what she wants because she follows my rules and obeys my commands. It's a reward for her obedience.

18

Aleksandra

I swear he's trying to kill me with lust.

The desire pools between my thighs, and his tongue brings me all sorts of heightened pleasure. But it isn't enough. With Antonio, it's never enough.

How can one man have such an effect on me?

I surrender my heart, body, and soul, giving him my everything.

His tongue does wonders, bringing me to the brink, teasing and eliciting a reaction that I'm not prepared to experience. Sweet release.

He's skilled with his tongue, fingers, lips, and all I want is more. More with him. More tonight. Just more.

I'm close, on the brink, but I can't quite fall into oblivion and let go.

He's the father of my children, which complicates matters, and he hasn't exactly let us go freely. Even when I don't want to be, I'm stuck in my mind.

It's all a heavy weight, like a fog, thick and dense. I desire him, but I can't forget what he did.

But am I so innocent, keeping the twins from him?

"Your mind is far from here, *Tesorina*," Antonio says.

He isn't wrong.

I have doubts, more than I'm willing to voice, and he must sense the frustration and fear, the worry that plagues me.

Antonio stands and reaches for my hand. "It's time to put you into bed," he says.

I reach for my clothes, but he snatches them before I have time. He hands me his dress shirt. "Put this on."

"Just this?" I squeak. "What if the guards see me?"

A wry grin meets his lips. "That's the point."

"You want to parade me around in front of your men?" I'm appalled at his suggestion.

"I want them to know that you belong to me, *Tesorina*." He pulls me hard and tight against his chest, his lips crashing against mine like he's claiming me.

I open my mouth to object, but his tongue finds its way past my lips as he holds me tight, his arm wrapped around my waist. My body melts into him.

Damn him!

I hate how easily he can conquer me, like I'm some plaything of his.

"I don't belong to anyone," I whisper as he finally releases me from his clutches.

"I beg to differ," he whispers, his eyes twinkling with mirth. "Come now. It's late." He guides me into the hallway, holding onto my clothes in one hand.

I hold my breath, waiting to see his men standing there, watching, but we're alone.

A breath of relief spills past my lips as his hand tightens in mine, leading me up to the third floor. I'm not being invited to join him in *his* bed.

I don't even know where he sleeps. I assume he has a bedroom somewhere on the second floor.

There are no guards outside my door. The house is quiet, as if the world is asleep. I'm sure there are guards at their posts, but I'm no longer being sequestered to the third floor or my bedroom.

He opens the door to my bedroom and gestures with a sweeping hand for me to enter.

"Not going to carry me over the threshold?" I'm baiting him. I don't even know why. I'm not sure what I want to happen. We've crossed a line downstairs that I swore I wouldn't engage in again with Antonio.

But my heart and body aren't in agreement with my mind.

He raises an eyebrow, drops my clothes in his hands, and with ease lifts me into his arms, sweeping me up under my legs as he carries me to the bed.

It takes every ounce of strength not to laugh and giggle. I will not wake the twins. They don't need to discover Antonio in my bedroom.

Gently, he places me down on the mattress, hovering above me, staring down, waiting.

What is he waiting for? Does he want me to make the first move? Is something on his mind as well?

"The door," I whisper, glancing from him to the adjoining door. It's cracked, just a bit, but I don't want to wake the twins.

He nods an affirmative and slips off the mattress. Antonio is swift and silent, securing the bedroom door and then the entrance to the hallway, giving us privacy.

Is this what he had in mind for 'tucking me into bed'? I'm not complaining; I wasn't sure what he wanted to do. However, downstairs had been a pretty good indication of something intimate.

My stomach fills with butterflies, and I nervously tug my bottom lip between my teeth.

Why am I nervous?

Why does Antonio have this power over me?

He stalks toward the bed like I'm his prey.

I exhale a nervous breath, and he continues toward me, climbing onto all fours, straddling me, trapping me.

"Antonio," I whisper, staring up into his dark, heavy-lidded gaze.

His lips fall back onto mine. It feels natural as our bodies meld together against the mattress.

The shirt that I'm wearing inches up at my thighs, and his fingers push the material back, exploring every inch of my bare skin beneath the white dress shirt that's missing half its buttons.

His hands are rough and strong, grazing my hips across my sides but waiting to reach the destination that I desire most of all.

He's my undoing every time.

I grow restless, antsy beneath him. I want him. One kiss yields two, and I'm pulling him closer, harder, tighter against my body.

"Slow down, *Tesorina*," Antonio whispers into my ear, bringing his teeth against the lobe, tugging playfully.

I groan at his insistence on teasing me to death. His knee slides between my thighs, mounting pressure against my core. I'm on fire, and he's adding fuel.

My fingers roam against his waist, pulling at his clothes, wanting to feel his skin against mine.

"Not yet," he says with more insistence and grabs my arms, pinning them together above my head.

Antonio is strong and forceful, but he doesn't take what I don't give him.

"You will not come until I give you permission," he whispers against my ear.

The ache builds inside of me at his command.

"No," I say and shake my head. He can't do that. Control me.

"Yes, *Tesorina*. If you want this, you will surrender to me."

I whimper in protest. My insides ache with intense heat, the throbbing sensation overwhelming as he thrusts his hips against mine.

"You're a fucking tease," I rasp, struggling to stare up into his gaze. It takes every amount of measurable strength to focus and not just give in to what I want.

He grins down at me. "The way I see it, you've been taunting me with that tight little ass and sexy as fuck hip sway every time you walk."

"You've been checking out my ass?" I can't help but laugh.

"I'm surprised you didn't notice," Antonio says as his lips trail a warm path across my neck and down my jawline.

One hand keeps my arms bound above my head, but his grip is looser than earlier. I wrap my legs around him and flip us around, taking charge, straddling him.

"My turn," I whisper with a sly grin as I crawl down his torso and remove every last inch of clothing from his body, as he lifts his hips for me to undress him.

He's sexy and well-endowed, more than even I remember since the last time we fucked in the shower years ago.

Just the sight of his cock makes me wet and excited.

Not that I want to divulge that little secret to him. He'll find out soon enough.

Easily, he can overpower me if he wants to, but instead, he lies there, letting me explore his body. I don't dare admit he could win the heart of any woman he desires with his looks alone.

But his temper might run them all away, and the fact he's a mafia don.

I trail my fingers over his abs and down the juncture of his stomach toward my intended destination when he grabs my wrist to stop me.

"Antonio?" I whisper, staring down at him.

Does he not want this?

Has he changed his mind?

He reaches up and grazes my cheek with one hand, bringing my mouth down to his. His hold against me is firm, and while I want to believe that I'm the one in control, it's only because he's given me the reins.

His other hand remains on my wrist, rolling us swiftly around. My back is flush with the mattress, the warm sheets against my skin.

Antonio brings my hand down to the mattress, his hands entwining with mine as our lips duel in a fiery kiss.

His fingers that were on my cheek glide down my torso, grazing my breast, and then he delves between my thighs, discovering my wetness.

My head is foggy from the alcohol earlier, but it's clear as day that he is what I crave. I lift my hips off the bed, grazing against him, wanting to feel him buried inside of me.

His touch is firm but gentle, rubbing and stroking, grazing my inner thighs with his cock.

"Condom," I say, breaking the momentary silence.

We already have two children, and I don't think either one of us is ready for that next step. I'm not sure we're even prepared for what comes after this tomorrow.

He grunts and shifts off me long enough to reach for the bedside table.

There's a bible that he removes from the drawer.

"That isn't going to keep me from getting knocked

up," I say. He doesn't think praying on it will keep a baby from happening.

"You don't say," he says with a smirk and opens it to reveal a hidden compartment containing a handful of oddities, including a few condoms.

"What? You didn't honestly think this is a hotel with a bible in every room, did you?" Antonio asks.

A small part of me wants to slug him, but I shake my head. "Your hospitality is nothing like a hotel," I say. I can't help the snarky tone or the bitterness that exudes from my lips.

"Better?" he asks, hopeful.

He can't be serious.

"Hotels don't usually involve being detained in your room."

He glances up at me before ripping open the foil packet.

I can't help but wonder if we're going to go through with sleeping together or this is about to fall apart, like my life at the moment.

"You wouldn't have been detained if you'd have followed the rules." He's not the least bit apologetic. He glances me over, curious if I'm about to object to sleeping with him now that we seem to be sharing a heated debate. "Are we doing this?" he asks.

"You tell me you're the one in charge," I mutter.

He pins me with his stare. "The way I see it, you've been hiding the twins from me. You're not so innocent, either, *Tesorina.*"

I reach for the storage book, the supposed bible, and toss it into the nightstand. Stuck to the bottom of the bible is that stupid business card the federal agent gave me just minutes before Antonio kidnapped me.

I had shoved it away, worried that if I'd have tossed it into the trash, someone might have gone through and discovered it.

My stomach flops.

Antonio's gaze hardens, and his nostrils flare. His breathing is louder, thicker, angrier.

Is he waiting for me to say something and explain? I should tell him that the feds came to me. I didn't tell them anything. How could I? Antonio took my phone.

Silence fills the room.

"Are you fucking talking to the feds?" He yanks the card and examines it to reveal the date, time, any pertinent information to interrogate me.

"It's not what you think," I whisper. My heart jackhammers in my chest, and I might toss up the alcohol that I drank a short time ago.

His laugh is dark, sinister.

A shiver courses through me, and I can't help but worry about what happens next. Will he put me in his prison, interrogate me, torture me until I tell him what he wants to hear?

"Then, tell me what the fuck you're doing with Agent Melinda Malone's business card," he says, reading the name on the front.

"She approached me," I say.

I have no reason to lie to Antonio. I haven't done anything wrong. I'm not the bad guy. He is.

"And you decided to what, spy on me for her?" Antonio asks, growling at me as he speaks. "I should have known you'd be up to no good."

"Me?" I can't believe the nerve of him. I reach for the bedsheets, feeling naked and exposed in front of him, and while he's not wearing anything, either, suddenly I'm uncomfortable. "I'm not talking to her. How could I? You took my phone!"

His jaw is tight. His gaze hardened. "It doesn't mean that the FBI agent didn't give you another phone."

"Go ahead, turn my room upside down if you have to. I have nothing to hide," I say.

He lifts the mattress, my ass hitting the floor as he topples the bed over to make sure there's not a phone hidden between the box spring and mattress.

"You asshole!"

When he's not satisfied finding nothing but air, he stomps toward the dresser, tearing every piece of clothing out from the drawer.

My voice is soft, fragile. "You're going to wake the kids," I say.

He'll probably wake the whole damn house with his tirade, but I doubt he cares about anyone but himself.

He glances at the children's room, and my stomach sours. Is he going to wake the twins and toss their room?

There's a moment of tension and silence.

Wordlessly, he fixes the mattress but leaves the clothes askew and exhales a heavy sigh, grabbing the condom and shucking it across the room. "So much for that happening tonight," he mutters.

"It's not my fault you ruined a perfect moment."

"Me?" He laughs darkly. "You're the one with all the secrets, keeping your relationship with Agent Malone a secret."

"If I was friends with her, do you think I'd still be locked up in your house? Maybe the secrets I keep are your fault. If you let me and my children free, I wouldn't be like this," I say.

He snatched me off the street at gunpoint. He can't pretend that didn't happen, that we're in a happy and healthy relationship. He's delusional if he thinks I love him and want to be here with him.

He reaches for his boxers and whips them back on before grabbing his clothes off the floor.

It's any wonder he can find them with all my stuff littered on the ground. "You're leaving," I say, dumbfounded.

Is that what Antonio always does, fight and run?

"Isn't that what you want?" He turns around to face me.

Oddly enough, it's not what I want. I want him, but he seems out of reach, a thousand miles away, even if he's just inches from the bed.

I want his apology. I want his anger turned from discontent to passion. I want to believe that he isn't a monster beneath his icy exterior.

I open my mouth and quickly shut it. What's the point of declaring anything when he's got a mafia to run, and I'm nothing more than a possession to him?

"Go," I say with as much conviction as I can muster.

I don't mean it.

I don't want him to go. The fight isn't over, but emotionally, I'm drained.

I want us to be tangled in the bedsheets and forget this stupid argument ever happened. I want to feel his lips against mine, telling me he's sorry, that he's wrong, that he trusts me because I haven't done anything to betray him.

But I'm not great at relationships. I have my own bratva family to thank for that, and now I've made a mess of whatever was finally transpiring between us.

I should have burned that stupid business card or, better yet, dropped it in the street when she'd given it to me.

Antonio undoubtedly will hate me. He will grow to despise me, just like my father did with my mother.

Antonio leans down, capturing my lips in one last fiery kiss. It's forceful and rough. His fingers tangle in my hair, pulling me harder and tighter with a brashness that demands control and power.

He's in charge, and he's making it known.

The kiss ends as quickly as it started.

I pull my bottom lip between my teeth. I can still feel him against my mouth, his breath lingering on my cheek, even though he's approaching the door.

I open my mouth, and I want to tell him not to leave, that I'm sorry, that he means more to me than I care to admit. I'm crazy for wanting him, even after the fight that just transpired.

But nothing spills out, and instead, I'm left in the cold, alone, with silence filling the void.

19
———

Antonio

I can't keep doing this, fighting with Aleksandra. It's not good for the twins, and it's certainly not healthy for my sanity.

And if there's any chance that she betrayed me, I want her out from under the roof of the complex.

I have a business to run, an enterprise that I need to focus on, and it's impossible with fleeting thoughts of last night bouncing through my mind.

She needs to go. And while I don't want her out of my life or my children never to know their father, what other choice do I have? Her poisoning them with ruthless thoughts, believing that I'm holding them captive, will only aid in her anger and relentless pursuit of escape.

What I desire and what I must do aren't mutually exclusive.

Sitting at my desk, I gesture Ardian into my office.

"You called for me, sir?" He stands with his shoulders back, his posture perfect like he's in the presence of royalty. And why shouldn't he? I'm the fucking mafia king of the castle. Even better, he respects my authority.

"Sit," I command and nod toward the chair opposite my desk.

He closes the door as he enters my office and slinks into the chair. He's more at ease than most men who work for me.

"Any word on the bratva?" I ask. He's in charge of surveillance and reconnaissance. I need to know that they won't be in further danger if I let Aleksandra and the twins leave.

"Mikhail has returned home," Ardian says. "But you already knew that."

I let him go. Not because I wanted to, but because it was the only way to ensure stability and peace between the Italians and Russians.

We forged a simple agreement. He and the bratva are to leave the other mafia families alone. Mikhail's feud is with me. In exchange, he's given his freedom.

It's as good a deal as we'd make, and putting the other families first, it's what a good don does, protects his people. My men realize we're at war and are prepared to weather the storm when Mikhail comes for retaliation.

And he will. Inevitably, the war isn't over.

"Any chatter on Aleksandra?" I ask.

I want to know if she is safe leaving the complex or will her brother go after her?

"I'm not sure what you're hoping to find, sir," Ardian says. "If you are suggesting that she leave, I suspect that she'll return home. She has nowhere else to go, and that would be reckless."

I realize that, and the thought of sending her to a safe house is briefly considered, but I don't imagine she'll go there or stay under my protection.

It's difficult to wipe the grimace from my face at the thought of something dreadful happening to Aleksandra, Liam, or Sophia. Mikhail wouldn't hurt his family, would he?

I run a hand through my hair, my stomach doing somersaults. Under any other circumstances, I'd hide my distress, but I don't fear Ardian's knowledge of my discomfort.

"Might I make a suggestion, sir?"

I nod for him to elaborate on whatever it is that he wishes to disclose.

"We have apartments in the city that can be monitored and are outside of bratva territory. It might be wise to offer her a place to stay and a stipend if you wish her to cut ties with her family."

I press my lips tight and mull over Ardian's suggestion.

It's not the worst idea, and I would know her whereabouts and ensure that she is always protected.

———

I knock firmly on Aleksandra's bedroom door before entering. I don't wait for her to tell me to enter. She doesn't get to give me permission. This is my house. She is my guest.

I'm waiting for an outburst, a shout for her to tell me to get the hell out, but instead, she's nowhere to be seen.

The bathroom door is shut, the shower running.

I poke my head into the twins' room, and they're playing on the floor with the new train set that I bought them, among dozens of other toys.

I study Liam and Sophia from the doorjamb. They barely even notice me. At least they don't pay any heed to the fact that I'm watching them.

They have no idea that I'm their father.

Do I tell them?

That would be breaking one of Aleksandra's rules.

What has Aleksandra told Liam and Sophia about their father? I imagine she's given them the same story that she's fibbed to Mikhail, that he's away fighting a war, a hero who will one day return.

But she never expected me to return or find out that she was pregnant.

"Antonio." Her voice is a whisper. It's soft and sweet as she stands behind me.

I spin around on my heel, glancing at her from head to toe. She's wearing only a towel, clenching it in her fist against her chest.

Her hair is dripping against the floor, leaving a puddle as she stands waiting for me to answer her.

"I want to have a word with you," I say and reach behind myself, closing the adjoining door, offering us privacy.

"Can I get dressed first?"

"I'm not stopping you," I say and can't seem to hide the smirk on my face.

Aleksandra rolls her eyes and pushes me toward the door, exiting the hallway.

I let her believe she has some aspect of control. If I wanted to overpower her, I could, easily.

Stepping backward, I approach the door, my back to

the wood, but I don't open it or step out into the hallway.

I'm not leaving that easily.

Her voice is terse, along with her gritted teeth. "Go!" she snaps at me.

This side of her is too enjoyable and endearing to walk away from. "I'd rather not," I say and fold my arms across my chest. "Besides, you have something of mine that I'd like back."

I don't honestly give a damn about the dress shirt. There are dozens more in my closet, and one shirt can easily be replaced.

"What?"

"My dress shirt," I say. The grinning grows even brighter as I stare at her.

She's flustered and hurries around to the side of the bed, bends down, keeping her towel grasped in her grip. Aleksandra retrieves my dress shirt and tosses it at me. "I don't know why you care so much about that thing. Plus, it's missing half its buttons."

It is missing quite a few buttons in the haste from last night's festivities.

"Yes, I suppose it is."

"Are you leaving now?" Aleksandra gestures with her free hand for me to skedaddle out of her bedroom.

Nice try, *Tesorina*.

"No," I say and let the white dress shirt fall to the floor at my feet.

Her eyes widen, but I sense it's more out of frustration and irritation for me than anything else.

The feeling is mutual.

I hope I don't regret my decision.

Her eyes narrow like she's about to yell at me or throw something, but the only thing in her grasp is the towel secured around her body. And it's unlikely she'll let that drop anytime soon. Her grip is like life or death, and she's not going to let me see her naked again.

"You're free to leave."

"What?" she asks.

My comment catches her off-guard.

"You and the twins are free to leave the complex if that's what you want." I won't hold her captive or against her will. Bringing her here had been for her safety, not that she'd ever see it that way.

"Just like that? No strings attached?"

She doesn't believe me, and why should she? I'm not the most forthcoming or honest man in New York City.

"I'll set you up with an apartment in the city, a place of your own. There will be a guard to ensure that your brother and his men don't cause you or the kids any problems. But I want to know my children," I say. "However, I won't keep them here at the expense of my selfishness."

Her eyes tighten, and her gaze flickers toward the adjoining door. "This isn't a trick?" she asks as she keeps one hand gripped on the towel and opens the adjoining bedroom door with her other hand.

She glances in on them, satisfied that they're playing quietly together.

"I can't promise that we'll share custody, but if you'd like to visit with them, we can make arrangements," Aleksandra says.

"I'll leave you to change and pack your things," I say, opening the door to the hallway.

"Antonio." Her voice is soft, pensive.

I glance back over my shoulder at her. "Yes?"

"Thank you."

I don't say a word. What can I say? I'm doing this for her, but I'm not entirely selfless. I shut the door and step out into the hallway.

Ardian is waiting for me. His expression is grim. I'm not sure whether he disapproves of my methods or there's something else he's keeping from me.

"Is it done?" I ask.

———

Aleksandra has no car, no mode of transportation since we abducted her. I hate seeing things from her perspective, realizing that she deems me a monster because I just might be one.

I'm the bad guy—the man of nightmares.

But I wasn't always this way. Roberto made me what I am, ruthless. I have him to thank for corrupting my childhood, stealing me from my biological parents, and raising me as his own.

My childhood was fucked up.

And I don't want that to be what Sophia and Liam experience.

Instead, I'll give them a place of sanctuary, a home of their own, away from the bratva and the mafia. They can have a normal childhood, away from fear, danger, and terror.

"Is that all you're bringing?" I ask, glancing at the twins with the clothes on their back. Aleksandra didn't bother to pack a suitcase for the twins or herself.

The clothes, the toys, all that I've purchased, she's chosen to abandon.

I don't know how she plans on stocking the apartment with clothes and toys. The stipend I've given her covers food and necessities, but not another wardrobe.

"We don't need anything else. Thank you," she says with a tight-lipped smile. It's an act. She's keeping it a show for the twins, like they chose to stay here for a while as if this was bed-and-breakfast.

I glance at Ardian.

If she doesn't take the suitcases, the plan will never work.

There's a bug and a tracker sewn into the luggage lining, just in case she bails the minute she arrives at the apartment.

"I would like to see you again," I say, pinning Aleksandra with my stare. This isn't the end, not by a long shot. Sophia and Liam are mine. Letting them go is the hardest thing I've ever done, but it's not without cause.

"That's probably not a good idea." She stares at me, her lips pressed together.

I lean closer, invading her personal space. I wrap my arms around her waist, hugging her goodbye, and let my lips linger beside her ear. "They are my children, *Tesorina*."

She pulls back, but I don't release my grasp from her hips. There's a flicker of fear behind her gaze. Does she worry that I won't let her leave with her children?

"We can arrange visits on holidays, birthdays, that sort of thing," she whispers. It's as if she's silently pleading with me to set her free and willing to give me a promise of anything to obtain her freedom.

But I don't want an empty promise.

"I would like that," I say, my gaze latched onto hers. "Stay right here." I untangle from her and withdraw to the living room to retrieve two teddy bears that I gave to the twins and were abandoned by the children amongst the mass of toys and children staying at the complex.

The stuffed bears aren't just any typical toy. While they look cute and cuddly, the black glassy eyes house a camera and two lenses to provide superior video footage. A microphone is tucked into each bear's ear and a tracker is nestled deep inside.

I bring the two toys to the twins, handing one to Liam and the other to Sophia.

"How about a stuffed animal to take home?" I say, offering the kids a warm and friendly smile. I've barely spent any time with the three of them together. It's no wonder they look timid in my presence.

Aleksandra opens her mouth but quickly shuts it as I hand the kids the stuffed animals.

"Thank you," Liam says.

"What do you say, Sophia?" Aleksandra says to her daughter.

"Thanks." Sophia cuddles the teddy bear, rubbing noses with the dark brown fur, and gives it a tight squeeze.

"You're welcome," I say and open the front door, leading them into the garage.

I hand Aleksandra a slip of paper with my cell phone number. "Memorize it in case you need anything," I say. While I doubt she'll call me, I want her to know that I'm available anytime.

"Thanks."

Mario is right on my heel, grabbing the keys and following us to the vehicle. He opens the back door for the twins to climb onto the bench seat. The vehicle is already running, and the garage is open, making it chilly inside, but the car should already be warm and toasty.

"You're not driving us?" Aleksandra asks as she stares at me, her voice soft, tentative. Is she making sure that no one overhears us?

"Mario will make sure that you get to the apartment safely," I say. "He has the keys and will make sure it's safe before you head inside."

She glances past me into the back seat at the twins. They're oblivious to the dangers of the world around them. But she can't be naïve.

"Thank you," she whispers, staring at me.

"If anything ever changes, you are welcome to stay here, with us, become part of the family." I'm making her an offer that I don't make to just anyone.

An invitation to become part of the Moretti family.

I don't expect her to take me up on the offer.

She lets out a soft breath and leans forward just slightly, closer. Her body language is speaking more than she is, like she wants me but is denying herself the pleasure of her desires.

"I can't do that," Aleksandra says.

I pull her tight against me, my fingers at the back of her neck as I crush my lips against hers. I want her to remember the feel of my body pressed against her, the warmth of my lips on hers, the heat shared between us.

The tension in her body dissipates against me as she doesn't fight the kiss like I first expect. Her arms pull me tighter and closer, deepening the kiss.

There's a spark, a flicker of fire still burning bright between us.

It will never be extinguished, so long as we're both alive.

I should break apart the kiss, send her on her way, and vow never to see her again. But I'm not ready for goodbye.

My hand at her lower back glides up beneath her jacket, pressing her against me, wanting her to feel the desire building between us. I drag my tongue against her lips, and she instantly parts her mouth, granting me entrance inside.

It's not the only thing I want inside of her, but I can't fuck her in the garage with Mario and our children watching.

But for the briefest of moments, I don't give a damn about the twins in the car or Mario waiting for orders to return her home.

I want Aleksandra.

The desire to ravish her is insurmountable. Like an avalanche, I can't stop. The truth is that I don't want to. I desire to take her, fuck her, break her, and make her mine.

But she's already broken, and it's my fault.

Snatching Liam.

Kidnapping the three of them.

It's any wonder she hasn't coldcocked me and wished me dead. I don't blame her for hating me, but perhaps one day, she will find forgiveness inside of her for what I've done.

I break the kiss, ending the sizzling heat surfacing between us.

She whimpers, but I barely hear it. "Goodbye, *Tesorina*," I say as I gesture for her to climb into the back seat with the twins.

Her lips are ruby red, swollen, and glistening from the heated exchange. She doesn't say anything. Her gaze moves to the vehicle, and she slips into the back seat wordlessly.

I shut the door and let her leave, granting Aleksandra her freedom.

The pain inside of me burns. I don't dare admit to anyone what she means. It's a burden to feel, to love, to know joy because my greatest enemy has the power to take it all away.

20

Aleksandra

We head away from the compound, the vehicle's engine humming as we drive away from the city.

I sink into the comfortable leather seat and try to relax. The weather is chilly, the sky a dull gray expanding as far as the eye can see. It feels like snow, bone-chilling cold. Dreary.

Traffic whizzes by us on the highway. The driver is moving at a decent clip, but we're not leading the parade by any means, either. It's like he's trying not to be noticed. That's probably typical considering he's mafia. Does he have a dozen arrest warrants out for him, and he's evading the police?

I don't exactly know how to get to the apartment, but we've been traveling for a while and appear to be heading out of the city. Didn't Antonio mention it was in New York City?

My stomach bubbles, and I clear my throat, doing my best not to show any sign of fear.

"Where are you taking us?" I ask the driver.

Liam and Sophia are cuddling their stuffed animals, babbling to each other, oblivious to the potential danger that we are in. They are full of smiles and life.

Will the man driving the vehicle snuff the light right out of them?

Antonio told me he was letting us go. Did he give different orders to his colleague?

I shouldn't have blindly accepted Antonio's offer to leave. It's not like I plan to stay at the apartment, but it gives me a place to crash while I find out who is in charge of the bratva compound.

The driver doesn't answer my question.

I press my lips together, trying to remember the driver's name. And while I want to reach for the handle to the back door, I can't open it while we're traveling at high speeds. That's assuming the door isn't child-locked, not to mention the twins.

"Mario," I say, trying his name out on my tongue.

He glances in the rearview mirror at me. His gaze is cold and harsh, much like his demeanor.

It seems I've gotten his attention.

"Antonio mentioned that the apartment was in the city," I say louder and with a little more force and conviction.

I'm met with silence.

He offers up no excuse, no lame explanation about why he's taking a different route. He heard me, which means my children and I are in danger.

"Where are you taking us?" I ask, trying again to get an answer from him.

"Shut up!" he snaps and presses his foot harder against the gas pedal. The engine roars, and we whip through traffic, weaving in and out past other vehicles.

"Mommy," Sophia's eyes widen and glisten with tears. She wraps her arms around me, trembling in my grasp.

I pull her close and tight, wanting to protect her. Liam's eyes are bright and wide like a deer, but he doesn't scoot any closer. It's like he's trying to be brave.

Did he learn that from Mikhail or Antonio?

Liam hasn't been around either man very much. "It's okay," I whisper to the twins, doing my best to assure them that nothing is wrong.

Except everything is wrong.

We're heading far out of the city, and I have no idea where Mario is taking us.

———

I don't recognize the area or the exit that we take after driving for several hours at maximum speeds on the highway.

Are we still in New York?

Daylight has vanished, which gives me an excellent opportunity to see much of our surroundings. It's dark. There are no nearby lights outside, except for the stars. The sky is clear, unlike when we left New York City.

The vehicle comes to an abrupt halt after traveling on the back roads, through mountainous terrain I'm unfamiliar with.

Sophia's leaning against my side, her eyes closed, asleep.

Liam is resting his head against the door; he, too, has been resting for the past hour after whining about being hungry.

Mario kills the engine and steps out of the vehicle. He yanks the backdoor open. "Out!" he demands.

There's a gun in his right hand.

"Please, don't do this," I say, pleading with him not to kill me. If I'm dead, I can't protect my children. Is this Antonio's way of having access to the twins without my complication?

Sophia stirs awake as I'm yanked out of the back

seat. She sounds sleepy but fearful as her voice quivers. "Mommy?"

I want to lie to her, tell her to go back to sleep and that everything is all right. But it's not. Nothing is all right.

Liam stirs, and though he's pretending to be asleep, I can see the tremble in his hand as he reaches for the handle to the car door. He gives it a pull, but it doesn't open.

"You're a complication that we don't need," Mario says. He grabs me forcefully by the arm and tugs me up to my feet to follow.

He slams the back door shut, ensuring the twins don't leave the vehicle.

If I run, I abandon the twins. That's not an option.

"Let go of me!" I shout, stomping on his toe, fighting back. I jab my knee into his groin, wrestling for the gun.

His hold doesn't loosen in the slightest. The cold metal grazes my temple as he places the gun on my head. "You're making it easy for me," Mario says with a snicker.

It's hard to see much in the darkness, but my eyes have adjusted, and the car is still running, the headlights pointed in the opposite direction.

I can't see the twins from the car, and I pray they don't watch. If Mario kills me, I don't want them to witness my death.

"Why kill me?"

He hasn't pulled the trigger yet. He's had plenty of ample opportunities. Does he like dragging it out, making me beg for my life?

"You're clouding Antonio's judgment."

I don't know what he means. How have I interfered in his mafia dealings?

"Get down on your knees!" he shouts at me, pushing me into the dirt.

The ground is frigid like the air.

"Is this what Antonio wants?" I don't beg for my life, but I'm on my knees, my hands grabbing fistfuls of dirt. Anything that I can use to disorient him.

Mario refuses to answer me.

Antonio mustn't know what Mario is up to. Which means there's little chance of him being my savior. We're out in the middle of nowhere, probably so he can dump my body, if not all three of us.

He cocks the safety, the click sending a chill down my spine.

"Antonio will kill you," I say.

He murdered the last mob boss. Why wouldn't he take vengeance on a man who killed the mother of his children?

21

Antonio

Two hours earlier...

"Mario should have been back by now," I seethe between gritted teeth.

Pacing the length of the hallway, Ardian is leaning with his back against the wall, his arms folded across his desk.

"Maybe he had an errand to run?" Ardian doesn't sound convinced by his suggestion. His brow is furrowed, and he rubs at his jaw. "You gave the kids the teddy bears with the nanny cam installed."

It's not exactly a nanny cam, given that it also contains a tracking device, but I had that added aftermarket.

I hurry into the office with Ardian on my heel. I pull up the live streaming feed, but it's hard to see anything. The camera is dark; the video footage pixilated.

"Maybe back the feed up a bit?" Ardian suggests that I couldn't have figured that out on my own.

I pull up the tracking information on the web, and my stomach sinks at the fact that they're way outside the area they should be in.

"What the hell are they doing in Pennsylvania? Did you know about this?"

"Of course not," Ardian insists. "I'll call Mario and see what the hell is going on." He dials and waits, shaking his head.

He doesn't bother to leave a message. It's clear that Mario is attempting to go off-grid, but why?

What purpose is there unless he plans to dump three bodies? But then he could have done that in several other locations in New York. He didn't have to travel across state lines to find a place to dump the bodies.

I run a hand through my hair, my stomach terse. I can't think about what Mario might do. It sickens me to imagine that he might hurt my children or Aleksandra.

"I want the chopper ready in ten, and we're going after my family," I say, giving orders to Ardian to handle the specifics.

We have a helicopter pad in the backyard, and Ardian makes the arrangements so that we can be on our way.

I head to the armory and retrieve several guns, ammo, and a bulletproof vest that I put on under my jacket.

Mario's proven that he isn't to be trusted. If he's gone after my family, he's likely after my seat on the throne. I toss an extra vest at Ardian just as he ends the call and shoves his phone into his pocket. "You're coming with me."

"Chopper will be here in eight minutes, sir."

"Good. I need to know someone has my back," I mutter as we hurry to the back of the house. I secure the vest and then my black blazer over the top, doing my best to conceal my protection. The last thing I want is Mario aiming for a shot at my head because he notices that I'm wearing a vest.

I give orders to Gian and Monte before heading out of the complex and outside for the chopper.

"I should haven't sent Mario." Why didn't I drive her myself to the apartment to make sure it was safe and she was happy? It would have given us the opportunity for a proper goodbye.

The chopper's blades are loud and don't cease to die down as we hurry to the helicopter, keeping a low profile.

Our ride is waiting for us.

I climb into the back with Ardian, and we secure the headsets that help drown out the ambient sound around us and allow me to communicate with the pilot.

I've got a tablet shoved into my jacket pocket with a live feed for the surveillance and the vehicle's location as it heads west. I relay the information to the pilot while I try to sit back, but there's nothing capable of helping me relax.

My foot taps against the floor of the helicopter. Anxiety sets in, itching at me under my skin, making my heart race. The cabin is warm, my cheeks feel flushed, and I'm doing my best not to let panic set in, but the mere thought of Mario hurting my children or Aleksandra kills me.

Is that why he's doing this, to get back at me for killing Roberto? Is this vengeance?

"What's our ETA?" I ask the pilot.

"An hour and twenty."

"That's not good enough. They could be dead by then!"

———

I keep a close eye on the vehicle's tracking device, and as we grow near, the red blinking slows down on the map.

"It looks like they've stopped," I say, giving the exact coordinates to the pilot.

Although the video footage is pixilated and problematic, I can catch pieces of conversation, enough to know that Aleksandra is still alive.

I can't communicate with her through the device, but it offers enough hope that she isn't dead yet, nor are my kids.

"What's the plan?" Ardian asks.

From outside the window, the view is absolute darkness. There's no town, no lights, no nearby cities.

"Other than killing Mario?" I shoot a look at Ardian. The pilot works for the family, so I don't worry about him witnessing what we're about to do.

I don't care what excuse Mario has fathomed to try to weasel his way out of this fiasco. He's a dead man.

As we grow near, there is a vehicle's headlight, but it's difficult to see much else.

Ardian hands me a set of night vision goggles.

There are two darkened figures in the distance, one towering over the other, a more petite figure.

"Shit. He's about to kill her!" I scream and open the door to the helicopter on our approach, lining up my weapon to take the shot before Mario does first.

We're not the least bit silent or invisible on our approach. The deafening roar of the engine and propeller isn't the only thing to give us away. Our spotlight shines brightly below, lighting up the scene beneath us, giving me a clear shot of Mario.

He can't hear my threats and warnings about putting down his gun. There's no rational explanation other than his betrayal that makes any sense.

Spotting us closing in on him, he raises his gun, pulling the trigger, spraying the helicopter with bullets.

"I'm going to have to pull back."

"The hell you are! Put us down!" I shout at the pilot.

As the helicopter sways and shifts with the pilot's movements, there's a glimpse of motion in the forest down below.

Does Mario have backup?

Are there others working with him and betraying me?

Shots hit the helicopter from Mario's gun.

Every bullet he wastes on attacking me is one less to kill Aleksandra, Sophia, or Liam.

He can take as many hits at me as he wants.

The helicopter engine sputters as the tail whirls, and smoke fills the cabin.

It's dizzying, aiming the kill shot while the pilot loses control. We're still too high to jump without killing ourselves.

I line up the shot and pull the trigger, hitting Mario in the head. His body collapses to the ground.

"Brace for impact!" the pilot shouts.

There isn't much time to do anything but hold on.

22

Aleksandra

Is Antonio coming to rescue me or kill me?

I want to believe that he's here to save me, and the firefight seems a pretty good indication, but I can't help but worry that he'll hold me hostage inside his home again.

The helicopter goes down, skidding against the ground. It was already low when Mario shot several rounds at the engine, bringing it crashing to the ground.

A ball of fire rises into the sky.

Thankfully, the helicopter isn't near the vehicle.

With Mario dead at my feet, I reach for his gun and hurry to the car for Liam and Sophia.

The passenger-side door is open. The car is empty.

Shit!

"Sophia! Liam!" I shout into the void of darkness.

Without the helicopter's light, the only glow was from the blaze and the explosion when it landed unceremoniously on the ground.

Who was in the helicopter?

Antonio and his men or the bratva?

My head throbs and my stomach grumbles, but I ignore all of it, rushing around the vehicle, searching for the twins.

"It's safe to come out!" I can't see much of anything. It's a new moon, and the stars don't offer up enough light in the darkness.

Whether they're ten feet or a mile away, I can't tell. There's no rustling of leaves or twigs—just silence stretching onward in front of me.

Behind me is a crackling of the fire, the creak and

groan of metal crunching on the ground, the weight squeezing down, crushing anything in its way.

"Aleksandra!" Antonio's voice carries across the night from behind. I don't turn around to see if there are any more survivors.

I can't abandon the twins, but they could be anywhere. I need light, whether a flashlight or a torch, something to help me see the woods in front of me.

Behind me, is the clearing where the helicopter went down.

Heavy footsteps on the ground, boots crunching, and two adult shadows looming toward me.

Do I run?

The blaze offers enough light to examine the wreckage, but there's no sign of my children.

Antonio strides with a purpose, and one of his men is beside him, limping but hiding the pain well as he attempts to keep pace.

"Where are the kids?" Antonio shouts.

"I don't—they were in the car," I say, gesturing to the empty vehicle with the door ajar.

While I don't trust Antonio, what other choice do I have? I need his help in locating Sophia and Liam. It's cold, and they're not adequately dressed to be outside for an extended period.

Antonio affixes his night vision goggles and grabs my hand. He's forceful as he pulls me into the thicket of the forest all around us.

"Stay here," he orders at his comrade.

"What are you doing?" I seethe.

How can I trust Antonio after what happened?

"Taking you to the twins." He doesn't lighten up his hold as he drags me through the forest. "I can see their heat signature. They're moving north, back up toward the main road."

Twigs and leaves crunch under my feet. Low-hanging branches scratch my cheek as I follow close to Antonio.

"They're together?" I ask, breathing a sigh of relief.

"Yes, but they're not alone," Antonio says.

There's concern laced in his tone. Something he isn't telling me.

"Someone else is out there?" I don't mean to clench onto his hand harder, but I do.

"Yes," he whispers. "We need to hurry."

He drags me alongside him, through the forest in the darkness.

Up ahead, there are voices and chatter.

"Let go of me!" Sophia whines and struggles.

Is her brother with her? Are they both putting up a fight? Who is with them?

"Stay here," Antonio orders and releases his grip from my hand.

I don't listen. I'm just a few steps behind him, keeping him close, not wanting to get lost in the wilderness or let anything happen to my kids. How can he expect me to stand by and wait for it all to be over?

Sophia and Liam must be frightened.

"Stop right there," Antonio shouts.

While it's dark outside, my eyes have adjusted to seeing a shadowy figure between the twins. Whoever it is must have each of them gripping one hand.

"I don't work for you," his Russian accent permeates the air.

I'd recognize that voice anywhere.

Yuri, my brother's adviser, the Sovetnik. What is he doing in the middle of the forest with my children? Did he come to retrieve them from Mario, and if so, what the hell is going on?

"No, but you worked with Mario," Antonio says as he steps closer, his weapon raised at Yuri. "He's dead, and you're next."

"Wait!" I shout and hurry closer, wanting to see Yuri for myself, needing to know what the hell is going on.

"What are you doing?" Antonio isn't the least bit pleased that I'm not following his orders.

I'm not one of his men he can boss around.

I can't believe that Yuri would want to hurt the twins. Is he here to save them? Did he know about Mario's betrayal of the Italians? Did he come to take us home?

"He wouldn't hurt Sophia and Liam," I say. I'm sure of it. He's been good to the twins and me.

"She's right," Yuri says. He's quick to answer, trying to remedy an already tense situation.

"Why should I believe you?" Antonio seethes on his approach.

"You shouldn't."

Yuri releases his clutches from Sophia and Liam. They rush toward me, throwing their arms around my waist as I pull them against me, embracing them and rushing them out of danger. I walk with them several paces away from both men.

Neither of them seems trustworthy—the mafia or the bratva.

I may as well dig my own grave, putting my life in their hands, either one of them.

Antonio shoves the gun barrel under Yuri's chin, the safety cocked. "Tell me what the plan was. I want to know everything! Who else is involved in your little scheme to murder Aleksandra? What did you plan on doing with the twins?"

"I don't work for you," Yuri barks.

"Obviously," Antonio says. I imagine he's rolling his eyes, annoyed by Yuri's answer. But a man like Yuri doesn't divulge secrets. "Who are you taking orders from? Mikhail?"

How could he take orders from Mikhail? Isn't my brother dead or detained in Antonio's prison?

"Let me guess, you're betraying your boss just like Mario betrayed me," Antonio says. He slams his knee up into Yuri's crotch, watching the man double over in agony. He lands two more blows to his chest and another to his face.

Yuri doesn't fight back.

Why?

I don't understand it. I want to shield my children from the violence, the cruelty, and the horror of what they've already endured at the hands of men who want nothing more than blood.

There's no honor in any of it.

I grab the children's hands and hurry with them through the forest, away from Antonio and Yuri.

A gunshot rings out.

I freeze momentarily, stunned by the realization that one of them is dead.

Neither man would be callous enough to offer a warning shot. "Come on," I say, dragging Sophia and Liam through the forest and darkness, back toward the light in the distance. The blazing flame from the helicopter explosion offers enough of a glimpse to guide me along the way.

We are near the empty car with the headlights on.

I shuffle the twins into the back seat. "Stay here," I warn them. I shut the passenger door left open from their earlier escape and hurry around the vehicle for Mario's dead body.

He's not moving, but there's still a fear that ripples through me.

What if he's not dead?

What if Mario grabs me and attacks me?

I exhale a shaky breath and crouch down to the ground, searching Mario for his keys. His body is no longer warm. The cold air has helped chill him down. I dig my hand into his pocket and retrieve the car keys.

He doesn't move, doesn't flinch. He's dead.

"What are you doing?" Antonio's voice forces a shudder to run through me.

He's towering above me and could end all of this if that's what he wants to do.

"Do you plan on killing me?" I whisper, standing slowly as I turn around to face him.

I can't trust anyone but myself.

With the fire raging nearby, it's easy to see his facial features. His brow is furrowed, his jaw tight with a grimace. "No." Antonio appears both perplexed and insulted by my accusation.

There's crimson on his white shirt beneath the black suit on the collar. If there's also blood on the suit, I can't see it in the darkness.

"You murdered Yuri," I say, meeting his stare. I refuse to cower or show fear, even though I'm trembling inside.

"He had it coming," Antonio says and wipes his face with his hand. A smatter of blood that had grazed his cheek smears. "He wasn't innocent, *Tesorina*."

Is the blood from shooting Yuri, or is he injured from the helicopter crash?

"You don't know that!"

"I know that he and Mario worked together, which means they both betrayed their leaders," Antonio says. He doesn't appear the least bit apologetic for what he's done. "I was letting you free. Is that still what you want?"

"You lied to me. Is Mikhail alive? He's back at the Russian compound?" How could Antonio have kept this from me? Is it because he knew that'd I have wanted to return home?

Antonio reaches into his pocket and retrieves his cell phone.

"Perhaps you should call your brother and find out who is behind Yuri's orders," Antonio says.

I press my lips together. I don't want to believe Mikhail ordered Yuri to have me killed. "I'm not doing your bidding," I say.

"*Tesorina*, Mikhail doesn't just want you dead. He intended to sell Sophia and Liam. Yuri's here with orders to secure the twins and put them up for auction. Mario had orders to kill you and make it look like I was involved."

"And who gave those orders?" I shout.

"I swear on my life, it wasn't me," Antonio says.

I don't believe Mikhail would hurt the twins. And Antonio, it doesn't make sense that he'd order Mario to have me executed, either. Not when he could have done it at his compound.

"Then why not kill me in the back of the car?" I ask. "Mario could have murdered me without driving for several hours."

"It's too messy. Do you realize how difficult it is to get blood stains out of leather?" Antonio quips.

I can't tell if he's joking or not.

"How do you know Yuri intended to sell the twins and that Mikhail is involved?"

"Maybe it wasn't Mikhail. It could be someone wanting to take Mikhail's throne. Is there anyone you can think of who might want you dead?" Antonio asks.

"Other than you?" I quip.

He exhales a heavy breath. "I don't want you dead, *Tesorina*. And I would never put our children's lives in danger or sell them."

"But you would kidnap them," I say pointedly.

His gaze tightens. "That was different, and I apologize for what was done, but it's in the past."

Easy for him to say.

I don't answer, glancing past him at the car. The twins are inside, staring out the window at us, waiting for me to drive them home.

"Goodbye, Antonio," I say and stalk toward the car.

"Are you seriously going to leave us out here?" he asks, appalled that I'd bail on his ass. "Ardian needs medical attention."

I approach the front door of the driver's side and lift the handle, opening the door.

Fuck.

"Hurry up and get into the vehicle," I say, climbing into the driver's side.

Antonio helps support Ardian's weight as he escorts him to the car and the passenger side in the front.

As he approaches the car, it's obvious there's blood everywhere. His limp was the least of his concerns. He'll likely bleed to death if he doesn't get to a hospital soon.

Antonio guides him into the front seat, secures the seatbelt across his lap, and slams the door shut, coming around to the driver's side. He taps on the window.

"I'm driving," he says.

"The hell you are. Get in the back seat." I'm not happy that he'll be seated with the twins, but I don't trust where he'll take us.

When Antonio doesn't follow my orders, I press the gas and lunge the car forward.

"Fine! Fine! I'll get in the back," he grumbles.

I slam on the brakes and wait for him to climb into the back seat and slam the door before hitting the gas again, hurrying away from the destruction behind us.

I glance in the rearview mirror.

Antonio glances at his phone, the light from the screen illuminating much of the back seat.

"Where's the nearest hospital?" I ask, needing directions. I don't have a phone, so GPS is out of the question.

"We're not taking him to a hospital," Antonio says.

"He'll bleed to death if we don't," I snap.

How can he let his friend die?

"What's the plan? Let him bleed out and then bring his dead, lifeless body back to your house?" I'm short on patience, and Antonio is silent.

After several seconds, his response is terse. "Turn right at the fork in the road."

I follow his orders, not because I want to, but because I don't know where the hell I'm going, and I don't want to be responsible for a dying man.

Unlike Antonio, I'm not a murderer.

23

Antonio

I text one of my contacts and get the address of the nearest doctor who is willing to help us.

We don't drive for more than an hour before taking a side road covered in gravel. The ride is bumpy and jars the vehicle around. Ardian must be hiding his pain or unconscious, because I don't hear a peep from him in the front seat.

I direct Aleksandra to turn into an unmarked driveway a few minutes later.

Aleksandra is silent, and her knuckles are white on the steering wheel. Every so often, she glances at Ardian in the front seat.

His breathing is weak, labored, and he's lost quite a bit of blood. I hate to admit Aleksandra was right. Sending him to the hospital would have been a better choice, but that's not a viable option.

Doctors are trained to bring in the police, and they ask questions. At least medical professionals living off-grid keep to themselves, and the man we're heading to see, he's lost his medical license for killing a patient. His name was all over the news, and while I'd rather not bring Ardian to him, what other options are there?

We can't just wander into a local clinic without drawing too much attention to ourselves.

When we pull up at a remote cabin in the woods, my stomach flops.

"Stay in the car," I order Aleksandra. Hopefully, she doesn't leave Ardian and my ass behind.

The moment she stops, the engine is idle, and I jump out of the backseat, hurrying to the front door.

All I can hope is this isn't an ambush and the only man who betrayed me tonight is dead.

I pound aggressively on the front door.

There's a commotion behind the door, and the interior light flickers on behind the covered windows inside the cabin.

A gentleman opens the door. He's in sweatpants and a flannel shirt. He appears more awake than I would have thought, given the amount of time it took for him to answer the door. But he's not brandishing a weapon or threatening me for trespassing.

"Gian sent me," I say to explain my appearance at his front door.

"Where's the patient?" he asks, glancing past me at the running vehicle in the driveway.

Did Gian warn him that we were coming and for him to be ready?

"In the front seat," I say, and he follows me outside in his slippers to escort Ardian into the cabin.

The air is chilly, and our breath is visible from the cold.

There are lights around the front of his property, offering a slight glow along the driveway in addition to the vehicle's headlights that are illuminated.

Aleksandra doesn't say a word.

Sophia and Liam have fallen asleep in the back seat.

The doctor glances from Aleksandra to the sleeping twins before helping me carry Ardian inside. "Put him on the table," he says. He doesn't mention the kids or ask about Aleksandra.

How much did Gian tell him?

There's a kitchen table that's been cleared and on a nearby counter, medical supplies. He was waiting for our arrival.

I help Ardian onto the table, laying him down. Blood pools at his injuries, spilling past his torn and tattered clothing.

The doctor examines his wounds, ripping Ardian's pants further to expose the injury. Shrapnel protrudes from his flesh. I'm not the least bit squeamish, but watching the physician remove the metal shards isn't a favorite pastime.

I head toward the window, glancing out at the vehicle.

"How long will this take, Doc?" I ask, glancing over my shoulder as he tends to Ardian's injuries. The doctor already has an I.V. hooked onto Ardian's hand

and is sterilizing the tools to remove the pieces of shrapnel.

"Could be an hour," he says. "Depends on how bad the damage is after I remove the metal lodged in his leg. Right now, it's keeping him from bleeding to death."

I exhale a sharp sigh and pace the length of the cabin from the living room to the kitchen. The space is small, quaint.

"Do you have somewhere else to be?" the doctor asks.

I can't help but feel antsy, like a sitting duck waiting for the next target to strike. Mario wasn't working alone. That was made clear by Yuri's presence.

And if Yuri is working with someone other than Mikhail, who is it?

The squeal of tires kicking up gravel forces me to rush to the door, yanking it open, but it's too late.

Aleksandra is gone.

"Fuck!" I curse, standing with the cold wind in my face and the heat of the cabin at my back.

I dig out my phone from my pocket and step outside, closing the door behind myself to call Gian. I need a car and an additional set of eyes on Aleksandra.

"What's up, boss?" Gian answers. "You make it to Doc's house?"

"Yes, Ardian is with the physician right now. I need you to get a car for me at this location. Aleksandra left with the kids." I can track her with my phone, at least.

"Have you thought that maybe she doesn't want to be found, sir?" Gian says.

"It doesn't matter what she wants. Her life is in danger, and I don't want my children to end up in the wrong hands."

I'm finding it difficult to trust anyone right now, after Mario's betrayal, but all along, I worried about his allegiance to me after Roberto's death. He'd been playing with me, making me believe that I could trust him.

Are there any other mafia members looking to stab me in the back when I least expect it?

"Get me a vehicle," I say, ignoring his remark. I end the call and pull up the tracking software to locate Aleksandra and the twins.

They haven't gotten far, and I'm not sure how they plan on getting anywhere without a map or GPS to guide them.

Does Aleksandra even have any money to stop for fuel? What about a credit card for a hotel? Or will she return to Mikhail's after all that's transpired now that she knows he's free?

She'd do anything for Sophia and Liam, but returning to Mikhail's, that's the worst choice she could make.

The tracker blinks with their movement down the main thoroughfare we came upon. The vehicle stops, or the tracker has difficulties finding the signal as it flashes in the same spot for several seconds. It doesn't appear to be moving.

How long until Gian can secure a vehicle to my current location? He'll probably reach out to a local used dealership and have a car driven down to me. But that takes time, and I'm not the most patient man.

I head back inside the cabin.

The doctor is working tirelessly to save Ardian's life.

"I need to borrow your vehicle," I say to the physician.

He grunts and mutters something unintelligible under his breath.

"I'll buy you a new car and pay you double your fee for looking after my soldier," I say. It's not like I can't afford it. And while Ardian is more than just a soldier, I don't want to risk his life by letting the doctor that I barely know in on his position and worth to me.

He glares at me and then nods toward the front door. "The keys are hanging on the wall."

"Thanks," I say. It's not like he doesn't have Ardian as collateral as well.

I despise leaving my man behind, but he's in no condition to travel and needs to be stabilized before I take him home.

Threats have a time and a place; now isn't it.

I need to go after Aleksandra, Sophia, and Liam before she does something stupid.

———

In a matter of minutes, I'm following the tracking device on my phone, pointing me north on a side road.

Two sets of railroad tracks cross the main thoroughfare. And just before I approach, the red lights flicker on. I hit the gas, but there's no way I will make it before the train.

I slam hard on the brakes as I near the tracks, jolting the vehicle around a bit.

"Damnit!" I slam my fist against the steering wheel.

I'm lucky enough to get stopped not just by one train but two. The first whizzes by at lightning speed. The other on the second set of tracks crawls by at a snail's pace.

I examine the GPS maps, but there are no other roads that don't cross the tracks, and any other route will add at least an additional hour to the trip.

I flip from the GPS app on my phone to the tracking device with Aleksandra's whereabouts.

There's no sign of movement, which either means she discovered the tracking device or they're waiting for something.

Or someone.

I'm impatient, but there isn't much I can do but wait.

Finally, the tracks clear, and I hit the gas, hurrying as quickly as possible. But she's already had a decent head start.

Up ahead, as I close in on the last half mile until the destination, the sun has already come up. There's a small gas station on the right, and I recognize the car we were in earlier pulled over in the parking lot.

I hurry into the lot and shut off the engine before jumping out of the vehicle. I lock the doors and shove the keys into my pocket while heading toward the abandoned car.

It's empty.

I rush into the gas station, pulling open the glass door—the bell on the door jingles to announce my presence.

The place is small, and unless they're in the bathroom or intentionally hiding from me, it's not like I'd have difficulty spotting them, especially Aleksandra.

"My wife and kids just stopped in here, couldn't have been more than a few minutes ago," I say to the man behind the counter.

"I didn't see anything," he says.

He's lying.

He looks nervous, and his eyes are darting around, avoiding me. He glances at the trash briefly.

I stalk toward the bin and notice the stuffed animals torn to shreds. My mouth is parched at the sight of the destruction of Sophia and Liam's bears. She knows I was tracking her, watching her movements.

The attendant on duty must know something.

"I'll bet she spoke to you," I say and approach the counter. I flash my weapon holstered on my hip to let him know I'm not fucking around.

His gaze lands on the phone near the counter. "Did she ask to use the phone?" I ask, grabbing the landline before he can stop me. I hit redial, already suspecting that she's reached out to Mikhail.

"Aleksandra?" a Russian voice picks up the call. It sounds like Mikhail, but it could be any of his comrades.

I don't have to ask to know where they're taking her.

24

Aleksandra

Thirty minutes earlier...

A black SUV approaches the gas station, and the window rolls down on the passenger side. I step outside with the twins. They're whining and restless. I can't blame them for being tired.

"Get in," Luka says.

"I thought Mikhail was coming to get us." The sun begins to rise, casting light over the mountains and through the forest.

While I've always trusted Luka, I thought the same about Yuri.

"It would take Mikhail hours out of his busy day to come to get you. Let's just say I was in the neighborhood. Get in," he says.

I open the back door and let the twins into the vehicle. I make sure the child safety latch isn't enabled and then shut the door, opening the passenger side to sit up front beside Luka.

"Why were you in the neighborhood?" I ask.

"Mikhail wanted me to have Yuri followed." He glances in the rearview mirror at the twins. "Where'd they get those bears?"

"Antonio," I say and frown. "Why?"

He turns around and rips the toys from their hands.

"What are you doing?" I scold Luka. Does he know nothing about kids? He can't just steal their toys and not expect an outburst.

Sophia's bottom lip pouts, and she sniffles, hiding her tears.

Liam folds his arms across his chest, his nose twitching with a snarl. "That was mine!" he bellows out before the waterworks come at full force. "Give it back!"

Luka pulls out a pocketknife and rips along the teddy bear's spine. "What the hell are you doing?" There's no way the twins will settle down now that he's destroyed their presents.

He digs into the stuffing and yanks out a red flashing beacon. "The gifts are trackers. Possibly also surveillance equipment." Luka jogs into the gas station and tosses the teddy bears into the garbage.

He says something to the attendant on duty, but I can't hear the exchange. Luka doesn't appear the least bit calm or polite. He's probably threatening the man. That wouldn't surprise me in the slightest.

He hurries back to the vehicle.

"How the hell did you know there was a tracker in the stuffed animals?" I ask.

Is that how Antonio had been able to locate us last night? Maybe I should be relieved, but anger resonates throughout my body. What else had he seen? Witnessed?

How long had he been running surveillance on my children and me?

"I've seen something similar that was a nanny camera. You look like you've been through hell," he says, glancing me over.

He slams the door shut and jets off, whisking us out of the parking lot.

———

I try to remain awake on the drive back to the city, but I'm exhausted after staying up all night. Not to mention the adrenaline rush from the previous day.

It takes all of my strength to keep my eyes open.

It's hard to trust Luka after what happened with Yuri. I want to ask Luka about it, but I'm much too tired and struggling just to keep my eyes open.

While I don't know where we are, he's using his phone's GPS to take us back to the city, which offers me a tiny bit of comfort.

The ride is quiet and long.

It's a struggle to stay awake.

Eventually, I drift off to sleep, not meaning to let my exhaustion get the best of me.

The car comes to an abrupt halt, and my eyes flash open to see that we're just outside the gate entrance of our house.

The guards open the metal gates and allow us entrance inside the compound.

Home sweet home.

Mikhail waits outside the front door, his jaw tight and hands bunched at his fists. He doesn't appear pleased to see me.

I thought I'd feel relieved to see him alive, but my stomach bubbles with anxiety.

Luka brings the vehicle up to the front entrance and shuts off the SUV. I climb out and open the back door for the twins to follow behind me.

"Did the Italian prince break your little heart?" Mikhail quips. There's a brashness to his remark, his eyes narrow and fueled with something that I don't quite recognize.

He smacks me hard across my face, sure to leave a red mark on my skin.

I shield Sophia and Liam from him, protecting my children.

"Don't be stupid, Aleksandra. You want to come home, then you'll follow my rules. Get inside!" he barks and points at the door.

I escort the twins into the compound, and he's on my heels right behind me.

"Children, go upstairs to your room," he says. "I need to have a word with your mother."

"Yes, Uncle Mikhail," Sophia says. She latches onto Liam's hand, and they hurry up the elegant stairwell to their bedroom.

I watch, grateful that they are out of sight before Mikhail says or does anything else that might scare them. I'm not afraid of what he will do to me, only what might happen to the twins.

"Let me guess. You've decided you're finished playing house with Antonio," Mikhail snarls with disgust.

Exhaling a nervous breath, I ignore his remark. Maybe I should have heeded his warning at Antonio's and not come home.

I glance up into Mikhail's cold stare. "You should know, Yuri betrayed the family," I say.

All I can do is hope that Mikhail wasn't involved and had no knowledge of what happened. That he'd been in the dark, same as Antonio.

"You know nothing," Mikhail snarls, and his hand comes up a second time to smack me across the face, but this time, I pull back quicker than his blow. His eyes widen, shocked. "You defy me, little sister?"

"One of Antonio's men tried to murder me, and he teamed up with Yuri to sell the twins."

Mikhail snorts at my remark. "Sell the twins? You mean someone wants those pestilent little brats?"

"Don't speak about my children like that!" I snap, stepping toe-to-toe with him, unafraid. He very well might slap me again for my disobedience.

Mikhail rolls his eyes and ignores my remark. "Don't think that everything is all sunshine and shit with you coming home. You'll be sequestered in your room. You can come out for meals, but you are not to attend any lavish parties, no guests, and certainly no leaving the premises. And don't think you can wander freely without a guard. I don't trust you, little sister. And make one wrong move, and I'll let you sleep in the dungeon."

"Home sweet home," I mutter. "Will one of the guards be escorting Sophia and Liam to preschool?" Usually, I accompany them, but if Mikhail forbids me from leaving, someone else will have to make sure they are looked after when the twins aren't in the compound.

"Luka will handle it. Now, get upstairs," Mikhail grunts.

Nikita used to be responsible for escorting the twins to preschool, with me accompanying him. Luka can probably handle the task, but I've never seen him with the twins on his own.

I quietly head up the wooden stairs and down the hall toward my bedroom. It's early, and I'm beat.

The twins are across the hall in their shared bedroom, the wooden bunk beds against the wall. I crack the door open, and they're seated on the bottom bunk together, pulling the bedsheets down, making a fort.

I should scold them that it's too early, they haven't had enough sleep and should climb under the covers for a few more hours.

But I don't.

They're happy, cheerful, and don't have a care in the world. I don't want to take that innocence from them. Already, Sophia and Liam have been through so much. If they're filled with joy at home, who am I to take that from them?

They're quiet and seem to be staying out of trouble, so I leave them to play together. Shutting their bedroom door, I back away down the hall and retreat to my bedroom.

I open the door, and a waft of jasmine fills my nostrils. There's a broken perfume bottle lying on its side on the floor. The contents spilled and stained the wood. My room is in disarray and not the way that I left it.

The drawers are open; my clothes are strewn about as if someone was searching for something. Had the guards thought that I was involved in Mikhail's abduction? Is that why they ransacked my room and tossed my things all over the place?

Or had the rampage been when Antonio's men had torn the place apart, looking for Mikhail?

I don't bother to clean up the mess, not right now. I

shut the curtains and hit the lights. I climb under the covers and let my head hit the pillow.

I should feel at ease, relieved to be home.

But my stomach is in knots. I toss and turn, trying to get a few hours of sleep to ward off the impending headache that I already feel coming.

It's of little use.

All I can think about is *him*.

Antonio.

Why did he let us leave?

Why had Mario wanted me dead?

Are there others still after my children?

I roll onto my back and stare up at the ceiling. Pushing the blankets off, I sit up in bed. I want answers. No, I need answers, and while I don't think Antonio is the person to ask, maybe Mikhail or Luka can shed some light on what happened.

But I can't trust Mikhail to divulge anything more than what he wants me to know. He's not a man to slip up or spill anything that isn't intended to be told.

I slink out of bed and grab a change of clothes from the floor before heading for the bathroom for a hot shower. I'm covered in filth, both physically and emotionally. I wash all of it down the drain, standing under the hot spray until the water grows cold.

Retreating to my bedroom, I dress and clean up the mess left on the floor, putting my clothes away. There's little else for me to do cooped up in my room. The library is downstairs with a plethora of books to bide my time. There's no computer, no phone, or television in my bedroom.

I sneak out of my room and am quiet down the hallway, my footsteps silent. I remember which floorboard squeak and groan with years of living under the same roof. I avoid those as I wander down the stairs, careful not to be seen.

I often snuck out against my father's orders in my teen years. Mikhail probably remembers my rebellious streak, but he's not intelligent enough to put a guard outside my bedroom door.

Why?

Does he think I've come crawling back and am

begging for his forgiveness? I refuse to cower toward him or Antonio.

I breeze down the stairs and linger in the hallway near the foyer, waiting until the coast is clear before I dash past an open door.

A man behind me clears his throat.

If it were Mikhail, he'd have gripped me by the neck and thrust me around. I press my lips together and spin around, my hands in front of me, folded together.

Luka cocks an eyebrow as he glances me over. "You have orders to remain in your room."

"Unless a guard accompanies me," I say, allowing him to help me out.

He snorts under his breath. "Where are you heading?" he asks. He keeps his voice low, careful not to arouse suspicion from the men in the office just a few feet away.

While I wasn't eavesdropping, it wouldn't have been difficult to do if I hadn't been caught. "To the library," I say.

I don't have a destination in mind. I just want out of my room. I'd been cooped up already for too long and want to feel like I'm home, like nothing's changed and everything is all right.

Except it isn't.

Everything has changed.

Mikhail has discovered that I'm a liar.

The twins' father isn't a military hero fighting overseas, and I have no intention of marrying him. Not that I believe Mikhail would want me to wed Antonio, he'd probably have me executed before he'd allow me to marry an Italian Mafia leader.

"Mikhail is looking for a reason to punish you, don't give him one," Luka warns.

I hate that he isn't wrong. "You mean locking me up in my room isn't punishment enough?" I exhale a heavy breath, and he grabs my arm, yanking me quickly past the open office with the Russian soldiers inside.

Mikhail is hosting a meeting, but I don't know what they're droning on about, probably trying to get even with Antonio.

Will it ever end?

"Don't test your brother's patience," Luka warns. He whisks me into the library and closes the door behind us.

There's enough light from the windows pouring into the library that I don't bother to turn on a lamp or the overhead switch.

"I didn't tell Antonio anything about the family," I say and fold my arms across my chest.

Luka glances me over from head to toe. "If you had, Mikhail would have had you killed."

My mouth is dry, and I press my lips tight. "Someone wants me dead. Yuri was part of the operation, trying to sell my children." I step closer toward Luka. "Tell me what you know."

His shoulders relax, and while I'm tense, he doesn't convey the slightest bit of fear or anxiety. "I'm not surprised. You've pissed off many people. Your brother suggested that we wed when you return home."

"What?" I laugh at the absurdity of his suggestion. "No way. He wouldn't do that to you or me."

"He wants you out of his hair and out of trouble, away from Antonio."

I'm not marrying Antonio. Don't they realize that just because we shared one passionate night and two children, I'm not tied to the man?

"He wouldn't ask one of his men to marry me," I say, not wanting to believe it.

"It's been brought up a few times by your brother since you left and he discovered the children's father is an Italian."

"It's stupid how much the Russians hate the Italians!" I groan and stomp away from Luka, staring out the window. "I'm not marrying you."

"Yeah, I never thought you'd go along with it," he says. There's a hint of humor in his tone, like he's pleased that I don't bow down to the whims of my older brother. "But Mikhail doesn't exactly accept the word no for an answer."

Tell me something that I don't know. "Well, he can't force me to marry a man I don't love."

"He can," Luka says, staring at me disapprovingly. "You know he can force you to do anything that he wants, and if you disobey him, it gives him greater pleasure."

I grumble under my breath, "Mikhail is a sadistic asshole."

"You're not wrong," he whispers, making sure that no one can overhear us. There's a slight smirk on his face.

Although I don't imagine anyone is listening and the door to the library is shut. "But?" I'm waiting for him to stand up for his boss.

"He is your brother and wants you to be protected and your children to grow up with a father."

I tighten my gaze. "And you agree with him? That my kids need a father?" I can already feel the annoyance brewing at his remark, like I'm a prize to be bought and sold to a man who wants a family.

Luka clears his throat. "I never said that. Those are his words. I merely think it might be good for you to be out from under his roof, raise the twins someplace outside of the city."

"I thought you weren't intending to marry me?" I

can't help but wonder if he's trying reverse psychology on me.

"Oh, I'm not. I'm just stating the facts that Mikhail will always control you unless you get far from here, far from the compound."

I hate that he's right. I purse my lips and shuffle my feet. "Where am I supposed to go?" It's not like I have a dollar to my name. My money is tied up and only released in small amounts with Mikhail's approval.

Father didn't do me any favors when he died.

"If it were me, I'd have asked the father of the twins for child support. Demand a lump sum and then get as far from New York as you can."

This city is the only home I've ever known. Leaving without a job, a place to go, it's terrifying. "And why would Antonio give me a cent?"

"You could blackmail him," he says and shoves his hands into his pockets.

Did he seriously just suggest that I blackmail a mafia don? "You're crazier than Mikhail."

Is he trying to get me killed? I thought Luka and I

were friends. At the very least, he's always looked out for me and my best interests.

"What? He kidnapped you and your children. You could threaten to go to the police unless he gives you fifty thousand dollars."

"That's extortion." I'm not the most innocent person, but I'm not going to threaten Antonio or his family. I'd more than likely end up dead or with my children ripped away from me.

25

Antonio

Three weeks later…

Ardian is resting at the complex, with the best doctors and physicians looking after him since the helicopter accident.

I've been biding my time, keeping a close watch on the Russians. There have been no recent threats to my family or my extended Italian brothers.

All is quiet.

Almost too quiet.

I haven't seen or heard a word from Aleksandra. Not that I expected us to remain close, but she is the mother of my children, and I want to see Liam and Sophia.

But showing up at the Russian complex might be stupider than when I kidnapped her. It could start the next war between our feuding families, and right now, we've brokered peace. At least between the factions in the New York area.

It can't last, but I won't be the reason for its destruction. Not with my children under Mikhail's roof. There's too much at risk.

"Where are you off to?" Ardian asks. He's cooped up on the living room sofa, stretched out, supposedly healing.

He looks fine to me, but he does walk with a bit of a limp that he tries to hide. I'm sure it hurts like hell, but we've all got scars from battle.

"Who said I was going anywhere?"

The man can read me better than anyone else under my roof. At least Ardian, I trust. I've been wary of the others since Mario's betrayal. But all along, I suspected he might turn on me, betray me, and still be loyal to the man I killed, his boss.

"You're dressed sharper than usual," Ardian says.

I raise an eyebrow. "You're paying too much attention to me and not enough attention to anything else."

"Put me back in the field. Let me work, boss."

I can't do that. It's against the doctor's orders. He has at least another week to recover, if not longer. While he can handle some minor paperwork, surveillance, the type of work that can be done from his ass seated on the sofa, that's not what I'm about today.

"I need info on Aleksandra," I say.

He runs a hand across his face. Ardian is muttering something under his breath, probably about how I'm an idiot for loving a woman who could get me killed. He isn't wrong.

"There isn't anything I can find from this couch," Ardian says.

"I know, so I'm going out." I try to remain cryptic about where I'm heading. While I trust Ardian, anyone else could be listening in, and I don't need trouble to follow me. I already have enough of that daily.

Lately, the feds have been sniffing around the property, patrolling the neighborhood more than usual. Like they're looking for something, but they're too obvious for their own good.

They're probably rookies. Foolhardy, thinking they can advance their career with a massive takedown of the mafia.

Good fucking luck.

Could Aleksandra have snitched to that federal agent?

Doubtful. If she had, the feds would be all over the place with a warrant, knocking down the front door. At the very least, they'd have arrested and charged me with kidnapping. And since that hasn't happened, it means she's not talking.

Which is a relief.

Maybe I was wrong, and she wasn't going behind my back to Agent Malone.

"I'll be back in an hour, maybe two." I don't plan on being gone long. I want to see Aleksandra and the twins. I need to know they're all right.

I head down the hall and to the garage, grabbing a set of keys hanging. I hit the engine as I open the garage door.

The auto start is a nice feature, but I don't give it ample time to warm the car up before climbing into the front seat and heading out. Every so often, I glance at the clock.

The twins will be getting out of preschool soon. I'm familiar with their routine, and it's the perfect time to check up on Aleksandra.

Depending on if she's becoming accompanied by a guard and who will determine if I intervene or watch.

But either way, I need to see her and know that she's all right.

I hurry across town and pull up in a space near the back of the preschool where the playground is situated. There aren't any children outside playing. It's bone-chilling outside. Winter is brutal, and snow begins to fall and blanket the streets.

Snow is covering the windshield.

I pull on a beanie and gloves and step outside into the frigid air. It's well below freezing, and the snow is light and fluffy. The sun crests along the sky. Soon it will be dark and the roads icy and slick.

Stepping outside, the black boots help keep my feet warm. I shut the car door and shove my hands into my coat pockets.

A plow rushes down the street, kicking up snow and sludge. I hurry to get away before it kicks up against my dress pants, but I'm not quick enough.

I fucking hate winter.

The grumble of discomfort vanishes when I catch sight of Aleksandra in a deep red coat. It's long and thick. She has the wide hood pulled up over her head and winter boots to match.

She hurries across the street and then stalks along the slippery sidewalk in haste to get into the preschool.

"Aleksandra," I say, calling out to her.

She glances from her intended destination to me. Her eyes widen.

Is she afraid of me?

She shakes her head no and glances back over her shoulder. The vehicle across the street is lit up, the headlights on, the windshield wipers clearing the snow from the window as the SUV is parked with a driver behind the wheel.

She's being watched. I slowly head toward her and take a seat on the nearby bench. It's dusted with snow, which doesn't help me stay dry, but it's right near the school's sidewalk entrance.

I can no longer see the vehicle, which means they can't see me. Hopefully, they don't realize who I am. If they do, we're both screwed.

She approaches me and places her foot on the bench like she's lacing up her winter boots.

"I don't have much time," she says. "Mikhail's men are watching me. What is it?"

"I just needed to see you, to know that you're all right." I want to pull her against me, wrap my arms around her, and crush her in a hug. It's stupid and crazy, but she brings out something inside me that's foreign and unfamiliar yet warm.

Dare I say I might love her. I love Sophia and Liam. It's impossible not to love them. They're perfect. And the fact that she carried my children, it's my weakness, Aleksandra.

Her eyes are glassy and red. She has dark circles beneath them. Has she been getting enough sleep? Her cheeks are rosy, but that's probably from the cold. There's a scratch on her neck, but she wiggles her coat higher, and I can't see it any longer.

"I'm—it's complicated," Aleksandra says. "Mikhail is hosting an engagement party for me two weeks from Friday."

I swallow the lump forming in the back of my throat. Is this what she wants? "You're getting married?" I wish I'd heard her wrong, but I know what I heard, and it's unsettling.

Does she even love the man she'll be bound to?

She pulls her foot down from the bench and then lifts her other boot to do the same, retying her laces. They're long and lace from the heel to halfway up her knee, biding her a few moments with me.

It isn't enough.

I want to see the twins, hug them, tell them they can return home with me. But I'm not sure that's what they want, and I expect it isn't what Aleksandra desires, either.

"I don't want to, but Mikhail isn't giving me a choice."

"Why are you telling me this?" I ask. If I show up to the party, I'll destroy everything that I've worked to achieve. The peace between the Russians and Italians will be severed.

She pauses for a breath. I almost think it's because she loves me, but I'm not a fool to believe that she'll want to be with me after one night and forcing her to live under my roof.

"Because you're the father of my children, and I won't be in New York after I get married. He's shipping me off to Russia."

My stomach drops at the mention of her leaving the country. I'll never see my children again if she goes to Russia. "No, he can't do that."

She puts her boot down on the ground. She's out of time. Any minute, the guard watching her will be coming out of the vehicle if she wastes any more time with me. "I have to go. The party is in two weeks at the compound. It's at seven o'clock. Please,

I need your help."

"How am I supposed to get in?" I ask.

Every Russian will recognize me.

"I'll suggest to my fiancé that we make it a costume party," Aleksandra says. "Mikhail will listen to him." She hurries to the preschool entrance and presses the buzzer, waiting to be allowed inside to pick up the twins.

The bench is cold. The air outside is even chillier, but I sit and wait. I want to see Liam and Sophia, even from a distance.

Snow continues to fall, thicker and faster.

Several minutes pass before Aleksandra steps outside into the snow. On each side of her, are the twins, clutching her hands as she walks with them down the sidewalk and then waits for traffic to clear before crossing the street.

Sophia and Liam don't seem to notice me. It's probably for the best. It's not like either one of them can keep a secret, and I don't want Mikhail or his men to suspect that I'm coming for my family.

26

Aleksandra

The moment I return with the children from school, Mikhail is on me like I've just robbed a bank and taken hostages. "You left the compound without my permission?"

I remove my jacket and then my gloves. The items dried in the vehicle on the way back from the preschool, and parking in the garage helped keep me from getting a new dusting on my clothes.

My boots are still soaked, and if I track the mess through the compound, I'll never hear the end of it.

I help Sophia and Liam remove their wet winter gear

before they hurry up the stairs together to play in their bedroom.

After the children are out of earshot, I finally answer Mikhail.

He's standing there, tapping his foot on the wood floor, waiting for my response. His arms are folded across his chest, and he is every bit terse and uptight, worse than Antonio.

"I brought a guard with me," I say, as if that doesn't break the rules. "You can't keep me locked up forever."

He can, and will, if he wants to, but I don't think that's what he desires, or I'd be tossed out on the street. He is looking out for me in his strange way, but it doesn't mean that I have to bend to his will and do as he commands of me.

He grunts and shakes his head. "That engagement party that I had planned, you can bet your ass that it's going to be a wedding. And you're not leaving the house until there's a ring on your finger."

"What?" I can't believe him. "Mikhail, no, that isn't fair."

"I'm done with your childish antics. Running off, refusing to follow my direct orders. Your husband will get the privilege of disciplining you and believe me when I say it won't be soon enough."

My mouth is dry, my hands tremble, but I ball them into fists, not wanting Mikhail to witness my displeasure and discomfort with his threats.

"You're going to force me to marry Luka?" He isn't the worst choice. There are men whom I despise who work for my brother, but he isn't the warmest and most considerate man, either. He's also not particularly great with children.

"That isn't a surprise, little sister. Yes, you will marry Luka, and you will join him with your children in Russia."

I can't. I won't do that. "No, please don't do this," I plead with him to change his mind. An engagement gave me time to stall, to devise a plan to get out and away from Mikhail. I had thought that there'd be months until the actual wedding day and moving out of the country.

"It's already done. I decided while you were out

gallivanting with your children. The arrangements are made."

I purse my lips and need to devise a plan fast. I told Antonio that I would try to make the engagement party a costume ball.

"If it's my wedding, then do I get a say in the dress, the attire of the guests, the theme? I'd love to do an old-world theme with guests in elegant costumes."

Mikhail chuckles and shakes his head. "Sister, this wedding is for you. I'm glad you're coming on board, but no, your fiancé and my men will handle all the necessities. You needn't worry about a thing," he says, and his gaze tightens. "And there is no way in hell my men are dressing in anything other than a tuxedo. The last thing I need is you trying to dress up one of the maids to marry Luka."

"I wouldn't do that. I want to help plan my wedding," I say. If he disagrees with the costume party, how will Antonio sneak inside the compound?

"No!" Mikhail is firm and commanding, making it clear that he's the one in charge. "You will let Luka and my men deal with the arrangements. If I hear a word that you're involved in anything, I will lock you in the dungeon until you're wed. Is that clear?"

"Crystal," I seethe between gritted teeth.

27

Antonio

The night before the party...

I still can't wrap my brain around the fact that Aleksandra is getting married, and it doesn't sound the least bit consensual on her part.

Her bastard brother is selling her to one of his men.

At least that's my take on the entire scenario.

Maybe I'm wrong. He could be looking out for his little sister, but forcing her to marry a man she doesn't love and shipping their new family off to Russia sounds more like a present for Mikhail than for the new family.

Who is she marrying?

I want details. I still need to devise a plan, and I can't do that without a little more knowledge of the engagement party.

That's what she called it, but my gut tells me it's more than just an engagement party. If I were the one forcing someone to wed, I'd use the engagement party as a cover and intend for the couple to marry at once.

Mikhail isn't naïve. He must realize that she wants out, and the longer he waits, the more time she has to escape.

Everything I know from being a mafia boss tells me that the wedding is tomorrow. The party is a rouse to get Aleksandra to comply.

But I need more details. If it's a wedding, it's unlikely that the guests will be dressed in costume attire. I doubt her fiancé or Mikhail will go for that suggestion.

Ardian and I stumble into a seedy club across town. It's on Russian turf, and it's no secret that they do business at the strip club. It's not the least bit upscale or frilly. The place looks like a front for money laundering, and it probably is amongst other illegal acts.

Not that I care.

Ardian has been healing, and while he isn't up to the task of drinking tonight, he can help be my eyes and ears. Plus, I appreciate his company and watching my back.

And I'm sure he's thrilled for a night out admiring the ladies dancing.

Waltzing into Russian territory is dangerous, but it seems the only choice if I plan on getting intel before the party. As I suspect, whether it's an engagement party or a wedding, I need details.

The club is dark, and I pay the cover for both of us as we enter. I don't recognize the bouncer or the bartender when we enter. Not that I come here that often.

I'm not a fan of throwing my money at the Russians and their associates. But the place serves decent drinks, and the women offer a nice view. Plus, there's always an opportunity for a dance, and while I don't need to pay for a woman's attention, it's nice to enjoy the entertainment occasionally.

The lighting is dim, which helps us look inconspicuous as we enter. No one pays us any attention, and why should they when there are plenty of women dancing to capture attention?

We head to a corner booth in the back and sit. The waitress comes over, offering to take our drink orders. I get a scotch on the rocks while Ardian requests a ginger ale.

Usually, he'd drink me under the table, but between the pain killers and him driving us back to the complex when we're done, his ass will remain sober.

"I don't recognize anyone yet," Ardian says, taking a long look around the place.

"Does that include the girls?" I ask with a knowing smirk. I've heard that he's dated one of the dancers. I'm not sure if it's accurate, but rumors usually start with some merit of truth.

"Yes," he says and laughs, glancing away. His ears redden.

Ardian has slept with one of the dancers. I'm guessing she's not here, though, or his attention would be on *her* rather than on our mission.

"Anyway, how do you want to do this? Pay for a couple of lap dances and see if the girls talk? Or wait around for Mikhail's cronies?"

"It's still early. We can pay for a dance, but I wouldn't expect the girls to know much." I wave my hand dismissively. "Give it time." I have good information that the bratva frequent this place, specifically several of Mikhail's men. While I usually wouldn't travel onto their turf to get information, I'm coming up against a wall and need a breakthrough.

I can't show up to their complex without a plan in place to get Aleksandra and the twins out. The last thing in the world I want is to put their lives in further danger.

———

After having drinks, lap dances, and getting bits of information for over an hour and a half, the club manager visits our table.

"I hope you gentlemen have enjoyed the entertainment, but we're closing early tonight."

"Why's that?" I ask, offering a friendly smile. A place

like this doesn't just happen to close early when it's not even late yet.

"We're having a private party," the manager says. "A friend of the family has rented the club tonight for a bachelor party. Unfortunately, it's by invitation only."

As in, we're getting our asses kicked out.

"Are you sure we can't pay for a couple more hours? We'll be discreet and keep to ourselves." I yank out my wallet and reveal several crisp one-hundred-dollar bills.

I don't worry about Mikhail's men recognizing me.

Maybe I should be concerned, but we're in a corner booth in the back, the lights pointed toward the stage. In a dark corner of the club, we're just two men enjoying the show.

28

Aleksandra

The day of the wedding...

I have no way of contacting Antonio again. I still don't have a phone. Mine was abandoned at Antonio's home, and Mikhail has forbidden me from contacting the outside world.

The engagement party was a rouse.

I'm to marry Luka tonight.

And if that's not bad enough, we're leaving for Russia tomorrow. A country that I haven't visited since I was a child. It's not my home, and I suspect it isn't Luka's, either. But Mikhail has made the arrangements, setting us up with a place to live, travel documents, and transportation.

And Luka knows better than to defy Mikhail.

Unlike Antonio, who refuses to bow down to my brother or anyone else, Luka would never betray his boss.

To Luka, I will always come second.

It's never been about what I want. It's always been about what's best for Mikhail, and getting us out of the country and away from him is his priority. But it's not best for the twins or me.

The staff around the house are bustling around getting ready for the wedding. I'm trying not to puke.

Do I lie to Luka and tell him I'm pregnant with Antonio's child?

I doubt that would help. Luka has already agreed to be a father to Sophia and Liam. While he isn't particularly warm or friendly with the children, he isn't cold-hearted, either.

But he isn't their father, and I don't love Luka.

Will Antonio show up tonight, and if he does, will he arrive before the wedding? I told him seven o'clock, but the wedding has been moved up to two hours.

There's a wedding gown in my room, hanging on the back of the door.

The sun is setting, and all I can think about is taking the kids and running. But we wouldn't get far without help.

And Luka isn't going to help me flee.

While he doesn't love me, he won't betray Mikhail.

———

Day fades to night. I wear the dress required, not because I want to, but because there is little choice. Whether I wear a wedding gown, sweatpants, or nothing, I will still be forced to endure a wedding against my will.

The dress fits well, considering I had no say in picking it out or trying it on previously. There are plenty of gowns in my bedroom closet that they likely used one to determine my size.

I'll require help with zipping the back, but I refuse to struggle and try to do the task on my own.

"Mama!" Sophia shouts as she beats on the door with her fist, and it flings open in haste. The girl knows to knock, but she doesn't understand the principle of waiting to be let inside. And there's no lock from the inside on my door.

Anyone can come and go as they please, which irritates me to my wit's end.

Sophia is dressed in a daisy yellow dress. It's frilly and fancy, and she twirls around to show me the new gown that she's been gifted to wear tonight. "I look like a princess!" she squeals with laughter.

Liam tramples into the room a few moments later. He looks incredibly dashing in his black suit and white dress shirt. His face is wearing a scowl, his cheeks red.

He stomps on the wooden floor and hands me his matching daisy yellow tie. "Help," he says, thrusting the bowtie at me.

Liam doesn't appear the least bit pleased to be dressing up for tonight, and I'm not sure if he even understands what's going on, that his mother is being forced to marry a man she doesn't love.

I've tried to shield my children, but it's not like I've spoken to them at any length about the wedding or Luka.

They must have questions.

"You both look incredible," I say, and I kneel to Liam's level, securing the bowtie to finish his ensemble neatly. If I weren't being forced to wed, I'd soak up the experience a little more, but all I can do is a glance at the clock.

Will Antonio show up when it's too late, and I'm married to Luka?

What happens then? Will Antonio fight for me or let me go?

A heavy set of boots trample down the hallway. I glance up at the impending figure in the door. I half-expect to see Luka, but it isn't him.

Mikhail is always dressed in his black suit, white dress shirt, and shiny black shoes.

"Sister," he says with his thick Russian accent. It's thicker than mine. I've spent years trying not to sound like the family and blend in with those in the city.

I pinch my lips and rise to my feet.

Sophia hurries behind me at Mikhail's presence. Can she feel the danger brooding right off him?

Liam stares up at Mikhail, not the least bit afraid or intimidated. "Why do I have to dress like you?" Liam asks.

Although I imagine it isn't intentional, Mikhail glares down at Liam, snarling. It's just his way. He's not the least bit great with kids. I don't know how Liam isn't terrified of Uncle Mikhail.

"You don't like the way I dress?" Mikhail asks. There's a hint of amusement in his tone, and I worry how Liam answers.

If he insults his uncle, he very well could be disciplined, and I don't want that to happen to my child. But if I intervene, the punishment will be ten times more severe for both of us.

"It's hot," Liam says and wiggles in his suit. He pops the bowtie off and unbuttons his suit coat.

"Do you hear this kid?" Mikhail jabs at Liam. "One day, you'll be expected to wear a suit and dress like the family when you take on the business."

I don't want my son to become like his uncle or father, the head of the bratva or the mafia. But I hold my tongue. I know better than to start a war with my brother. At least I don't want him to know that I'm about to betray his plans to marry me off to Luka.

The least I can do is keep my head down until Antonio shows up. If he comes to help. There's no guarantee he'll get in through the front gates, let alone be able to help me.

"I want to be an astronaut," Liam says, staring up at Mikhail. "Your job is boring."

Frankly, Liam has no idea what Mikhail does for a living.

I'm grateful that I have been able to shield Liam as much as possible while living under Mikhail's roof. The bratva aren't the least bit secretive about their orders or what they do to prisoners.

Eventually, Liam and Sophia won't be blind to the violence. Another reason I have to get out while I still can, and moving to Russia would only be worse.

Maybe Luka won't be directly taking orders from Mikhail, but there are other bosses in Russia. The bratva doesn't only do business in New York City.

Nikita wanders down the hallway. "Boss," he says, poking his head into my room.

"Do you hear this guy?" Mikhail jabs a thumb in Liam's direction. He gives a hearty laugh like he's not the least bit offended. I don't know if it's a show he's putting on for his men, like Nikita, or he's not the least bit bothered by Liam's remark.

I hope it's the latter, but I'm not confident.

"What is it?" Mikhail asks, glancing at his employee.

"There's an uninvited guest downstairs," Nikita says, glaring at me.

Could it be Antonio? He wouldn't waltz up to the front door and expect a warm greeting.

Unless he's trying to plan a diversion.

29

Antonio

I didn't come alone to the party, not that Mikhail and his thugs know that I brought company.

Two of my men are in the trunk. They can pull the lever in the rear to let themselves out when no one is watching.

The moment I drive in through the open gates, there's a swarm of men with guns surrounding the vehicle.

One guard shouts at me, his gun raised at the side window. "Get out, slowly!"

I smile, pleased at how easily the guards take the bait. I'm a wanted man by the bratva, and Mikhail's soldiers are all too gullible.

As long as they don't search the vehicle. But they have me, what they want, and I won't put up a fight.

"I'm not armed," I say and keep my hands up so they don't inadvertently shoot me. They're the kind of men who shoot first and then clean up the mess after burying the body.

"I don't care. Get out," the Russian says. He grunts his answer, his beard thick and his brow tight. He doesn't appear the least bit pleased to see me, like I've ruined the party.

Good.

They have no idea what's on the agenda. I intend on ruining their day.

I wasn't sure that I'd make it on time. Aleksandra had made it clear that I should arrive at seven o'clock, but it didn't take much to hear the whispers of Russian men bragging about a wedding and sending the children off to boarding school.

My children.

Luka, her fiancé, enjoyed his last night of freedom at the club.

But something tells me a man like Luka isn't going to stop himself from having any woman he wants, married or not.

Why is he marrying Aleksandra?

She's made it clear that she doesn't love him, but what does he get out of the arrangement?

I'm yanked from the vehicle and thrown down onto the grass, face first.

I spit out the clump of dirt that finds its way into my mouth. I'm grateful there isn't snow or ice on the grass.

The Russian pats me down, making sure I'm not carrying a weapon before he hauls me back to my feet and thrusts me inside the front door.

"Aleksandra!" I shout, hoping to garner her attention. I want her to know that I'm here and that the plan is in motion.

"Shut up!" the Russian grabs my hair and yanks my head back. His gun is tucked under my chin.

One of the soldiers hurries up the stairs on a mission if I've ever seen one.

Is he securing Aleksandra to ensure I can't get to her, or retrieving Mikhail?

"On your knees." The Russian with the gun pushes me back down to the ground.

I'm not a man to kneel, not to the Russians or anyone else, for that matter.

But he forces me onto the wood floor, and my legs buckle. If I end up shot, or worse, dead, I'm of no use to Aleksandra.

"I've been waiting for this day," Mikhail says as his eyes glint under the pendant lighting in the foyer. He stalks down the stairs like a man on a mission.

Is that mission to marry off his sister or murder me? Perhaps he's pleased that he believes he has the opportunity to do both.

Have my men managed to sneak out of the trunk of the car without being caught?

"Waiting for what? To kill me?" I ask. I attempt to rise to my feet, but the Russian knocks me back down, slamming his fist into my stomach and sweeping his leg under mine.

"Don't hurt him!" Aleksandra hurries down the stairs past one of the Russians, who is grumbling something under his breath.

Mikhail doesn't so much as look over his shoulder at her. "You are supposed to be upstairs!"

"I love him!" Aleksandra hurries down the stairs, yanking herself free as another guard grabs her by the arm. "Let me go."

She's feisty and vibrant, a force to be reckoned with.

I try not to smile at her, the sight of her in a gorgeous wedding gown, her cheeks rosy, and a scowl on her face.

She's beautiful.

And I intend to make her mine.

"You love this fool?" Mikhail raises an eyebrow and jabs his thumb at me like he can't believe the spoken words.

I'm not sure she means them, either, but it's clear

she's willing to say anything to get out of marrying Luka and moving to Russia.

I don't blame her. I'd do the same.

"He's the father of my children, which you already know," Aleksandra says. She glances at the tall Russian thug who keeps grabbing her by the arm, attempting to silence her and put her in her place.

The girl doesn't listen.

Fiery.

Fierce.

Exactly the woman I want to claim.

Mikhail's expression is grim, and his nose twitches with a snarl. "You'd rather marry Italian scum and be disowned by the family than accept Luka's hand?"

"She's not moving to Russia," I say. Whether she marries me or not isn't the point. I'm not letting my children get on an airplane and move halfway across the world.

"There will be a wedding," Mikhail says.

Before he can say anything further, I interrupt him. "Aleksandra will marry me."

"What?" she says, glancing at me with wide, doe-like eyes.

"Yes, excuse me?" Mikhail tilts his head slightly as he ponders the idea. He glances at his little sister and back at me. "Are you expecting my blessing?"

"I'm hoping you won't kill us."

He chuckles like I've just made a joke, and he folds his arms across his chest. Mikhail strokes his long, thick beard as he considers my request.

"What might I get in return for you marrying my baby sister?" he asks.

It's clear he wants something, but I'm not sure what that entails. I never did find out what Luka was getting out of the arrangement, other than a family and a new distant home.

I won't give up any of my turf. If that's what he's hoping to conquer, we'll sooner start a war between our families, again. But I'm trying to be civil, remain calm, and while I don't appear to have the upper hand with my knees on the floor and my gaze staring up at Mikhail, my men must surely be upstairs by now rescuing my children.

I'm buying my men time.

And I would marry Aleksandra in a heartbeat.

Mikhail waits for my answer.

"Two goats and an ox," I say.

He snorts and rolls his eyes at my remark. Mikhail doesn't have a sense of humor.

"I'm not for sale," Aleksandra says. She's insulted.

Good, then my offer was believable.

"On the contrary," Mikhail says with a wicked smirk. "I was paying Luka to take her off my hands."

"What?" Aleksandra's eyes widen.

How could she not realize the marriage arrangement had some form of monetary value?

Luka wasn't wedding her because he loved her or was trying to save her from her older brother. She couldn't be that naïve to think the marriage was anything more than a bargaining tool.

"Do you think I enjoy keeping you and your rambunctious little brats under my roof? I tolerated you because you are family. But after running off and betraying your flesh and blood, I've had enough."

Aleksandra's jaw drops. "That's not fair! That isn't what happened," she says, quick to clarify that she didn't betray her brother. Is it because she wants to mend the tear between them or something else?

Mikhail waves his hand dismissively at Aleksandra. "I don't care about your excuses. You will marry Luka unless Antonio wants to hand over control of his kingdom."

"He'll never do that!" Aleksandra pushes closer to her brother, coming to stare up into his stone-cold gaze.

She's right, and I'm not about to turn over control of my empire to the Russian bratva. But I need to stall. I'm waiting for my smartwatch to buzz with a coded message, a text to let me know my kids are safe.

There's been no alert and no message yet, so I try to delay the inevitable. Besides, the longer I'm in the foyer, I'm not being detained in their prison, or worse, dead.

"Surely, you could use more money," I say.

"You want to buy my sister?" Mikhail asks with a hearty laugh. "I never took you for the kind of man who would pay for sex."

"I'm not paying for one night with Aleksandra. I'm paying for every night with her for the rest of my life."

Aleksandra flinches, her eyes tighten, and I can't quite read her emotions. Is she angry at my suggestion?

"How much?" Mikhail asks. He nods for his man to bring me to my feet. "I don't do business with men who beg."

I wasn't begging or pleading for my life, but it's not worth the argument or the waste of breath.

"One hundred thousand. It's enough money to fund your extracurricular activities," I say. It's no secret that the bratva delves into illegal arms dealings.

Mikhail pulls Aleksandra closer, and his fingers tangle in her hair. "She's my only sister. You're going to have to do better than that," he snickers.

"I'll double it."

Mikhail drops his hold on Aleksandra and strokes his jaw, considering the offer. "Two hundred thousand. Plus, I want a ten percent cut on your gross business assets and an apology for kidnapping my family."

He's insane, asking for a percentage of my business. I ignore his request for an apology. Dons don't apologize or grovel, even when they are fucking wrong.

"Two hundred thousand, and we walk away without starting the next world war," I threaten.

The Russian boss snorts at my suggestion. "War? You can't win a war with the bratva. Don't you remember what happened the last time, what we did to your families?" There's a sneer on his face, a glint of glee in his eyes.

It's evident he enjoys torturing women and children, helpless victims. He'd go to great lengths to hurt those closest to me, and I wouldn't put it past him to do the same to Sophia and Liam.

But if survival means ignoring his remark and

rescuing my children from the bratva, then I'll have to lose this battle to win the war.

"Do we have a deal?" I ask curtly. Behind him, at the top of the stairwell, there's a dash of movement. It's Sophia and Liam, I'm sure of it.

Are they with Ardian and Monte? If I can easily spot the twins, any number of Mikhail's men could also notice them.

"Mommy!" Sophia squeals and hurries down the stairs with her brother right behind her. She's wearing a bright yellow dress, and her hair is a bit disheveled—the matching yellow ribbon in her hand.

My men are nowhere in sight.

They couldn't have been caught, or Mikhail would have been informed.

Are they still searching the property for Sophia and Liam?

Liam hurries to Aleksandra's hip, securing himself at her side when smoke begins to waft from the stairwell.

The fire alarm blares with a high-pitched annoyance that is deafening.

"Dmitri and Nikita, find out what the hell is going on. Everyone else outside," Mikhail shouts over the ear-piercing alarm.

Aleksandra grabs Liam, clutching her leg, and I reach for Sophia, lifting her into my arms as we head out the front door with Mikhail and most of his men leading the way.

Two of his guards head up the stairs toward the smoke, coughing, guns held up in unison.

Did Ardian and Monte set off a fire upstairs? Is that why they sent the twins downstairs to protect them from further danger?

Is there a fire, or is it just a rouse?

My men can easily handle two of their soldiers, but why defy a direct order to retrieve the twins and get out of the building?

"Did you do this?" Mikhail snarls and juts his finger at me as we hurry outside.

The air is frigid, and Sophia is shivering in my arms.

I remove my black blazer and slide it over her shoulders to help warm her.

Liam has his face buried in Aleksandra's chest. His hands are tucked against her dress, doing his best to keep warm.

"Let us go," I say. "The kids are freezing. Let me put them in the car and take them home."

"Home?" Mikhail chuckles with his thick Russian accent. "And you think that's with you?"

Aleksandra approaches her brother and rests a hand on his arm. "Let me go with him."

"I promised our father that I'd see to it that you're taken care of. That means you're getting married, little sister."

Mikhail has his head wrapped around the idea of Aleksandra being a bride, whether she wants to wed or not.

Sophia shivers in my arms. My blazer isn't enough to keep her warm with the sun setting. The last thing I want is for my children to get sick from being out in the cold.

"Let me marry your sister. I've already made you a generous offer," I say.

What will it take to convince him that Aleksandra and the children are better off with me?

"Please, Mikhail. He's the children's father," Aleksandra pleads with him.

"Mikhail!" Nikita calls, hurrying outside.

Mikhail grumbles, pulls out of Aleksandra's grasp and stalks up the stairs toward his soldier. "What did you find?" he asks. He's loud, abrasive, and I can't help but wonder if my men got out already. Perhaps the fire was a diversion for them to sneak back to the vehicle.

But that wasn't the plan. Something must have gone awry.

"A candle was knocked over in Aleksandra's room. Dmitri and I put out the fire, but her room has significant smoke damage," Nikita says. His white shirt is dirty, covered in smoke and grime from the fire upstairs.

"Get yourself cleaned up," Mikhail orders. "Everyone back inside. It's fucking cold out here."

I don't follow his command. I'm not one of his men. "I'm taking Aleksandra, Sophia, and Liam home with me." I'm done stalling for time and trying to bargain with a man out for blood.

My men must have set fire in Aleksandra's bedroom in their own attempt to escape.

Mikhail glances from me to his sister. "Is this what you want? Once you leave, there's no coming back, Aleksandra."

She steps closer beside me, her body brushing against mine. "I love him, and the children deserve the chance to know their father."

Sophia's cheeks are red. She pulls back slightly to stare at my face. "You know my daddy?" she asks.

"I'm your father," I say, staring into her pale blue eyes. She has Aleksandra's matching gaze.

Sophia's cheeks are red, and she shivers in my embrace. I don't wait for Mikhail to answer. I clutch the little one tight against me and grab Aleksandra's arm, tugging for her to follow me to the car. The back door is unlocked, and I hurry around to open the door, shuffling Sophia inside while Aleksandra helps guide Liam into the other side.

The hem of Aleksandra's gown is dirty, the back zipper undone halfway down her back. Her hair is messy, her makeup smeared. She's beautiful, and she's fucking mine.

30

Aleksandra

Did I tell Antonio that I love him?

He carries Sophia to the car, and I guide Liam into the back seat before climbing into the passenger side.

In the back, are two booster seats. Antonio prepared to bring the twins home. Does he know what he's getting himself into, having a family? Is he ready to be a father to my children?

I can't stop shivering from the icy chill in the air. My dress is not the least bit practical to wear in winter. Not to mention my lack of footwear.

Antonio starts the engine when he's in the driver's seat and cold air thrusts out of the vents. I push the vents away, aiming them anywhere but on me.

"It'll warm up soon," he says.

Soon can't come quick enough. I'm freezing, and my hands are red and numb. I glance back at the twins as they buckle their safety belts. They know the routine.

Although I'm not sure they understand what's happening, one day I'll be able to explain it to them when they're older.

"Are you my daddy?" Sophia asks.

Antonio hits the gas, and the engine roars. "I hope you boys are back," he says.

What boys? Did he bring his men with him?

There's a muffled response, and I glance around, wondering where the hell that came from.

The trunk?

Antonio glances at his watch as it buzzes with a text message. I can't read it from my seat, but I imagine it's some type of indication that it's time to go.

Mikhail just let us leave. Something feels amiss. No guards are chasing us with guns drawn, and as Antonio lurches the car forward toward the gate, the guard on the opposite end opens the metal doorway, letting us leave.

We breeze past the guard gate, and I glance in the side mirror.

Mikhail is nowhere to be seen.

"That was too easy," I whisper.

"Agreed," Antonio says as he grips the steering wheel, his knuckles white. Every so often, he glances up in the rearview mirror, like he's looking for Mikhail or his men tailing our ass.

But they know where he lives.

It won't be difficult for them to find us. And it isn't over; I know my brother. He's not going to leave things unsettled.

———

We arrive back at the compound. The house is just as we left it, except my bed has been made, my clothes put away, and the sheets changed.

I never thought I'd be relieved to be here under his roof. But maybe I was wrong, and Antonio isn't so bad.

"Thank you," I whisper, staring at him as I linger in the entrance to my room.

He's in the hallway escorting me upstairs, but I'm not sure why. Does he intend to lock me up, or does he have something he wants to say in private?

Sophia and Liam are playing in their bedroom, preparing for a talent show. Though what talents they have, I don't have the slightest notion. It's sweet that they want to perform for us and have shut the door, making us promise not to come in because they want it to be a surprise.

"Can I come in?" Antonio asks.

I give a mere shrug and a faint smile. "It's your house," I say. If he wants to come into my room, nothing will stop him.

"Listen, I know you may have said what you did to get out from under your brother's hold. You're welcome to stay here as long as you'd like, but I'm not going to force you to move to Russia," he says.

I breathe a sigh of relief. "Good, because I'd have to slug you if you planned on us moving anywhere outside of the country."

"Even Italy?"

"Tell me you're joking." I don't have it in me to kid around about moving to a foreign country after the crap Luka and Mikhail put me through recently.

Antonio offers a warm smile. "Can I come in?" he asks again.

"Yeah, sure," I say and step farther into my bedroom, shuffling toward the bed.

Antonio follows behind me and closes the door. "Listen, I meant what I said to your brother. I would like us to be a proper family."

"Proper? Who are you, and what have you done with the man who kidnapped me?"

He doesn't so much as crack a grin.

"Bad joke?" I say and chew on my bottom lip. I plop down onto the edge of the mattress at the bottom of the bed. The anger I harbored for Antonio has begun to fade. There's no resentment for what he did, kidnapping us.

Antonio approaches and comes to stand over me, hovering, looming. He has the uncanny ability to make my stomach flop.

I suck in a nervous breath and pray he doesn't notice. My heart hammers in my chest. He's the only one with the ability to render me speechless.

"Bringing you here the first time, it was to protect you," he says. He leans closer, and his hand guides my chin up so that I stare into his gaze. "I'm sorry if I made you uncomfortable."

That's the least of what he's done, and I open my mouth to retaliate, but his lips are on mine the moment I do.

The kiss is hot, passionate, and fierce.

Antonio is strong, and the magnetism between us is forceful.

One kiss leads to two, and I'm clutching him against me, pulling him down onto the bed. I've never felt so needy or desperate in my life.

Maybe I do love him? I certainly desire him, and I love the feelings he stirs inside me. Even in anger, there's a heated intensity that never fades out.

"I shouldn't have left," I say. I'm not an idiot. I knew there were risks involved with returning to the bratva's compound. I'd been naïve in hoping that my brother would let the past be forgotten.

And worse, I'd put Antonio's life in danger.

He rests his forehead against mine, capturing my lips in another searing kiss before laying me on my back. With ease, he guides me up to the head of the bed before straddling me, pinning me beneath him.

Already, I feel the bulge in his pants, his desire burning for me.

His eyes are dark. A deeper and richer hue of chocolate that melts my insides as he grinds into me.

Fuck.

He's going to let me die a slow and sensual death.

I want to feel him, touch him, taste every inch of his body. My fingers trail along his arms, and he grabs my wrists, pinning me forcefully onto the mattress.

"You're mine," he growls. "I get to do what I please with you."

A shudder courses through my body.

The one night we shared years ago wasn't quite like this, but I hate to admit I'm dying inside, aching to explore his body. The way he talks dirty makes me so easily come undone.

I won't crumble under his strength, his power.

"No one owns me," I say, staring up at him, challenging him. There's no anger or resentment. No hostility, except that he's stronger than I am, and I'm fighting for control sexually.

He leans down and playfully bites on my bottom lip, tugging it between his teeth.

Does he realize how easily he can make a girl shudder?

My breathing comes out labored as I rock my hips against his. His knee offers friction between my thighs, the dress awkwardly placed with the back still half-unzipped, and the skirt hiked up to my knees.

"Not yet, *Tesorina*," he whispers and grins down at me, pleased with himself.

"Please." I sound needy, breathless, and my desire is

fueled by the fact it's been too long since I've had a man in my bed.

My body pulses and trembles as he grinds against my hips, a knowing smile at the satisfaction of what he can do.

"I want to see you come," Antonio breathes.

His words are my undoing.

My toes curl, and my insides clench down, wanting to feel him inside of me. Fully clothed, I shudder and spasm, my body taking over, finding release as I arch my back into him.

He holds me tight, and I'm unable to deny the physical attraction, the desire ebbing and flowing through me. Not that I'd want to, either.

I want this with Antonio.

I want him.

My heart races as my body finally settles down. He lifts off me long enough to help remove the dress, shedding me of the unwanted gown but leaving my panties on.

Antonio kisses along my stomach, inhaling my scent as his nose grazes over my panties. "You're soaking wet for me," he whispers with a knowing smirk.

"Pleased with yourself?"

"I consider it an accomplishment, making a beautiful woman come in my arms, with her clothes still on," Antonio says.

My cheeks flame.

"It's nothing to be ashamed of," he says and scoots off me long enough to shuck his clothes to the floor with my gown. "Although I should suggest that we wait until our wedding night."

I groan at the mention of us getting married. I'm sick and tired of discussing weddings. Why do I have to tie myself to anyone for the rest of my life?

"You're cruel," I seethe. Is he playing games, trying to rile me up again? Because it's working.

There's a knowing glint in his eyes. "Why? You already had your first orgasm of the night," Antonio says. "If anything, I'd be halting my pleasure. But I get it. You want more of me."

"I want every inch of you," I whisper, staring up into his darkened gaze.

"Where do you want it?" Antonio asks. He leans in, and his tongue traces over my top lip, not giving in quite yet. It takes everything in me not to come undone, just feeling him tease me, his body above mine.

I whimper in protest. This man will be the death of me.

"You're killing me," I moan, pulling him closer and tighter, wanting to feel his cock inside of me.

He smiles down at me, dropping soft, feather-light kisses against my lips. "You're exaggerating."

"I never thought you'd be such a fucking tease," I grumble.

His lips shut, but a smirk adorns his face. "And you like it," he whispers down at me. "Your body doesn't lie."

I lean up to capture his lips and roll us around, desperate to take control, to dominate him.

But he won't have it.

The moment I attempt to overpower him, he's pinning me down, reminding me that he's in charge.

"Your desperation is sexy, *Tesorina,*" Antonio says. "The blush spreading down your breasts. I'll bet you're aching inside for me. Aren't you?"

I snarl-up at him, but he chuckles before leaning down, sucking on my neck. "I swear if you leave a mark," I grumble, but my resolve crumbles. He's made me weak at the knees, and the throbbing sensation between my thighs has heightened to a desire I don't recall experiencing before.

"That's the point. I'm marking you, claiming you," he says. "Let every man see that you belong to me."

His words ignite a fire building inside of me.

"Don't come yet," he warns. "Not until I give you permission."

A whimper spills past my lips because I'm already teetering on edge. And he won't let me fall into oblivion, at least not yet.

"Please." I'm no longer above begging for what I want. Is that what he likes to hear? "I want to feel you inside of me."

"Good girl," he whispers, and I feel him tease my entrance. "Now, was that so hard to say?"

My eyes slam shut, and I bend my legs, giving him ample room to fill me. There's an ache that builds, but it's a good kind of pain. He stretches me to accommodate his size.

I forgot how big he was and how his cock feels inside me.

The last time we were in the shower, it was swift and rough.

He's no less rough this time, but he's also attentive to my needs. But I want to be focused on him. He saved me tonight, rescued me, even offered to marry me.

I shift on the bed and wrap my legs around him, dragging him deeper inside of me.

"Fuck," he grunts. His face is red, and he thrusts faster, harder, driving his cock farther into me.

"I want to watch you come," I say, staring up at him. I guide my fingers along his back, my nails scratch over his skin and down to his ass, marking him just like he marked me.

"Come with me," he grunts.

Each thrust brings me closer toward the edge.

My back arches, and my toes curl as he pounds into me deeper than ever before. I shudder and clench onto his cock. My insides tremble and quiver as he spills himself inside of me.

"Shit," I curse, realizing that we forgot to use protection.

It takes Antonio a minute to realize I said something. "What's wrong?" he asks, moving off my frame.

I climb out of bed and head for the bathroom to clean up. Not that it'll do much good to prevent another pregnancy, but it can't hurt. "We didn't use a condom," I say over my shoulder as I shut the bathroom door behind myself.

31

Antonio

A condom. That's what she's worried about?

It's probably the fact that she could end up pregnant again. But I've already told her I'd marry her, and I want to be in Sophia and Liam's lives.

She opens the bathroom door when she's finished. Aleksandra is stunning. There's a glow about her, and the fact she's naked makes me hard. I can't tear my gaze away from her body.

"Would that be the end of the world?" I ask. "If you got pregnant again?" It's not like we're trying to have another child, but I missed out on all the firsts with the twins. I wouldn't miss out again.

I climb off the mattress and pull her into my embrace, wrapping my arms around her.

"Again?" she laughs, glancing down at my cock.

"It's your fault; you look so goddamn beautiful." There's a gruffness, a heat that sizzles between us, even now.

"And what would you have me do differently?" she asks.

I whisk her toward the bed, pulling her down onto my lap. "Absolutely nothing," I say and crush her lips with mine. I want to devour her from head to toe, discover every freckle and blemish that makes her truly unique.

And I intend to do just that.

"Mama!" Sophia pounds on the adjoining door.

The little tiger bursts in without waiting and stares at us with wide, confused eyes. We're not the least bit dressed or decent.

"Get out!" I bellow, pointing at the door.

Sophia's eyes turn into two waterfalls as she tears back into her bedroom.

"Look what you've done," Aleksandra scolds as she pushes me away and stalks across the bedroom towards the dresser. She doesn't put the wedding gown back on. It lays in a heap on the floor.

I grab my clothes scattered on the floor and pull my boxers on first.

"Me?" I ask. "She tore in without waiting for permission."

"She's a child," Aleksandra says and rolls her eyes. Already dressed in her bra and panties, she slides her pants up her hips.

It's impossible not to stare at the sexy as hell woman just a few feet away from me.

"Relax. It's not like she had any idea what she saw," she says.

I yank on my trousers and then my dress shirt. "Are you sure about that?" I run my hand through my hair. The last thing I need is to traumatize the kid.

"Let it go. If she starts asking questions, I'll deal with it," Aleksandra says.

"Good, because I'm not ready for the sex talk with the twins."

"And you think I am?" She emits a heavy sigh. "Thankfully, we have a few years until that discussion happens."

While I button my dress shirt, Aleksandra pulls her blouse on over her head. It takes all my strength not to stalk over and rip her clothes right off.

She opens the adjoining door and disappears into the kids' bedroom.

I exhale a heavy breath and wait a beat before following. I can't help the grumpiness and irritation that exude from within me. It's not like I'm used to being around kids, let alone my own.

This is all still new to me, foreign.

I approach the open door and lean against the doorjamb, poking my head into the room.

Aleksandra is kneeling on the floor beside Sophia. Her voice is soft, and while I can't hear what she's saying to our daughter, it seems to be helping soothe the little tiger.

Am I really cut out to be a father? Or am I making things worse by keeping them here under my roof?

"He yelled at me," Sophia says, her cheeks rosy and the biggest pout on her face.

"And your daddy is incredibly sorry for yelling at you," Aleksandra says, glancing at me over her shoulder.

My mouth goes dry at the sound of daddy on her lips.

I stand there in awe at the realization that I have two children. They're my flesh and blood. Sure, I've known for some time now that I've had kids, that the twins were mine, but it hasn't settled in, the fact that they're going to look up to me, that I can shape and influence their future.

It's a fucking lot to take in and accept.

"I'm not sorry," I grit between clenched teeth.

Sophia's eyes glisten with tears.

Fuck. I'm about to make the kid cry again.

Aleksandra stands and spins around on her feet. "I'm going to have a word with your father," she says. She moves at lightning speed toward me, grabs my arm, and knocks me back into her bedroom.

She closes the door with her foot, making sure the conversation is between us.

Good. That's fine with me.

"Am I supposed to be scared of you?" I ask. There's practically steam emanating from her, and the passion in her eyes makes me want to pin her against the wall and show her who the fuck is in charge.

She groans. I have the uncanny ability to frustrate her or maybe fluster her. Probably a bit of both.

"The kids aren't used to your brashness. You need to tone it down, or they'll never connect with you."

I try to be gentle, but I'm not the kindest and most considerate person. Running the mafia doesn't let me be sweet and warm. "You don't think I realize that?" I ask, my voice louder than I intend.

She's backed up against the door, and I lean forward, shoving my hand against the wooden material, trapping her.

"I'm doing the best I can," I say.

"Well, do better," Aleksandra quips. Her eyes are locked on mine. "Now that they know you're their father, you're going to have to man up and act like a dad to those two kids in there."

"What do you think I've been doing since the day you moved in?" I ask. I had my men secure the twins toys, clothes, anything that they wanted was brought to the complex.

"The day I moved in?" She laughs under her breath and realizes that I'm not smiling. "You have a funny way of thinking, Antonio."

I lean closer, my breath mingling with hers. But I don't kiss her. "I just want what's best for my children," I say.

"Our children," she corrects me and shoves her hand forcefully against my chest, pushing me back several feet. "You need to learn to tone down your anger, aggression, whatever the hell it is that keeps you in charge of the mafia. The twins don't need to be part of that hostility."

I take a step back, out of her reach.

"You're right."

It burns me how right she is, and the anger rips me apart inside. I'd kill to protect my children and

Aleksandra. The mere fact that I brought Sophia to tears makes my heart race and my stomach somersault.

I head for the main door out of the bedroom to the hallway.

"Antonio," Aleksandra says, calling after me.

I approach the door, my hand on the doorknob. I don't turn around, but I wait. I give her time to say whatever needs to be said.

Will she ridicule the way I dealt with Sophia?

"Are you always going to run away from me?" she asks.

I scoff at her suggestion, and I can't let it go. I turn around to face her and lean with my back against the door. "When have I ever run? If I recall, you pushed me away. You kept the fact that you were pregnant a secret. Tell me, Aleksandra, when have I run away from you?"

She stalls for a second.

There was an instance where I left after finding that FBI agent's business card, but she told me to go.

Her tongue darts out and swipes across her top lip. "You're right, but you're running now. Having children isn't easy. Don't just walk away because you screwed up and yelled at our daughter. Accept responsibility."

She sounds just like a mother, scolding a teenager. But I'm not her child, and I'm not in adolescence.

"You're going to make mistakes," she says, her voice softer, gentler, and calmer. If one of us is rational, it's Aleksandra. She steps closer toward me and untangles my arms folded against my chest.

"I don't make mistakes," I grunt.

I'm waiting for her to roll her eyes, but she's far more patient with me than I'd expect. It's hard to argue with her when she's not fighting me. This calm demeanor throws me askew.

"Of course, you don't," she says and raises an eyebrow. Her gaze is locked on mine, waiting for me to say something.

She probably wants me to apologize.

Damnit.

I don't make apologies. It's a sign of weakness amongst the family, my mafia family. But Aleksandra is part of my family now, too, and Sophia and Liam.

Sighing, I squeeze Aleksandra's hand and bury the anger, silencing it within me. No one can ever know the secret power that she holds over me. My men wouldn't pay me the proper respect that I've earned. But my daughter fearing me is the last thing I want to happen.

32

Antonio

Two weeks later...

Situated behind my desk, Ardian comes blazing into my office. "Sir, we've got company."

Before he can further elaborate, Mikhail pushes past him and strides into my office. His bodyguard accompanies him, blocking the door.

Ardian hurries down the hallway, and I can only assume to gather reinforcements and weapons.

"How'd you get in past the gate?" I ask.

Did one of my men agree to let him inside? I can't

help but wonder if anyone else has betrayed me since Mario.

There's a wicked grin on his face. "Don't mind yourself in such untrivial matters, Antonio." Mikhail steps closer, approaches my desk, and finally sits across from me. He kicks his legs up on the wooden desk, his boots filthy and tracked with snow that he leaves behind on the papers strewn about.

I push my laptop aside, out of his way, and shut the lid.

"What do you want?" I seethe. He's not here for a pleasant visit. That doesn't exist between us and never will.

"I've come to collect what's rightfully mine. I gave you my sister and her children. You've yet to pay me the two hundred thousand, let alone a percentage of your empire."

I scoff at his idea of a deal. I'm a man who keeps his word, but I have a feeling he's not here just for the money.

"As soon as you give me the routing and account number, I'll transfer you the funds that we've agreed upon," I say. I'd do anything to protect my family, including Aleksandra, Sophia, and Liam.

"Good, because I'd hate to do anything drastic," Mikhail says and snickers. "I've got two men watching the twins at their preschool, and another has a gun on your girlfriend. Don't do anything foolish."

Mikhail reaches into his pocket. "I'm not going for a weapon," he assures me and reveals a handheld tablet. He flips it around to show me the screen.

There's surveillance footage of the twins on the playground at the preschool, and his men are visible just outside the gate. He flicks the screen with his hand and shows me the second set of footage, with a gun poised on Aleksandra.

She's in the back of a vehicle. It's dark. There's duct tape on her lips, and her hands appear bound behind her back.

"Let her go!"

"As soon as we get our money, every penny," Mikhail says. He hands me a slip of paper with his routing and account numbers to transfer the money to him.

I exhale a heavy breath. Is this what I get to look forward to every month?

Extortion and threats to my family.

I refuse to bow down or cower to men like Mikhail. But I have to tread carefully to ensure that Aleksandra and my children are unharmed.

"Do you mind?" I say, gesturing to his sopping wet boots on my desk.

Mikhail chuckles and removes his feet from the wood, sitting up straight. "I never thought you'd be this easy to extort," he says. He doesn't even try to hide the fact that he's gloating underneath his calm exterior.

I open my laptop and sign into the computer. I'm opening a web browser to transfer the funds to his bank account a moment later. It's probably an offshore account, untraceable.

"You are never to come near my family again," I warn.

It was too easy for Mikhail to get to the twins, to Aleksandra, to waltz right into my office. How many of my men have betrayed me? I can feel the treachery burning inside of me like a raging inferno. Mikhail is waging war, and my men have proven disloyal.

"You needn't worry yourself, Antonio. If you continue the monthly payments, you'll never see me again," he says.

I exhale a heavy breath. "How much are we talking?" He'd asked for ten percent gross, but it's not like he has direct access to my financial records and receipts for transactions. There's no paper trail in the business I'm in, and he knows it.

"Twenty percent," Mikhail says. "Is that going to be a problem?"

His bodyguard stands in the door and glances from the hallway back toward his boss and then at me. He clears his throat at Mikhail. I can only assume it's a signal, but of what?

His bodyguard's gun is poised at his hip. The reflection of metal catches my eye. He isn't holding it, which means I could reach for my spare gun under my desk and take out Mikhail or the bodyguard. It's unlikely I'd make both shots before getting hit myself with a round or two.

And I'm more concerned about Aleksandra and the twins. If I make one wrong move, they could die.

I press my lips together. I don't like shakedowns. While I'm a man of the mafia, I'm also a man of my word. "We agreed to ten percent," I say. Technically, I wasn't happy about that arrangement, but I'd have said anything to get Aleksandra and the kids away from the Russian mobster.

Mikhail leans back in the chair. He stretches his arms and puts his hands behind his head. "Well, the price went up."

"Excuse me?"

What's saying he won't raise the price again in a month. He's just as bad as the cable provider that fucking hoses me. At least with cable, I get a service. What do I get from Mikhail? Certainly not him leaving us alone.

"You left with my sister and didn't pay."

He thinks he owns me. "You're a dead man!" I threaten, my heart pounding against my ribcage.

"Remember who started this war," Mikhail says. "You brought death onto your doorstep and into the homes of your mafia brothers. Are you sure you want to do that again?"

My top lip twitches with a snarl. "You're a monster."

"No worse than you kidnapping my nephew and working for Roberto." Mikhail can't let that go.

"Do you see Roberto running the mafia around here?" I won't confess to murdering Roberto. I can't take a chance that Mikhail came in here with another agenda, wearing a wire, and trying to incriminate me.

He glances around my office from his position in the chair. "Seems you've done well for yourself. Let me give you a piece of advice, *brother*." There's disdain in his tone, arrogance, and anger simmering at the surface.

"I don't want your advice," I snap.

"But you should take it," Mikhail says. His demeanor is calm, and why shouldn't it be? He's getting everything he fucking wants. "Don't fuck with the bratva unless you're prepared for war. Your predecessor was foolish, believing he could sell Liam, and for what, a couple hundred thousand to a wealthy family who wanted a Caucasian son? You nearly destroyed your own family, and you didn't even know it."

He's right, I fucked up, started a war, but we put it all behind us. Didn't we? We'd made a truce, a cease-fire, and the arrangement had been to let Mikhail return to the bratva under the condition that he and his men leave the other mafia families alone. His war was with us.

"I paid you your money," I say, turning the computer screen so he can see the receipt for the transfer of funds. "I want Aleksandra released and you to leave my children alone."

33

Aleksandra

My mouth is covered in duct tape, my hands bound with a zip tie behind my back.

"I'm sorry, Aleksandra, but you're marrying me, and we're moving to Russia," Luka says.

I've never known him to be a monster, but he works for Mikhail.

I try to scream, plead for Luka not to do this, but the duct tape makes it impossible for me to say anything intelligible. Every word is muffled and mumbled. He could easily silence me with his gun, but he doesn't seem to want me dead.

We're in the back of an SUV, parked across the street from the children's preschool. Two of Mikhail's thugs are just watching my kids play outside the gate.

I kick and fight back with my body, not letting Luka have control of me.

They've already slaughtered one man, Gian, my bodyguard who had accompanied me to pick up the twins from preschool.

He's lying dead in the vehicle behind us.

After Luka shot Gian in the head, he dragged me out of the SUV and thrust me into the back of his vehicle. I should have put up a bigger fight, but the other two men with him, Dmitri and Nikita, made it clear that they'd kill Sophia and Liam.

With Dmitri and Nikita across the street, I take the opportunity to slam the full weight of my body into Luka.

He curses in Russian and snarls at me, grabbing me by the neck. "I'm trying to protect you."

Luka is a liar.

If he wanted to protect my children and me, he'd leave us alone.

He relinquishes his grasp on my neck long enough for me to use my legs to beat him in the chest. My aim is for his crotch, but he's a moving target, making it difficult to land a blow every time I attack him.

"Antonio will hurt you," Luka says, like he can reason with me, and he's not physically hurting me. I want to scream at him, but the duct tape makes it difficult to say anything out loud.

I back myself up against the car door and slam my legs forcefully across the backseat at Luka. I'm trying to reach for the door handle, and I manage to yank it open. I can almost reach the sidewalk if I can thrust my body out of the car.

As soon as I'm up on my legs, I can run.

But Luka has other ideas.

He grabs my legs and yanks me farther toward the opposite door, my back against the bench seat as he towers over me. His hands come up around my neck, choking me.

I scream and plead against the duct tape, but he can't make out a word I'm saying, and no one else can save me, either.

The back door is slightly ajar, and I'm struggling to get away, but without my hands, I can't fight back, and his body pinned against mine makes me unable to move.

"You're going to die, Aleksandra, and then we're going to slaughter your children," Luka threatens. His face is red, his eyes black as night. There's a darkness behind them that I've never seen before.

Tears burn my eyes, and my vision goes blurry and then black.

For a second, I think I might be dead.

That it's all over.

There's a rush of commotion, of noise, of voices that I don't recognize. All I hear is ringing in my ears, and I can't focus on the sound.

Luka is no longer holding me down. Someone is pulling him out of the vehicle.

Is it Antonio? Did he come to save us?

"Aleksandra," Agent Melinda Malone's voice clears through the fog. She removes the tape from my mouth and helps me sit, unbinding my hands. "It's a good thing we put a surveillance team on the preschool."

Are they after Antonio or Mikhail?

I gasp for breath, glancing out past the FBI agent as a team of her men has the Russian members of the bratva in handcuffs: Luka, Dmitri, and Nikita.

"Sophia and Liam?" I need to know they're safe.

"They're inside the preschool with all the other kids," she says. "You can relax. It's all over."

Is it over? What about Antonio?

I need to know that Mikhail isn't holding him hostage, harming him. If they went after my children and me, why wouldn't they go after him?

But I can't bring the federal agents to his compound without betraying his trust. I chew on my bottom lip and step out of the vehicle.

"Can I see the twins?" I ask.

"Of course." She takes me across the street, and I ring the buzzer, stepping into the building. Agent Malone waits outside. She speaks with another agent while I enter the preschool.

I shut the door behind myself and am relieved when I'm granted entrance inside and the twins are oblivious to the drama that just unfolded. They both embrace me with a hug and ramble on about their exciting day, how they fingerpainted trees and learned about growing vegetables.

It's a relief that they're safe.

"Give me a second," I say to the twins and approach Kira, the director of the preschool.

"Do you know what's going on?" she asks. "We've had a few parents commenting on an FBI bust outside. They're afraid to leave with their children."

It's easy to lie. "I don't know anything," I say and hope there's no evidence of the duct tape that was on my face. My wrists are sore and bruised, but she can't see the marks left behind with my winter coat on. "Can I borrow your phone? I left mine at the house," I say.

I need to get hold of Antonio and ensure that Mikhail isn't inside the compound.

"Of course," Kira says. She pulls out her cell phone, and I dial Antonio's number. I'm grateful he gave it to me and told me to memorize it.

It rings, and I hear a gruff Russian, "Hello?"

My stomach drops, and my hands tremble at the sound of his voice.

It's Mikhail.

I roll my lips together and end the call. I quickly block the number I just called and hand the phone back to the director. If Mikhail attempts to call the phone back, hopefully, he won't get through.

"Thanks," I say and offer a weak smile.

I escort the twins outside, and Agent Malone stands just a few feet from the entrance conversing with another FBI agent.

"Agent Malone," I say and bring the children with me. I don't want to say much in front of Liam and Sophia, but we need a ride back to Antonio's, and I need her help.

———

Antonio is going to hate me. He may never forgive me, but the way I see it, his safety and his life are worth more than any amount of anger that he could bestow on me.

The twins are seated in the back of the FBI squad car. I'm situated with them, and as we round the corner to the compound and approach the guarded entrance, I lean forward.

"Open the window and let me do the talking," I say.

As far as I know, they don't have a warrant. They're here because I invited them and asked for their assistance.

The automatic window is rolled down as we slow down and come to a crawl.

"Aleksandra? Where's Gian?" one of the guards asks, confused why I'm not with their associate.

"The Russians killed him," I said. "Mikhail is answering Antonio's phone. Did you let Mikhail and his men inside the compound?"

"Of course not!" the guard quips, appalled by my suggestion. He holds a hand and picks up the phone to connect with the compound. When no one answers, he buzzes us through.

"Stay in the car," Agent Malone says as they pull around to the front entrance.

"I'm coming in with you." I refuse to let the feds bully me into sitting on my ass in the back of their car. "Antonio won't know to trust you, and Mikhail is my brother. I'm the best negotiator that you have, and I know the layout of the building. You need me," I say, insisting that they let me accompany them inside.

She pauses for a second, considering my request. "Your kids stay in the vehicle," Agent Malone says. She climbs out of the car and opens the back door, letting me out.

"Stay here," I say, giving the kids a quick kiss before jumping out of the backseat and shutting the door. "Lock the car." I don't want to take any chances that Mikhail will escape and kidnap my children from me.

"Already done. Do you think we don't know how to do our jobs?" she asks. She's brandishing her weapon and gestures for me to get behind her as we stalk up the stairs. "You really should be waiting in the car. This is against protocol."

I snort at her remark. "You wouldn't be going inside if it wasn't for me," I remind her testily.

"We're on the same side," Agent Malone says. "But I can't be responsible for you if you get shot."

"I won't blame you or sue you if that's what you're worried about," I snap.

Is she trying to dissipate the brewing tension between us because it's not working?

Just wait until Antonio discovers I let her in through the front door.

34

Antonio

"Do you think a measly payout every month will let you keep your family?" Mikhail chuckles. "Thanks for the little bonus today, but Luka will marry Aleksandra, and they will move to Russia," he says.

"Get out of my house!"

"You're not in charge here anymore," Mikhail says. He stands and gestures for me to get up from my desk.

"You're fucking crazy if you think you're taking over the mafia," I say. "Let Aleksandra and the twins go."

"Up!" Mikhail bellows and thrusts his gun in my face.

I reach under my desk and retrieve my weapon, brandishing the metal right back at him, cocking the safety off.

Little good it does. His bodyguard is on me with a gun, and now I have two weapons pointed at my head.

"Luka will send your little brats off to boarding school the moment the plane lands in Russia. You're lucky that was his idea. I told him he should kill them," Mikhail says.

"No one will touch my children, or I'll burn you and your men to the ground!"

Mikhail grins at my threat, not the least bit intimated by my words. "Promises, promises. Now, up!" He shouts the command for me to get out of my chair.

I snarl as I move away from the desk.

Where the hell is Ardian? Where are my men?

Mikhail climbs into the leather chair, pretending to be the boss of the mafia.

That's all he can do, pretend. My men will never bow down to him or accept his orders.

Gunfire erupts down the hall, and I exit my office in a rush, a rash of bullets spraying down the hallway.

Bodies are lying at the opposite end, dead. They appear to be Mikhail's men.

Ardian is taking cover at the study entrance, along with Monte and Otello.

"What the hell is going on?" I bark as I stand at the opposite wall in the study with them.

"Mikhail brought his whole fucking army," Ardian says.

I glance down, realizing there's blood on the floor and four more bodies. I grab a weapon from one of the deceased individuals. It's not like he's going to miss it.

"Who the hell let them into the complex?"

"They climbed over the fence, turned off the security footage long enough to let their men scale the perimeter," Monte says.

"Fuck," I grumble. They were waiting for us. "Any word on Aleksandra or the kids?" I need to know they're safe and alive.

I shoot several rounds at the Russian men invading my home.

If Luka wants to marry Aleksandra, then at least he hasn't killed her. What about Sophia and Liam?

"Nothing. Gian hasn't answered his phone," Ardian says.

"That's because they took Aleksandra hostage." I rattle off what little information I have and take several more shots as the assault on the complex continues to rain down on us.

There's movement at the front door.

"More reinforcements?" It isn't my men. They're hauled up inside the complex, fighting for their lives.

When had the Russians grown their empire to such a magnitude?

"FBI!" a woman shouts, her gun drawn as she enters my office with a team behind her.

Did the fucking Russians bring the feds to my house?

"I'm not going to prison," I say, staring at my men.

"Don't be stupid. You have a family," Ardian warns me. "If you kill a fed, they'll put you in federal max."

Ardian shouldn't be calling the orders, but he's right. He's sensible, and he's got a level head. I can't think straight right now.

"Ardian's right," I say and put down my weapon, holding my hands up. "We surrender and figure this out together."

The federal agents swarm the complex. Several more teams arrive, tearing through the building.

We're forced onto the ground, our hands bound behind our backs until the federal agents determine who they're after.

I'm just not sure which side they're here to protect, the Russians or the Italians.

One of the FBI agents hoists me to my feet. She's young and probably still early in her career.

"Antonio!" Aleksandra rushes past the FBI agents.

The female agent glances me over. "This is him? Antonio Moretti?" she asks.

"Yes, Agent Malone," Aleksandra says.

Anger burns through me. "Agent Melinda Malone?" I repeat the name, remembering it from that business card I found upstairs.

"That's correct," she says. "You're a tough man to find. Turn around."

I do as she instructs, and she removes the handcuffs.

Aleksandra brought the feds to my house?

I want to be angry, to scold her for putting all our lives in jeopardy, but the agents aren't arresting my men. They're taking away the Russians in handcuffs —every one of them.

"Where are Sophia and Liam?" I'm relieved that Aleksandra is safe, but I need to see my kids. I need to know that they're alive and well, unharmed, without a doubt.

"I'll take you to them," Agent Malone says, escorting Aleksandra and me outside.

It's frigid outside, and neither of us is wearing a coat. I remove my blazer, draping it over Aleksandra's shoulders as we are escorted to the FBI agent's vehicle.

Several vehicles line the front lawn. From the back seat of each car, Russian Bratva has been apprehended. I'm relieved to see Mikhail handcuffed, but how long will he remain behind bars in prison?

Sophia has her nose pressed against the glass, watching the commotion. Liam is on his knees, watching from the back window.

Agent Malone unlocks the car, and I open the back door.

Aleksandra is right at my side. I breathe a sigh of relief.

Sophia and Liam climb out from the backseat with wide, curious eyes.

"What happened?" Liam asks.

"That's a story for when you get older," I say.

EPILOGUE

Aleksandra

The federal agents want me to testify against my brother, Mikhail, and my Russian family. I've been told that my testimony will keep him and his men behind bars for a long time with both kidnapping in the first degree and unlawful imprisonment charges.

Do I put my older brother behind bars?

I want to feel relieved. I want to be free of Mikhail, Luka, and the other bratva members and not have to constantly look over my shoulder, worried that they're coming for me, that my time with Antonio is over.

But it also feels like a betrayal to the family that I was born into.

Antonio and I are alike in that way that the only family we have now is each other. He's spent time researching his heritage and discovering his birth parents, only to find out that they died ten years ago in an automobile accident. He has no siblings, and while there are aunts and uncles out there, he doesn't seem ready to reach out to any of them.

I don't blame him. Especially when he discovered his mother's lineage was Italian, but his father was Russian.

It's not a story he shares or speaks about, not even with his men.

"Are you ready?" Antonio asks, poking his head into my new home library.

On the third floor, he's given me not only a playroom for the children but a room for myself, a library, packed floor to ceiling, where I can be left alone whenever I desire.

He let me pick out the paint, the furniture, pictures on the wall, and of course, all the books.

I exhale a nervous breath and cling to the latest novel that I'm reading, a sweet romance that lets me escape from the harsh reality of my dark life. My story isn't one that anyone would want to read. But a world unlike my own is something I can truly immerse myself in.

He waits by the door, tilting his head at me. Antonio is dressed in a formal business suit, as he always is, professional.

I'm wearing a suit with a pencil skirt, my hair is tied up in a messy bun, and I've yet to slip on my heels.

We're going to court.

I'm dreading testifying against Mikhail, Luka, the entire Russian Bratva, but it's something I'll do because I want to protect Sophia and Liam. I need to know without a doubt that they'll be safe and left alone.

I grab a bookmark and slip it into the book before shutting the binding. Standing, I stretch, stalling for just another moment at home, where it's warm and safe.

I don't want to face any of them in court, but what

choice is there? Someone has to stand up to them, and I'm not doing it alone.

Antonio is testifying against Mikhail that he had a hand in my kidnapping, coming to the office to extort money and essentially pay a ransom for my release. It will ensure Mikhail spends life in prison as opposed to only a few years for kidnapping in the first degree.

"Are you sure Ardian can watch the children?" I ask Antonio.

"I have a surprise for you," he says.

I'm not sure I can take any more surprises. "A good surprise?" I ask. My stomach is already assaulting me. I'm beyond nervous. I'm terrified to go under oath. What if they ask me about the mafia and Antonio?

While I know Antonio isn't under the spotlight and on trial, I can't help but feel nervous.

"Come on," he says and takes my hand, leading me down two flights of stairs.

"Kira," I say and smile, surprised to see the preschool director in our foyer.

"I've hired her to watch the twins while we're in court today."

I'm both shocked and in awe of all that Antonio's done. He leans in, pressing a chaste kiss to my cheek. "You don't have to worry while we're gone. Sophia and Liam are in excellent hands," he says.

———

"Mama!" Sophia squeals as she comes running toward me with red and blue fingers from painting on the canvas in the playroom.

Liam doesn't pay me the slightest bit of attention. He's with Kira, building a massive building block set.

"Let's get you cleaned up," I say with a slight chuckle before she gets her dripping paint on my court outfit. Hopefully, I won't have to return to court, and Mikhail and his men will be behind bars for a very long time.

Antonio heads into the playroom to pay Kira for babysitting the twins and escort her outside and down to her car.

After the paint disaster on Sophia is cleaned, I give her the biggest hug and bring her downstairs with Liam for lunch.

The counter is clean and empty. I grab bread from the pantry and peanut butter and jelly to make the kids sandwiches.

Antonio saddles up right behind me in the kitchen, his arms around mine, making it difficult to prepare a meal for the two kids.

"We have a chef who can handle that," Antonio says. His hands run up and down my arms. His breath teases my neck.

"I don't mind. Besides, it gives me some level of normalcy," I say.

"Whatever you want, *Tesorina*." He presses a soft kiss on my cheek and pulls away.

The kitchen feels icy and cold without his body wrapped around mine. Already, I miss his warmth, body, and breath against my skin.

I glance over my shoulder to see what he's up to. Antonio grabs two glasses from the cabinet and retrieves the water pitcher from the fridge, filling them for the twins.

Sophia and Liam sit at the counter, climbing onto the stools. They're quiet as they eat, devouring every bite of their favorite sandwich.

"Do you want me to make you a sandwich?" I offer. My stomach has been gurgling since court. I'm not the least bit hungry, but Antonio probably has an iron stomach.

"I'm good," he says and grabs my hand, nodding for me to follow him into the hallway.

"Finish your lunch. I'll be right back," I tell the twins.

There's an errant smile on my face. "What is it?" I ask. Why does he want to get me alone? Besides, the hallway isn't the least bit alone when it comes to guards roaming the halls.

He's clasped his hands around mine like he doesn't want to ever let go.

"Are you okay?" I ask. I've never known him to be nervous, but he seems mentally distant, like he's lost in his thoughts.

"I'm perfect," Antonio says with a warm, reassuring smile. "I'm relieved it's all over, but I think we should talk."

My stomach flops. "Talk," I repeat. Nothing good ever comes from those few words.

He offers another smile and releases my hand long enough to run his fingers through my hair. He's pushing a strand of hair behind my ear. His attention is solely on me. It's as if the rest of the world doesn't exist for one single moment.

"I want you to be happy, Aleksandra."

"I am," I whisper, staring up at him.

"I don't want you to be here out of obligation or because I forced you to live under my roof. I want this to be where you want to live, where you're happy to return after a long day out," Antonio says.

I exhale a heavy breath. I don't know what to say.

His fingers tangle in my hair at the nape of my neck. "I want this to be your home, *Tesorina*. I want us to raise the twins together as a family. One day, I want to be your husband," he says.

My mouth goes dry. "You want to marry me?"

A crooked smile adorns his face. "One day," he says. "I don't think either one of us is ready for that yet."

He's right.

If he proposed today, I'd likely panic and freak out on him. But I do want to spend the rest of my life with him. I know he's not a sweet, innocent Italian. He's ruthless, cunning, and will do whatever he must to keep his family safe.

It's one of the many things that I love about him.

"I'm not going anywhere," I say. I've burned bridges with the Russians. They're no longer my family. Antonio and the twins, they're my family.

"Good," he whispers, and I turn my face up, brushing my lips roughly against his.

I want him more than I've wanted anything in my life. I need him, and I'm pretty sure he needs me, too.

———

Mikhail should have gotten the book thrown at him, life in prison, but it ended up being a hung jury.

How the hell did they manage that?

Did Mikhail pay off one of the jurors?

It can't be a coincidence that two of the men on the jury were Russian. While I didn't recognize them from the family, that doesn't mean there aren't connections. He could have easily paid them off or threatened their families.

He needs to be stopped.

"I can't believe he got off," I say and throw my hands into the air. "He's going to come after me. It's not over."

"I won't let that happen," Antonio says, pulling me into his arms. "He's not stupid enough to lay a finger on you or our children. The feds are watching him, and my source tells me they have an agent willing to go deep undercover. They're looking for information to lock him away for good."

I press my lips together. I want to believe him that we're safe, that it's over, that the madness and chaos will be put to an end.

"I don't want to live in fear, Antonio."

He pins me with his stare. "And you don't have to. I've already tripled our number of guards, increased our security, and upgraded our weapons. I've polygraphed everyone who works for me and had those who failed or had inconclusive polygraphs interrogated. You have nothing to worry about."

He has taken additional measures to ensure our safety and the safety of his men. Mario was the only Italian to betray Antonio and the family. When Ardian dug a little deeper into Mario's background, there was evidence that he was working with Roberto's partners from The Cradle, who have since disappeared. We suspect that Yuri had been part of the operation and stealing funds from the Italians for years.

"I'll protect you and our family at all costs."

————

And Antonio does protect us.

While still out there lurking in the dark shadows and ruling the city of Chicago, Mikhail doesn't reach out to us.

I don't know what trouble he's involved in, and I do what I can to avoid any Russian chatter. I don't want to know what's going on with them.

Antonio is able to keep his word, protecting us, no matter what, from any and all danger.

But knowing Mikhail is out there, alive, being a savage and brutal boss is enough to make sure I bring a guard with me everywhere I go.

A bodyguard is also with the twins when they start attending kindergarten in the fall at their new school.

While Sophia and Liam don't know or understand what their father does for a living, they recognize that he's important to his men and, more importantly, to them.

Antonio is a good father, warm, caring, and responsible. It's strange to see a gentle side to the same man who kidnapped me and held me against my will quite some time ago.

With the children, he doesn't let them see his work's brutal and ruthless nature. He shields them from the darkness and viciousness of the mafia underworld.

Being a father comes naturally once he learns to open up to the twins and them to him.

And I regret not telling him sooner that I'd been pregnant, hiding the twins from him for the first four years of their life. But he's forgiven me more than I've forgiven myself. Antonio won't miss out on another day with them, and when I conceive again, he won't miss out on my pregnancy or the birth.

————

Thank you for reading Ruthless Vow.

Want more?

Read Mikhail's story in BRUTAL BOSS.

I know what betrayal feels like. And how to punish people for it.

You don't get where I am—at the very top of the infamous New York City Bratva—without making at least a couple of enemies.

And I've made way more than that.

I might try my best to protect people from con artists and cartel bastards, but that doesn't mean I'm any better than them. When the lights go off, you can't even tell us apart.

Madisyn sure can't.

The first time I see her at Steele Concierge Medical, I think she's just a nurse. Innocent. Oblivious. Unsuspecting.

The second time I see her, standing right in front of my compound in the pouring rain, I think it is a mere coincidence. Her car has just broken down, and she is helpless. Clueless. Vulnerable...

Now, I know she is anything but.

You don't get where I am without being a manipulative savage. And Madisyn just messed with the wrong mafia boss...

One click BRUTAL BOSS now!

———

Sign up for Willow Fox's newsletter

And I'm thrilled to offer a sneak peek of Expose: Jaxson, a steamy slow-burn romantic suspense featuring a former special forces hero in a small town.

————

I ran for my life, and it was all *his* fault. Secrets had brought me over a thousand miles from home. I fled with only one thought in mind: a second chance. Starting over was my only option for survival.

I squinted through my sunglasses, shucking them to the empty passenger seat, finding it difficult to see. My vision adjusted, but the night was setting in fast as daylight fell over the horizon.

I struggled to see the narrow, snow-covered road ahead.

The streets at the bottom of the mountain had been freshly plowed and salted. The headlights on my five-speed were angled at odd intervals, casting shadows over the road covered in potholes beneath the slush.

The car jolted and bounced with my foot on the gas, splashing my scalding, stale coffee from the cup holder.

My eyes burned and welled.

"Shit!"

Tears threatened the surface, but I wouldn't cry. It wasn't the sting of blistering liquid that hurt. I'd done this to myself. I blamed him, but it was as much my fault.

Secrets surrounded my past. Benjamin Ryan had been part of those secrets, but there was more than even he knew. There were secrets I could never tell him, even as he was whisked away in handcuffs.

I packed my car with my possessions and hurried out of the state of New York. Of course, not before finding a small log cabin in the woods that I could afford in cash, sight unseen.

I also lined up a job interview at a nearby resort, but there was no guarantee of landing a position right away. My last one had ruined my life, and I couldn't even put it on my resume.

I'd have to be frugal with the few dollars left to my name, which consisted of a few ones in my wallet.

Was I bitter?

Sure as shit, but I moved on, started over, and prayed for a second chance. A fresh start is what I did, what I craved, and the only way to get that was to move.

I went back to using my maiden name: Ariella Cole. I wasn't in hiding per se. After all, I had done nothing wrong or criminal.

I couldn't say the same for him.

I didn't want to get mixed up in his illegal affairs.

I had planned on arriving at my new home before dark, but the interview had been in the afternoon at Blue Sky Resort, a ski lodge just outside of Breckenridge, Montana.

It was for a position covering other worker's shifts, everything from waitressing at the restaurant to doing housekeeping tasks and handling the ski rental equipment. I'd take whatever I could get.

The interview had seemed to go well, and they had asked to run a background check. I wasn't keen on it but I didn't have a choice, so they'd see that my ex-husband, Ben, had run up our credit. They couldn't deny me a job because of that, right?

He was serving time in federal prison for several felonies. That couldn't count against me, right?

When I'd left the resort, with my piping hot, burnt coffee, it had grown dark. The front desk attendant had given me directions since my phone died, and GPS was sketchy as to whether it worked in the mountains.

I headed for my new house, weary, tired, and worn after a lengthy interview and an even longer drive across the country. I wanted to discover my new home, climb into bed under the warm covers and sleep for a week.

The interviewer informed me they'd run my references, and I had to submit to a background check.

It sounded all good, and while I hoped the job was mine, there were no guarantees. They hadn't offered me anything yet.

I downshifted my car, but I struggled to get up the mountain.

The bald tires spun as I white-knuckled the steering wheel. The back of the vehicle fishtailed.

I downshifted again and stomped on the gas to climb the godforsaken beast of a mountain when the car slipped and slid backward downhill.

"Shit!" I screamed and stomped on the brakes hard, which only had me doing donuts as I spun and slid down the icy path of the mountain. I would have braced for impact if I had known how, but I just wanted to survive. I needed to survive.

My stomach ached with dread. My palms were sweaty, and I clung to the steering wheel, attempting to maneuver my car out of danger.

I had no control over the vehicle, like it had a mind of its own.

The car spun and smacked into a tree. The window smashed. It wasn't enough to stop the momentum from sliding down the mountain, and the back wheels skidded off the road.

By some miracle, the vehicle came to a halt. The back wheels teetered off the edge of a ravine.

The car's front appeared stable, but would it propel me downward and into oblivion if I made any sudden movements?

I glanced in the rearview mirror.

It grew darker by the minute, and I couldn't ascertain how far down the ditch went, but given the fact the entire drive up the mountain was switchbacks and dangerous, without a doubt, it was deadly.

Exhaling a soft, slow breath, I couldn't stay in the car. I needed to get help.

I hadn't seen a car on the road since I attempted to climb the damned mountain. Was there a reason for that? Did anyone live up in Breckenridge, or was I the only one crazy enough to head up there on the cusp of winter?

I probably should have traded my car in for a vehicle with all-wheel drive or a truck, but it wasn't like I could afford it.

I was strapped for cash. I spent every dime on getting to Breckenridge and paying cash for the cabin I found on one of the realtor sites online.

The place looked like a gem, backed up to a gorgeous river, and within walking distance to a few local shops in town.

This had to mean I wasn't the only one in Breckenridge, but they were smart enough not to travel at night up the mountain.

My phone was dead, and even if it had any juice left, I knew without a doubt there would be no cell service around here.

There had been no service at the bottom of the mountain. That had been when my phone still had a tiny amount of battery power.

Not that I didn't have anyone to call. My sister would expect to hear from me, but we weren't on the best speaking terms. She was pissed that I moved to Breckenridge instead of staying in New York with her.

I couldn't stay. I had to get as far away from New York and the enemies we'd made.

I glanced behind me at my knapsack. I couldn't risk reaching for it. Not until I was out of the car.

With slow precision, I unlocked the door and eased the driver's side open. I made no sudden movements.

While I'd have preferred to stay in the confines of the car that offered shelter, it teetered on the edge of a ravine. I wasn't ready to meet death.

The car creaked and groaned as I was careful to shift my weight from one foot and then the other out from the vehicle.

The vehicle didn't launch off the cliff as I had first feared. I shivered and pulled my jacket tight.

I couldn't easily open the back door from my position. The snow was several inches thick, and I had stuffed my boots in the trunk.

There was no way I could maneuver myself to grab my warm and comfy shoes. My fancy heels would have to suffice because I wasn't going barefoot. That would be even stupider in this weather.

"Okay, I can do this," I said to myself.

There wasn't another soul on the road, and I didn't even want to consider what wild animals like bears or wolves come out at night. I hadn't the slightest idea if they were nocturnal. I hoped I didn't run into any creatures because I had nothing but my hands to protect me, and well, I may as well just lie down and play dead.

Okay, so getting my bag from the backseat wasn't as easy as I thought. I exhaled a nervous breath, my stomach in knots as I climbed back into the driver's seat, reached for my knapsack in the back, along with my purse on the passenger seat.

I didn't make any sudden movements, and I backed away from the car, shut the car door, shoved my purse into the bag, and swung it over my shoulder.

My hands shook from the cold and the adrenaline coursing through my veins. I dug into my pockets, retrieving a pair of leather driving gloves. They would have to suffice.

With daylight nearly gone, I headed for the main road of the mountain.

I kept to the center of the snow-covered path. I'd probably hear something long before I'd see anything, but I wasn't holding my breath.

The moon offered the faintest bit of light to illuminate the snow-covered road.

I had no flashlight, and the darkness of night seeped in, which reminded me there wasn't a town for miles because there were no city lights nearby.

I glanced up at the heavens, the frigid night air offering way to a sparkle of stars peppering the night sky. It would be a beautiful sight if it wasn't so cold and I didn't worry about freezing to death.

My lungs hurt from the cold. With each breath inward, a thousand knives were stabbing at my lungs.

With my jacket zipped up tight, I leaned my head down toward my coat. I needed to find shelter. With sundown, the night would only grow colder.

My hands trembled even with the warmth of my gloves. The edge of the road was difficult to see with no light. It seemed even more impossible to determine if there was any evidence of shelter.

I kept walking up the mountain. The only way I could tell I was headed in the correct direction was because the wind assaulted my face, and my footprints were evidence of where I'd been.

I could no longer see my car in the distance. The broken windows may have offered little shelter from the wind, but I could have been warmer had I stayed inside the vehicle. I could also have been catapulted down the ravine had I so much as shifted the car's weight.

There was no use second-guessing my decision. I just hoped that the main road would lead off to a driveway, a house, a cabin, or some sign of civilization.

The chill of the cold brought tears to my eyes, freezing my eyelashes, stinging my cheeks. My hands were numb, and my knapsack offered no clothes. Frozen inside and out.

I stumbled over my feet.

My toes burned from the frigid air that assaulted every inch of my body. The sensation went beyond numb and tingling.

I tripped and braced myself as I hit hard-packed snow on the road, eating a mouthful. I spit out the contents as best I could.

My lips were numb, along with my cheeks.

I shivered and curled up in the fetal position in the middle of the snow-covered road. I buried my face away from the chill.

Shielding my cheeks from the cold, getting an ounce of warmth and a reprieve from the elements. I pulled my bag closer to protect me from the wind. I shut my eyes.

My body trembled, but I wasn't cold. Not like I had been earlier. Numb. Nothing but emptiness, a cold and lonely existence stabbing at me.

One-click Expose: Jaxson now!

ABOUT THE AUTHOR

Willow Fox has loved writing since she was in high school (many ages ago). Her small town romances are reflective of living in a small town in rural America.

Whether she's writing romance or sitting outside by the bonfire reading a good book, Willow loves the magic of the written word.

Visit her website at:

https://shopwillowfox.com

ALSO BY WILLOW FOX

Dangerous Boss

Bossy Single Dad Series

Billionaire Grump

Mountain Grump

Bachelor Grump

Ice Dragons Hockey Romance

Faking it with the Billionaire

Daring the Hockey Player

Arresting the Hockey Player

Looking for kinkier books? Try these spicy stories written under the name Allison West at shopwillowfox.com